SEA TO SEE

A Rome London Novel

XANN-SHAPELLA SMITH

Amazon KDP

This book is a work of fiction. Any reference to historical events, real people, or real places are used fictitiously. Other names, characters, places, and events are products of the author's imagination, and any resemblance to actual events or places or persons, living or dead, is entirely coincidental.

Copyright © 2017 by Xann-shapella Smith

All rights reserved. No part of this book may be reproduced in any form or by any electronic or mechanical means, including information storage and retrieval systems, without written permission from the author, except for the use of brief quotations in a book review.

Cover design by Doug & Sherry Walker and Xann.

ISBN:
978-0-9992027-0-8

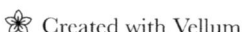 Created with Vellum

Acknowledgments

With gratitude and appreciation, I dedicate this book to all those who opened the door to Rome London's world and jumped in with both feet. Seeing your eyes light up when sharing your thoughts about *Block by Block* has been a humbling experience. Your enthusiastic comments, both verbal and written, have been a blessing in my life—for "a kind word [truly] is like a spring day." So here's to all my wonderful readers, fourteen to ninety-six and every age in between, who journeyed alongside Rome on her first travel adventure. This book is for you!

I would also like to thank my own team of superheroes who give so generously of their time and talents in support of myself and my writing. With special thanks to Doug for the captivating cover and Dave for using a lifetime of experience to advise on scuba diving. Lastly, cheers to Sherry and Tel—you know what you've done—as well as Saafe' and others who continue to help and encourage along the way.

Prologue

Current Assignment: Vacation.

*L*ogistics/Itinerary: Hobart, Australia, to Sydney, private jet, 2 hours, conversation with Heath. Sydney, Australia, to Honolulu, Hawaii, first class, 10 hours, traveling alone. Too much on mind to sleep. Honolulu to Lihue, Hawaii, 40 minutes. Take taxi from airport to town of Poipu on the South Shore, 25 minutes. Locate Heath's beach house. Sleep.

ROME SLOWLY WOKE TO A BRIGHT, sun-lit room, listening to the sound of wind chimes swaying in the breeze. She was certain the couch wasn't the most comfortable place in the house to sleep, but it's as far as she made it before collapsing from exhaustion. Her plane arrived on Kauai late, and by the time the taxi dropped her off at the beach house, she was so tired she could barely get the key in the door. Heath had some business to take care of in Sydney but promised to join her in forty-eight hours or less. Rome was glad for the head start and planned to use the alone time to rest up from the globe-trotting of the past few weeks.

    Sitting up, she located a clock and began counting the hours with her fingers. "Ten hours. Not bad." It was her first day on the beautiful Hawaiian island of Kauai and all she wanted to do was sleep. Jet lag had finally taken its toll and her body had won the argument. Grabbing the bottle of water she purchased at the airport, Rome guzzled the entire thing then walked to the nearest bedroom, closed the shades and crawled into the wonderfully comfortable queen-size bed. It didn't take long for her to drift into a peaceful slumber. Her vacation had finally begun and sleep was her only objective.

Chapter One

A barrage of artillery lit up the night sky as cannons fired from a British warship. Rome quickly covered her ears to protect them from the deafening noise, making it difficult to tread the deep water. The explosions continued with no distinct pattern or rhythm, filling the air with smoke and the pungent smell of gunpowder. Finding it hard to breathe, she watched from the water as the larger of the two ships pummeled the smaller, her masts falling into the ocean like trees in a forest, her white sails slipping beneath the surface, signaling defeat but not surrender. Taking all she could, the battered ship began her descent, the mermaid figurehead leading the way. Diving into the deep, she guided the ship on her final journey, leaving nothing but a pool of debris as the only evidence of her existence.

Instinctively, Rome pushed herself beneath the surface and swam as fast as she could toward the sinking ship. The darkness made it difficult to see, but she continued to propel herself deeper until she collided with an unexpected object: a dead man. She quickly pulled back and let his lifeless body continue on its path. Hit from behind, another body grazed her back. Rome had seen enough, but before she could start back to the surface, she came face to face with a third dead body: a face she recognized immediately.

"JAMIE!" Rome screamed as she abruptly woke from her sleep. This was the third time in twenty-four hours that she had the exact same dream, ending with the death of her ex-boyfriend. But this time when she opened her eyes, she saw a person run from the bedroom. Or at least she thought she did.

"Heath?" called Rome as she cautiously crawled from the bed, made her way to the open door and looked down the hallway. Nothing appeared out of the ordinary, but at a small five-foot-five, she wasn't going to leave the bedroom unarmed. Choosing a two foot statue of a tiki mask for a weapon, she left the bedroom ready to swing at the first thing that moved. The face on it alone could frighten off an intruder. Catching her reflection in a mirror, she realized the tiki had some competition as she looked at the state of her hair: a brown, bejumbled mess resembling a poorly-crafted bird nest.

Squinting from the light, Rome began to slowly walk through the house. "Heath, is that you?" She waited for a response, but again, no reply. The house was silent with the exception of the now-familiar sound of wind chimes dancing outside the window. As she made her way through the house, she was glad she wore her shorts and T-shirt to bed, rather than a nightgown. She felt more appropriately dressed for confrontation.

After a thorough search turned up no one, her mind started to wander to other possibilities. "No! I refuse to go there," she said out loud, unwilling to entertain the idea of a spirit being present. "I'm on vacation."

Needing some fresh air, she placed the tiki on the counter, opened the french doors and stepped onto the deck, allowing the warm breeze to greet her. As she stared out at the ocean, Rome retraced the steps of her vivid nightmare. She hadn't seen nor heard from Jamie since he stopped by her office in New York and that was over five days ago. So why the dreams? And why would Jamie be involved in a centuries' old battle between two ships? None of it made sense.

Her mind filled with unanswerable questions as she tried to discover the possible reasoning behind the persistent nightmare. "What's the connection? Is it guilt over the break-up? Am I subconsciously missing him?" Finally she asked herself the one question she did not want to consider: "Has something happened to Jamie?" Growing more anxious by the minute, Rome became determined to resolve the situation. Walking back into the house, she scooped her phone off the counter and dialed his number. It went straight to voicemail. Not surprised, Rome left a message asking him to call her back as soon as possible—a process that was all too familiar.

Weary from the energy consumed by her nightmares, Rome collapsed on the couch and took a moment to study the room's male-dominated decor. The walls were decorated with several tiki masks, a set of two beautifully-carved Hawaiian story boards and a variety of wooden war clubs and spears, some embedded with sharks' teeth and feathers. The shelving was made of bamboo which fit perfectly with the hand-woven blinds and the wooden-carved hula girl table lamps with painted palm trees on the shades. The only nicknacks to be found was an impressive collection of large shells and Japanese glass fishing floats. There was no denying that the Jones' beach house was a bachelor pad—a thought that made her smile as she drifted off to sleep... again.

"JAMIE, NO!" shouted Rome as she awoke from the same nightmare and quickly sat up on the couch.

Not expecting to see Heath sitting on the coffee table in front of her, she let out a second scream. "You almost gave me a heart attack."

"I just arrived to the sound of you calling out your old boyfriend's name. Who's giving who a heart attack?"

"It was a nightmare," she assured him, still trying to shake it off. "How long have you been sitting there?"

"I just walked in."

"You weren't here earlier, were you?"

"My plane landed about a half hour ago. What's going on?"

"I thought I heard someone in the house a few hours ago."

"Dead or alive?"

"I refuse to answer that," she said before taking hold of his hands and pulling him toward her. "Come here."

Still skeptical, Heath leaned forward but stopped just short of the kiss. "Are you sure there's nothing to be concerned about?"

"Not in the way you're thinking." With that said, they greeted each other with a long-awaited kiss.

Rome thought it best to wait and see if she heard back from Jamie before revealing the extent of her nightmares. The last thing she wanted to do was make her ex-boyfriend part of the equation. Three's a crowd, after all, and this was a vacation designed for two. It was an opportunity to get to know each other better before they return to the demands and restraints of their individual lives—a time to deepen their relationship. It was also the first time they were alone together without having to deal with her job as a travel writer for Trekking the Globe or Heath's family problems, both living and dead.

"So now that you're here, what's on the agenda for today?" she asked running her fingers through the locks of his sandy blonde hair, noticing a few more gray strands than when they first met.

"Beings it's 6:00 Hawaii time, how about dinner?"

"Is it really that late? I've totally lost track of time."

"That is the point of a vacation. What do you feel like?"

"I could eat anything."

"I know the perfect place."

"Let me grab a quick shower first," said Rome as she kissed Heath then quickly left the couch.

"I'll take care of some business while I wait."

Rome stopped in her tracks. "Business? I thought we were on vacation?"

"With the departure of my uncle as COO, I'm the only one at the helm of Jones Shipping."

"How is your uncle?"

"Still in the hospital. Heavily medicated."

"Nervous breakdown?"

"They haven't had a chance to evaluate him yet."

"Strange."

"He just keeps rambling on about ghosts."

"You don't think?"

"After what I've seen... anything's possible."

"So how much business will you need to do?"

"Enough to keep the lights on."

"Do you have a replacement in mind for COO?"

"I have some options I'd like to kick around with you."

"With me?" asked Rome, surprised by his desire to include her in a business decision.

"It's either you or my butler Sheldon and he's not here."

"I'd love to help," responded Rome enthusiastically as she grabbed her suitcase and rolled it toward the bedroom. Their relationship had just advanced a level and Rome couldn't be more thrilled. Pausing in the doorway, she watched all six foot three of him step out onto the deck and begin pacing back and forth as he took care of business. If someone had told her a month ago that she'd be vacationing in Hawaii with the Australian man she'd fallen in love with... she would have laughed them off the planet. But that was the chapter she was beginning and she couldn't wait to write the rest.

DUE TO HER inner clock still being a bit off, she'd woken up early and decided to take a morning swim. The water was amazing and the physical power that it took to fight the waves was the perfect morning exercise. Her sleep had been peaceful and free of nightmares which left Rome wondering if it was Heath's presence that made the difference.

Dressed in an athletic-style, black swimsuit beneath a bright lava lava tied around her waist, Rome walked along the beach letting the water wash back and forth over her feet. "Relaxation at its finest," she thought to herself. The beach was practically empty, making it feel like her own private paradise. Thoughts of a wonderful evening with Heath swirled around her mind as she happily relived the previous night's events.

Before her swim, she tried calling Jamie for the fourth time, but still no answer and no return call. She now had a sense of what Jamie must have felt when he was trying to contact her in Tasmania. But that's the past and Rome was looking to the future.

Out of the blue, a young woman, barely out of her teens, approached Rome from behind. To say she was strikingly beautiful would be an understatement. Her unconstrained wavy, black hair extended to the small of her back. She was taller than Rome by at least four inches and wore what appeared to be a vintage white chemise with a wide neck tucked into a skirt that looked like a petticoat layered with lace trim just below the knee.

"Good day to you," spoke the mysterious woman. "How's the water this fine morning?"

Not only was Rome surprised by her sudden appearance, but she was also intrigued by her use of a brogue English accent. She recognized a portion of her dialect from her time spent in the south of England and the other part from work in the Caribbean. "Perfect. Are you planning on taking a swim?" replied Rome.

"Nothing would make me happier, but my plans are fixed."

"It's not like the water's going anywhere."

"You swim with great strength."

"Thank you," responded Rome, slightly alarmed at being watched by a complete stranger.

They continued to walk down the beach in silence until it became clear that the woman had no plans for leaving her side. Fortunately, Rome had the gift of conversation down to a fine art. "Are you vacationing or do you live on the island?"

"I've come to visit someone."

"When did you arrive?"

"Only two days past."

"Then we're both new to the island. How long do you plan to stay?"

"Time has grown short. My departure is imminent."

"Why the short stay?" asked Rome curiously.

"Many are in need of help."

Intrigued by her answer, Rome stopped walking and turned to the woman for more clarification. "Here on the island?"

"Far away."

"And you're leaving to help them?"

"I came here to help them," replied the woman.

"I don't understand."

"You must return with me."

"Me?"

"Time is growing short!"

"Am I the one you came to visit?"

"Indeed."

"How can I help?"

"You're the only one who can."

Needing to confirm her growing suspicion, Rome slowly reached out and took hold of the woman's hand. The touch was a familiar one: substance, but not like flesh and bones. The woman was a spirit. An apparition. Rome closed her eyes as her physical connection transported her into the woman's mind. Shocked by the familiar images of the battle at sea, Rome broke free from her grasp and stepped away from the woman. "The nightmares... they've come from you."

"I needed you to see."

"See what?"

Just then Rome's cell phone rang. Looking at the screen, she saw it was a D.C. number with a familiar prefix. "Finally!" she said with a sigh, "Jamie must be back from his vacation and calling from work." Excited to hear his voice, she answered the phone and cut right to the chase, "how was the Caribbean?"

But it wasn't his voice she heard. It was Ross, Jamie's good friend and coworker at the State Department. Rome's heart immediately sank as she braced herself for what might be coming next.

She quickly learned that Jaime had been missing for nearly seventy-two hours. They found the boat he chartered adrift with no one aboard.

"This can't be happening," Rome thought to herself as the news went from bad to worse. They had found the body of a fellow diver, a policeman, floating about a mile away from the boat, but Jamie, his young captain and his sister had not been found.

"How did the policeman die?" asked Rome, scared to hear the answer.

"Gunshot to the chest."

"Gunshot?" repeated Rome, shocked by his answer.

"The autopsy showed he was dead before he hit the water."

Rome sank to her knees as she continued to listen to the findings of the joint US Navy and FBI investigation. She wanted to cry, but the shock of Jamie's disappearance kept her from producing a tear. Ross went on to explain all that they were doing to try and locate Jamie and the others, but she could tell by the tone of his voice they weren't holding out much hope. Finally, he summed up the conversation with the main reason for his call. "Jamie made me promise that if something ever happened to him and the case couldn't be solved, to contact you and you'd know what to do."

"How would I know what to do?" responded Rome, surprised by Ross' declaration.

"I don't know, but I told him I would," assured Ross.

Before ending the call, Rome thanked Ross then asked him to keep her updated on any new findings. Staring out at the ocean, she mentally went over the facts of the investigation, including the timeline of events and Ross's final words. "What would make Jamie think I could help him?" she questioned. "What can I do that the US Navy, the FBI and the State Department can't?"

A realization that Rome never considered hit like a ton of bricks. "Jaime knows about my gift. But how?" Rome quickly stood up and began looking around for the spirit with the thick black hair, but she was nowhere in sight. Heath, on the other hand, was on a direct course to her location. He waved from up the beach and Rome waved back, wondering how she would break the news that Jamie was encompassing her every thought. "Okay, so maybe that's not the best way to put it," noted Rome, "nor the right way to begin a romantic getaway." Her only hope was for a moment of brilliance to strike within the next thirty-seconds, but she wasn't holding her breath.

"You should have woke me," hollered Heath, within earshot.

Rome waited for him to get close then wrapped her arms around him. "I peeked in, but you were sound asleep." She greeted him with a good morning kiss.

"Like that's stopped you before."

"It's a whole new me."

"Not so fast... I'm kind of partial to the old one."

"That's good, because there's something I need to tell you that involves the old me and I'm not sure where to start."

"We are on vacation, remember."

"About that..."

"Don't tell me there's some emergency in the world of travel," said Heath, half joking, half serious.

"This has nothing to do with my job."

"Is it my job? Are you upset I'm doing business on our vacation?" inquired Heath.

"No, but my news will impact our vacation."

"Are you leaving?"

Rome took a deep breath as she looked into Heath's caring eyes. The last thing she wanted to do was hurt the man she'd fallen head over heels for, but she could no longer shield him from the truth. "Jamie needs my help."

"Jamie? As in your superhero, secret agent, ex-boyfriend?" responded Heath.

"He's missing and it doesn't look good."

Heath could hear the worry in her voice, so he dropped the jealous boyfriend routine and quickly came to her aid. "What happened?"

"He was on a scuba diving trip in the Caribbean and disappeared. They found the boat he chartered adrift and the body of a fellow diver floating about a mile away. Gunshot to the chest. Jamie and two others are still missing. It's been almost three days and they still can't find him."

Heath held her tight, giving Rome a safe place to fully react to the news, as well as time for himself to digest the new development. Jamie Webb becoming the focal point of their vacation was not part of his Hawaiian plans, but that's exactly what was happening and he'd have to dig deep for the strength necessary to support Rome in her time of need.

The walk back up the beach was long and quiet as both Rome and Heath remained lost in thought. When they reached the deck of the beach house, Rome took Heath's hand and sat him next to her on the hammock-style porch swing. She had dropped the bomb about Jamie and now it was time to fill in the details. "Since I arrived in Kauai I've been having these bizarre nightmares."

"About what?"

"They're confusing but consistent. The dream begins in the middle of a battle between two ships."

"What kind of ships?"

"Old ships. One had three masts and looked like a smaller, race-built galleon, but it was hard to tell with all the cannon smoke."

"Race-built galleon?"

"In order to make some of the galleons faster for military purposes, the British removed the upper portions of the aft and stern castles where the captain and crew had their quarters. They left a one-level captain's quarters with a small poop deck on top at the very stern."

"You know your ships," responded Heath, impressed by her knowledge.

"My Dad was in the Navy, remember? He also loves to build models of ships. I used to help him glue the pieces together, listening to him describe the different boats and their place in history."

"And the other ship?"

"Larger, with four masts and a high aft castle. Most likely a Spanish galleon or a British man-o'-war. It was hard to tell from my position in the water. Everything was happening so fast. Cannons were firing relentlessly from the larger ship, but very little return fire. Then the smaller ship starts to sink. Next thing I know I'm under water running into dead bodies until I come face to face with one of them... it's Jamie." Rome paused for a moment as she linked her nightmare to the current situation involving Jamie. "I wake up when I can't save him."

"What does Jamie have to do with a battle between two old ships?" asked Heath, confused by the mixing of two different time periods.

"I don't know."

"And it's the same dream every time?"

"Yeah, but I no longer think they're dreams."

"What do you mean?"

"I'm pretty sure I'm watching a past memory."

"From another life?"

"Not my memory," reassured Rome, "someone else's."

"Like with William and Helen in Tasmania?" confirmed Heath.

"Exactly."

"Which means there's a ghost living in my beach house."

"More like visiting."

"Have you seen it?"

"She approached me on the beach this morning and asked me to come with her."

"Where to?"

"She didn't say. Our conversation was cut short by the phone call about Jamie. But if I had to guess, it would be the Caribbean."

"The Caribbean's a big place. Where do we begin?"

"Jamie and I had been planning our trip for a year, so I have a head start. He's using the Isla de Providencia as his base of operations. Ross confirmed that was the case. It's a small island about halfway between Jamaica and Costa Rica. That's where he chartered the boat."

"Isn't that the island that Henry Morgan used as his headquarters when he was plundering the Spaniards?"

"You know your pirate history," applauded Rome.

"They say some of his stolen treasure is still buried on that island."

"I wouldn't doubt it."

"So when do we leave?" asked Heath.

"I'm not dragging you all the way to the Caribbean, especially when you have a business to run."

"Thanks to modern-day technology, I can run my business there just as well as I can from here."

"I'm serious, Heath, you really don't need to come."

"I'm not letting you go alone."

"You do recall I travel the world for a living?"

"You're still not going alone."

"Why not?"

"Four little words... gunshot to the chest."

"I'll be fine," said Rome reassuringly as she reached over and took his hand in hers. "I promise."

"So what are you going to do when you get there?" replied Heath, testing the credibility of her plan.

"After the spirit tells me where to locate Jamie, I'll pass the information on to the Navy and the FBI."

"How are you going to explain where you got the information?"

"If they find Jamie, none of that will matter," argued Rome.

"Oh, it'll matter," warned Heath. "If you don't tell them about your gift, they'll think you're involved in some way. And if you do tell them about your gift, they'll think you're nuts, or worse yet, lock you away in some secret government test site so they can study you."

"What?" responded Rome astonished by his extreme scenario.

"How are you going to prove you're not involved?"

"Jamie will tell them."

"If they find him alive."

"He's got to be alive or why would the spirit want my help?"

"How are you going to keep your gift a secret when they start interrogating you?"

"Interrogating me?"

"You know... small room, bright lights, people smoking in the shadows."

"No one is going to find out about my ability, Heath."

"How can you be sure?"

"Because we're not going to tell them," responded Rome.

"Who's we?"

"Jamie has to know about my gift. It's the only way any of this makes sense."

"He is a spy."

"Are you done yet?"

"Not until you say yes to me coming with you," answered Heath, posing an ultimatum.

"Fine."

"Great. I'll book the tickets and let Sheldon know where we're headed," he said, jumping up and walking toward the door.

"You can't be doing this because you're jealous," demanded Rome, expecting more superhero and secret agent remarks.

Heath walked back toward Rome, took her in his arms and kissed her. "I'm only going to help. I want to find him too." With that said, Heath left her side and walked back toward the door. "And by the way, I may have lied when I told you I wanted to take scuba lessons. You can't grow up on a sailboat next to the great barrier reef and not learn to dive."

"I know."

"How?"

"Sheldon."

"So you let me lead you on?"

"I knew you'd come clean."

"I'm never going to be able to surprise you, am I?"

"You already have... on a castle tower in Tasmania."

"I surprised both of us," he said smiling then entered the beach house.

For a brief moment Rome forgot about Jamie as they shared the memory of the night Heath declared his love. It was unexpected and Rome had to dig deep to find out if the same were true of herself. After a series of discussions and debates, mostly with herself, she arrived at a similar conclusion: she was falling for him as well. Hawaii was the first opportunity for them to be alone without any distractions—and for Rome, a chance to test the waters. Hopping a jet to the Caribbean was not part of that itinerary.

She had mixed feelings about Heath coming with her but couldn't be more thrilled by his willingness to help—more proof that he was in a hundred percent. Not bad for only knowing each other less than a month. Once again, they were headed into the great unknown, just as they had done on the Isle of the Dead. Still, in the back of her mind, she wondered what type of impact her search for Jamie would have on their relationship. Only time would tell.

Chapter Two

Shipwreck of the Maiden's Return

Caught in the glow of artificial light coming from deep inside the chasm, grains of sand swirled through the seawater like the inside of a snow globe. Thirty feet below the sea floor hung the Maiden's Return, a seventeenth-century British race-built galleon that had the good fortune of being wedged between the walls of a deep fissure that ran along the ocean floor. It was as though she'd been steered into place by the captain herself. Hanging by her sides, the boat appeared to be afloat at the bottom of the sea, adding a haunting eeriness to the legendary ship.

When first discovered, the outside wood of the Maiden's Return was carefully examined along the bottom of the hull. The last thing the treasure hunters wanted was to be trapped inside if the shifting of weight broke her free from the walls holding her in place. It was nothing less than magical for the divers to float beneath a shipwreck as though she were suspended in air or on display in a museum. It was an experience they would never forget or ever repeat in their lifetime.

Then began the excavation. The amount of drifted sand covering the top deck amounted to nearly three feet and helped to keep her hidden from the world of amateur and professional treasure hunters alike. Repeatedly, they emptied buckets of sand over the bow and into the seemingly bottomless chasm. It was a slow, messy and arduous process that had begun three days prior.

Today their search would take them inside the hull of the ship for the first time. Beneath the light of several subsea luminaries attached to the eight-foot-tall center mast, most likely blown in half by the strike of a cannon ball, three men in scuba gear worked to remove the last of the sand blocking the entrances to the two sets of stairs. They had already searched the contents of the diminished fore and aft castles and had come up empty-handed. From the furniture found, it appeared the aft castle housed the captain and one other person: most likely the legendary mermaid said to have brought good luck to the Maiden's Return.

One of the men communicated through his VOX, voice-activated system, as well as by hand signal, that he was ready to access the stairs to the next deck, commonly known as the gun deck. Although the divers were leery of swimming below after witnessing so many strange occurrences on the top deck—including the four strange deaths of their fellow divers—the possible reward dramatically outweighed the risk.

Floating headfirst through the hatch leading to the companionway, the first diver used his hands to pull himself down the stairs. He was happy to find the gun deck covered with only a few inches of sand, but the ship's furniture and twenty-four cannons had rolled from their positions during the final battle, causing a series of blockades. Aware of the possible dangers to his hoses and equipment, he carefully used his dive lights to watch for clearance as he began his search of the crowded deck.

Meanwhile, the two divers left up top listened intently to the diver below describe his discoveries. They also monitored the sound of his breathing as a way to tell how he was doing mentally. Heavy, quick breathing was usually a sign of panic setting in and at that point the other divers would begin talking him down.

The information was intermittent, with more being heard than not, the breakup most likely due to the confined space of the lower deck. Knowing that each would have his turn, the two divers paid close attention to the details of everything their associate encountered until it came time for the second diver to access the stairs near the front of the ship. As he made his way down the stairs, he reported the same findings and conditions as the first diver. All in all, the second deck was a mess.

Left alone, the final diver, who'd been added to the dive team after the deaths of the first four divers, began checking the dive computer on his wrist. While examining the technical data and gas numbers on the screen, he felt something swim past. Pulling the handheld light from his belt clip, he pointed it in the direction of the movement but saw no physical sign of sea life. Again, he felt something pass from behind and quickly turned to catch a glimpse. Still no visual evidence of anything physical could be seen under the light of the luminary attached to the broken mast.

Scenes from every underwater science fiction film he'd ever watched flashed through his mind as he waited for it to happen again, but nothing came. Finally, he chalked it up to a strange anomaly, then turned off his flashlight and hooked it back to his belt.

Without warning, he felt the same force come at him again, but this time multiplied in power. Wrapping his arms around the center mast, he hung on for dear life as it spun around him like a tornado, physically bunting him back and forth. The thrust was strong and caused his arms to slip, leaving his hands as the only tie to something solid. Feeling his glove-covered fingers slipping, he fought the urge to panic as his strength was put to the test.

Eventually, the swirling force split in half and left without warning. He watched as the water's movement showed the path of the invisible power entering the two companionways leading to the lower deck. Sporadic screams from his dive partners burst into his face mask, but the words were too broken to understand. For the first time in his career, the diver up top had no idea how to respond. After one of the longest minutes of his life, a high frequency squeal sounded inside his mask, then everything went silent. No screams. No breathing. No voices. Just silence... deadly silence.

Instantly, the diver tried to make verbal contact but received no response. The sight of steady air bubbles escaping each staircase told him everything he needed to know. Even with the certainty of his associates' deaths, he felt inclined to confirm his conclusion. Checking his air and gas level, he'd used up more than he should have during the strange attack. He had enough to investigate the lower deck, but only briefly. Cautiously, he made his way headfirst down the set of stairs near the stern, unsure if the force was waiting for him or if it had left the ship.

It took him a while to maneuver around the cannons and other obstacles in his way, but eventually he came within sight of the first diver's fins floating motionless ahead of him. Gently, he grabbed hold of the man's ankles and pulled his body toward him, finding the breathing hose to his face mask torn open. Jamie concluded that in his struggle with the invisible entity he caught the hose on something and ripped it. The look on the dead man's face was one of horror, taking the surviving diver back a few years to when death was a more prevalent part of his life. He had seen men, women and children die in more ways than a person could imagine, and after a sixteen-year military career, he had grown somewhat used to it. But that was not the case today. He was rattled by the frightened look on the man's face and reminded of his own mortality. "This could easily have been me," he thought to himself. "Lying dead in the hull of three-hundred-year-old ship."

Leaving the dead man behind, he made his way back through the maze, up the stairs to the top deck and down the other side. There he found the second diver had met the same fate. Unfortunately, the video camera attached to the living diver's face mask would not have captured the force that attacked the ship, but it was evidence that he had nothing to do with their deaths. Chilled and alone, he returned to the upper deck and tried to contact the surface to confirm the divers' deaths, but no response came. He would float to the top alone, the only diver left alive.

Just as he reached to turn off the lights, his plans quickly changed as he noticed the water moving off the stern of the ship. The mysterious entity had returned and was on a direct intercept course. Grabbing onto the mast, he looked behind him to see the same thing coming from the opposite direction. With no possibility of escape, he had no other choice but to brace for impact.

To the surprise of the diver, the separate forces entered the two companionways of the ship instead. Within seconds, he witnessed the force shoot out from the open hatch near the front of the ship, carrying one of the dead divers. Up and over the bow it went, taking the body into the abyss. Turning his head, he watched it happen near the stern of the ship. The second diver's body met the same fate as the mysterious force disappeared over the stern, carrying the body to its watery grave.

Immediately, he turned off the subsea luminaries, flipped on his dive light and ascended the walls of the gorge. Once he reached the sea floor, he adjusted his buoyancy control devise and propelled himself toward the surface. With the help of his dive computer, he continued to ascend at the proper rate and speed to avoid decompression sickness. Thoughts of how this latest tragedy would play out up top kept him busy as he made his ascent. He had no idea how to explain what he saw. Worse yet, he doubted anyone would believe him.

Eventually he made it to the surface, but not to the usual extraction point between the two hulls of the large catamaran-style ship. Removing his face mask, Jamie Webb felt the sun for the first time in three days and the vitamin D felt good. More than good. Man was not designed to live in the dark. Returning to the ship would mean providing an explanation for the deaths of his fellow divers. The only thing that made sense was labelling them accidents, as was the case with the four others. There was no way of proving differently, and even if he tried, no one would believe him.

As expected, a small rescue boat carrying three men immediately left the ship and headed straight for him. Bobbing up and down with the waves, he had no other option than to let them come.

Within no time they had him aboard, then circled back to the catamaran. Jamie had no idea what this latest development would lead to or how it would effect the search of the Maiden's Return, but there was no doubt in his mind that he was about to find out.

Chapter Three

It had been a long flight from Hawaii to San Jose, Costa Rica: thirteen hours to be exact with one change of planes at the George Bush Intercontinental Airport in Houston, Texas. Add in the four-hour time change and Heath and Rome arrived in Costa Rica just in time for lunch. They both grabbed a smoothie as they made their way toward the terminal where they would catch their next flight to the small Columbian island of San Andres.

It was a long trip, but they only took carry-on luggage which made navigating each of the airports less time consuming. Once they arrived in San Andres, they stopped at a bank to convert their money to the Columbian peso, then located the charter air service that Heath had booked to transport them to the neighboring island. After a quick thirty-five-minute, less-than-smooth flight, they touched down safely on the beautiful Isla de Providencia.

Before exiting the airplane, Rome took one last look through the window and was surprised to see a younger man with hair the same length and color as hers standing to the side of the landing strip. He was wearing a loose white shirt with the drawstring stretched open at the neckline and tan-colored pants with no shoes. As they exited the plane onto the runway, Rome tried to locate him but had no success. Her thoughts of the uniquely-dressed man quickly passed as she turned on her phone and saw she had two missed calls from her mother. "I'll call her back tonight," she thought as she followed Heath from the runway.

Providencia had all the charm of a traditional Caribbean island, yet was remote enough to avoid the cruise ship circuits and hoards of tourists that come with them. Due to the impromptu nature of the trip, there were no hotel rooms, cottages or cabanas available. Stopping short of buying a machete and building a hut, they took the advice of a local and travelled up the mountain to a guest house. The drive took them into the lush and beautiful rainforest that makes up the center of the island. Turning off the main road, the smiling driver with a mouth full of teeth, stopped at the end of what appeared to be a driveway that disappeared further upward into the trees. After unloading their own bags, Heath handed a large bill to the grinning driver and then watched with surprise as he happily sped off down the road.

"What? They don't make change here," he said placing his wallet back in his pocket.

"How does he expect any return business operating like that?"

"We're tourists, Heath."

"What kind of business model is that?"

"Things like this happen when you travel."

"I travel."

"In a controlled environment. First-class seats, five-star hotels, upscale car services... "

"All I'm saying, is that he could benefit from a business seminar... or two."

"Can we go?"

"Go where? We're standing in the middle of a jungle."

"Up the driveway," said Rome, pointing behind him.

Heath followed her finger to the narrow, steep driveway that disappeared into the trees. "How do we even know he dropped us off at the right place?"

"There are only five thousand people on the entire island."

"What if we're lost?"

"On an island this small?"

"It happened to Jamie."

"He disappeared off a boat, remember?"

"Probably captained by that guy's business partner."

Rome let go of her bag and approached Heath, taking hold of his upper arms. "Do you feel that, Heath?" she asked in an attempt to calm him down by changing the subject.

"Feel what?"

"The laid-back vibe of the island. That's why people travel. That's why they come to the Caribbean. Let it go," suggested Rome, then she returned to her bag and headed up the steep driveway.

"Sorry," hollered Heath from behind. "I guess I'm a little out of my comfort zone."

"You'll get used to it," responded Rome as she continued to climb.

"Great," he said to himself as he grabbed the handle to his suitcase and followed in her footsteps.

After a ten-minute climb on a humid, thirty-degree-Celsius day, they reached their destination: a multi-colored house reflecting the brightness of the Caribbean. The home had several entrances due to the apparent number of add-on rooms, but thankfully, a bright, hand-painted arrow pointed them in the right direction.

Before they reached the door, a voice called to them from around the back. "Alo. Come see the beauty of Providence." Rome and Heath followed a path through the bushes which ended with a breathtaking view. The house was built on a cliff that overlooked nearly half of the Isla de Providencia and the small neighboring island of Santa Cantalina. Simultaneously, Rome and Heath wrapped their hands around each other's, confirming that there was no one else in the world they would rather be sharing this moment with.

"What brings you to the island?" asked a voice from behind them.

Heath and Rome turned around to see a man with shoulder-length, salt-and-pepper hair, most likely in his early-fifties, lying in a hammock stretched between two trees. He appeared completely at peace wearing an oversized cotton shirt, shorts, a colorful headband around his unkempt hair and a dark pair of sunglasses.

"We're looking for a friend," responded Rome.

"Then you've come to the right place."

"What do you mean?" enquired Heath.

"There is no friendlier place than Providence. It is the island way."

"Our friend has gone missing and we're here to help find him," clarified Rome.

"One of the men on the boat?"

"Yes," confirmed Heath.

"He may be lost to the water."

"We're not giving up on him."

"That's the spirit. Believe it to happen and it will happen."

"The island way?"

"If you believe it to be. My name is Jonah. Welcome to my home."

"I'm Rome and this is Heath. Thank you for allowing us to stay at the last minute."

"Thank you for climbing the mountain," said Jonah as he crawled out of the hammock, took hold of a gnarly, well-used stick and began walking toward the small path previously travelled by his visitors. "Come. See the room where you will sleep, then we will have a meal together."

"The view from your home is spectacular. Have you lived here long?"

"I was born in this house, when it was much smaller."

"What a beautiful place to spend your life," responded Rome as she and Heath followed Jonah down the trail to one of the many colorful entrance ways. "I'm sure that view never gets old."

"My eyes no longer see, but the beauty lives on in my memory."

Not sure how to respond to the news of their host's blindness, Rome and Heath followed in silence, finally reaching a bright purple door with green trim.

"Behind this door you'll find clean towels, clean bedding and all the charm of the Caribbean."

"I'm sure it's perfect," said Rome.

"You'll also find an informative brochure with contact information for the businesses on the island that cater to tourists."

"Including dive shops and boat charters?"

"Of course. Providence has everything your heart desires. Settle in, then return down the path. Brunch will be ready in ten minutes."

"Thank you, Jonah," responded Heath as he watched him turn and walk away.

"This is so much better than a hotel."

"Agreed," said Rome as she waited for Heath to open the colorful door.

Entering the room, they found themselves immersed in authentic Caribbean decor, from the rattan blades of the ceiling fan to the dark wood of the furniture. The rugs, bedspread and bedding were a blend of orange, yellows and reds, adding more than a splash of color. Rome collapsed onto the double bed, grateful to have finally reached their destination, while Heath removed his outer shirt, revealing a much cooler white T-shirt.

"I'll ask for a separate room," said Heath as he walked toward the bed.

"All right," responded Rome spellbound by the rotations of the ceiling fan.

"Don't fall asleep, Rome."

"Okay," she said closing her eyes and drifting away.

"Rome!"

"What?"

"Get up before you fall asleep," requested Heath as he pulled her into a sitting position.

"I don't think I can make it ten minutes."

"Sure you can. Let's get you unpacked."

"I just need a few seconds, Heath."

"You need to eat something."

"You eat while I take a twenty-minute power nap."

"He's expecting both of us."

"Apologize for me."

"You need to keep moving."

"At this point, nothing can move me."

Suddenly, Heath yanked Rome from the bed and kissed her passionately, his arms holding her tight to his body. Surprised by his boldness, Rome pulled away just far enough to catch her breath.

"Feeling moved?" he asked with a self-assertive tone and twinkle in his eye.

It took Rome all of two-seconds to know what she wanted and that was Heath. She jumped in with both feet as she wrapped her arms around his neck and kissed him back.

Neither of them had felt anything close to this intensity since the day they spent together on the sailboat touring the Tasman Peninsula. And even that paled in comparison. Their unrestrained impulsiveness was exactly what Rome needed to release some of the stress and worry she had bottled up since Jamie's disappearance.

The ten-minute waiting period would have come and gone without either of them caring, but Rome happened to glimpse the time on a colorful frigate bird clock staring at them from near the bed.

"We have to go!" said Rome as she pulled herself away from Heath and walked to the bathroom to check her hair in the mirror. "We don't want to be late."

"Now you want to eat?" responded Heath out of desperation.

"I didn't realize how hungry I was until I worked up an appetite," answered Rome on her way back, taking hold of Heath's hand and pulling him toward the door.

"When you die, I'm going to donate your brain to science."

"Funny."

"You think I'm kidding," responded Heath as he allowed himself to be pulled out the door, grabbing the information brochure on his way.

DURING LUNCH, Heath and Rome got the lowdown on the island

from Jonah, and not wanting to waste any time, they decided to begin retracing Jamie's steps. "Our first move should be to charter a boat," said Rome. "I called Ross from San Andres to check in and he gave me the GPS coordinates where they found Jamie's boat anchored. He was about a mile off shore and the diving depth to the sea floor is around a hundred feet."

"The Navy would have dove for bodies."

"They did. But we're not."

"Then what are we diving for?"

"Whatever Jamie was diving for."

"A hundred feet's a deep dive," pointed out Heath.

"I've been that deep. You?"

"Close to eighty."

"I'll need the right mix of gases and all the tech for deep diving," said Rome as she looked at her watch. "It's still early enough in the day to get in a dive or two. Why don't you call down and see if there's any boats left to charter? I'll call the dive shop and make sure they have the equipment I need."

"Good thing I brought the brochure," remarked Heath.

Jonah listened to them make their separate phone calls while sizing up their personalities and the nature of their relationship. It was a force of habit he couldn't help. Heath ended his call and waited for Rome to wrap up hers. "I got us a boat and they're even sending someone to pick us up."

"I confirmed the equipment I need so we're set."

"You need? What about me?" asked Heath.

"One of us should stay on the boat... just in case."

"In case of what?"

"In case something goes wrong."

"I can handle a hundred feet, Rome."

"This way's safer."

"Are you sure you're not too tired?" asked Heath, concerned about her solo dive.

"I got my second wind. We better get changed."

"Catch you later, Jonah," said Heath as they left the back patio.

"I'll have dinner waiting," Jonah hollered in return, amused by their unique relationship. He hadn't had guests this entertaining in a very long time and was looking forward to their company and hearing the outcome of the search.

AN HOUR LATER, Rome and Heath reached the coordinates where Jamie's chartered boat had been discovered. The weather couldn't have been more cooperative as the sun's rays danced across the turquoise water. If the circumstances were different, she would be perfectly content to spend the afternoon relaxing on a pillow top hammock after a good swim or dive. But this was no vacation and relaxing would have to wait until Jamie was found. Contemplating what she might find at the bottom of the ocean, Rome began gearing up for the dive.

"Did you call your mom back?" asked Heath as he helped her on with her wetsuit.

"I sent her a quick text. I'll call when I have more time to talk."

"Do they know you're in the Caribbean?"

"I told her I'm traveling. I'll fill in the details later. They'll get a kick out of knowing where we are since they spent their honeymoon down here, boating from island to island."

"So your parents have a boat?"

"A friend loaned them theirs for a few weeks as a wedding gift."

"Nice."

"From all the stories I've heard, it was quite the adventure."

"Did your dad teach you to dive?" enquired Heath, breaking the silence.

"After his promotion stationed us in Jacksonville, Florida, Dad was no longer shipping out to sea, so he wanted to do more stuff as a family. During summer break between eighth and ninth grade, he had me take scuba lessons from his friend, a dive instructor in the Navy."

"I bet that was intense."

"He believed physical fitness plays a major role in scuba diving, so I spent most of that summer swimming against the waves, doing calisthenics, running and lifting weights. I felt like I was in basic training. After that, Dad and I started taking the occasional weekend scuba trip."

"Does your mom dive?"

"My mother prefers a good book and a comfy deck chair beneath a large umbrella."

"Did your parents ever buy a boat?"

"Oh, no. We'd go on organized scuba tours. Dad wanted me to get experience in a more controlled environment."

"Safer that way for a kid."

"Teenager."

"Barely. Have you dove much with Jamie?"

"Just off the coast of Florida. He came with me a couple times to visit Mom and Dad. Quick visits over three-day weekends."

"Did 'Mom and Dad' approve?"

"Two Navy guys together swapping war stories…"

"And your mom?"

"What's not to love?" As soon as the words left her mouth Rome realized she should have thought before she spoke. It was an off-the-cuff comment intended to be cute, but she hadn't taken the time to factor in how it would effect Heath. "So when did you learn to dive?" asked Rome in an attempt to change the subject.

"On break from university and only in controlled environments."

"Next time we'll dive together," Rome assured Heath as she began testing her equipment and tech to make sure everything was operational.

"What if you don't find anything down there?"

"Then we check it off the list and move on."

"What if you do?"

"That's the scarier question. Are you ready?"

"I'm not the one diving," responded Heath as he helped her step to the back of the boat.

Rome waved to Heath then stepped into the water, disappearing below the surface. It felt good to be back in the sea after being absent from one of her favorite hobbies for nearly a year. She had allowed work to consume her time and left very little for her private life. Having a workaholic for a boyfriend for the past two years hadn't helped either. It just made it easier to stick to her self-imposed schedule.

The descent to the bottom brought back memories of dives past and Rome felt a certain relaxation come over her that she hadn't felt in a very long time. On the other hand, it seemed strange to be diving in this location without Jamie. They had planned for this with enthusiasm. It was the vacation they both dreamed of yet put off to accommodate their careers. Chalk it up to one more of life's lessons learned the hard way. Shaking off memory lane, Rome returned her focus to the destination.

As she neared the sandy bottom, it wasn't long before the sea became darker, enough to require lights to examine the details. Although the fish and ocean life were beautiful, Rome worked to keep focused on the mission at hand. She was there to search for clues to Jamie's disappearance, and in the recesses of her mind, possibly even Jamie's body—a thought she did not entertain for long. Time passed as she searched in a large circular pattern, monitoring her dive gauges as she went. It was essential that she allow plenty of time for a slow ascent and not get too off course.

With the exception of a few beer cans and bottles, she found no evidence of man until Rome saw something in the distance. It appeared to be someone walking toward her along the sea floor. From what she could see, he was dressed in early eighteenth-century Spanish garb from head to toe. Rome knew he had to be an apparition. There was no other way a human being could survive without oxygen at the bottom of the ocean. Unsure of his intentions, Rome had nowhere to run. There was no way she could outmaneuver a spirit anyway or make it to the top quickly enough to avoid an encounter. Confused as to what to do, she watched him grow closer, her heartbeats increasing with each second that passed. It was likely he held the answer to Jamie's disappearance. If so, she needed the courage to find out.

It wasn't long before she came face to face with the ghostly Spaniard. Immediately, he reached toward her with both hands. By the look on his face, Rome knew he meant harm so she intercepted his grasp. His ghostly strength was no match for her human brawn as she held him at bay, her hands wrapped tightly around his wrists. Staring into his dark and disturbing eyes, she was instantly transported from the bottom of the sea into the ghost's memories.

Chapter Four

East Coast of New Spain (Mexico), 1719

Standing aboard a large Spanish galleon warship, Rome looked around to find them anchored near what appeared to be a tropical coastline. She watched as small boats rowed back and forth from the shoreline, transporting trunks, bags and barrels to the ship. It didn't take long for her to realize that the Spaniard from the bottom of the ocean was hiding in the shadows of the companionway leading to the decks below.

Dressed in plain crew clothing, rather than the elaborate and decorative costume adorned by his ghostly figure, he snuck onto the main deck of the ship and blended in with the crew. Rome watched him hide from the commissioned officers as he snuck through the maze of crewmen loading and storing supplies, fresh food and loot. Eventually, he escaped the ship by boarding a rowboat and heading to shore.

Along for the ride, Rome watched as he skulked about once he made shore, winding nonchalantly through the working sailors on the beach then disappearing into the forest. She could tell he knew exactly where he was going as she followed him down a lesser used trail. He moved quickly, then began to run until he ran short of breath. His journey continued until the sun began to set. She could feel his urgency to make it to a certain destination before darkness left him alone in the dense forest. With the disappearance of the sun, the trail became difficult to see, causing him to trip over roots and rocks.

Much to both their relief, the lights of a small village appeared at the end of the trail. The Spaniard rounded the outskirts of the small town and entered a house on the perimeter. Rome's curiosity grew as he greeted ten men with hugs and hardy handshakes. They referred to the Spaniard by his title and surname, Captain Mendivia, then invited him to join them for supper.

Rome knew enough of the Spanish language from her travels throughout Latin American and Spain to communicate well, but she thought their early eighteenth-century dialect would make it difficult to follow. Oddly enough, that was not the case. She had no problem understanding their conversation as they sat down to devour their meal.

Rome suffered through the sound of them stuffing their faces with food and drink, while following their dialogue exchange about Mendivia's escape from captivity. Finally, their consumption came to an end and they shoved the dishes aside, creating enough room to unroll the map pulled from inside Mendivia's shirt. Its aged appearance and the fact that it was drawn on the side of a tanned hide told Rome that it had been around for a while. The map became her visual focus as she studied the details while listening to the conversation.

"How long will it takes us to get there?" asked one of his men.

"Three days, maybe four, depending on the terrain. Burros would make it quicker," responded Captain Mendivia.

"That can be arranged. How did you come across the map?"

"It was discovered in a metal box next to the remains of my ancestor, Fernando Mendivia," replied the Captain. "He was accidentally dug up during preparation for a relative's burial—a regular occurrence in the old church cemeteries of Spain. Mother was superstitious and told me to destroy it."

"You kept it instead," concluded another man, fawning over Mendivia's diabolical nature.

"I spent the night reading his journal also found in the box. The very next day I signed on to sail west."

"And the map's origin?"

"Fernando accompanied Hernan Cortez on his exploration voyage from Cuba to the Aztec Empire in 1519. More than a year later, he returned to Spain with map in hand," answered Mendivia.

"Hernan Cortez? The great Conquistador who brought the Aztec Empire to its knees?"

"The very one," replied Mendivia with pride. "The Aztec Empire's capital city of Tenochtitlan was rumored to be a magical city, showered in gold, and Cortez was determined to find it. He even sank his own ships to squelch a mutiny and avoid returning to a sentence of imprisonment or death for defying the Cuban governor's orders."

"Sounds like a certain captain we know," said a third man at the table, garnering nods from the others as Mendivia reveled in the camaraderie of his men.

"My ancestor, Fernando, and many others were angry with Cortez over the sinking of the ships but had no choice but to follow him. They began a two-hundred-mile march toward the capital city, making allies with members of a different tribe along the way."

"We all know of the legend of Cortez," responded the first of his men. "The gold they found in the city was plentiful, but not as much as they expected."

"After the Massacre of the Great Temple, the natives rebelled against our people," shared a second man.

"We're all familiar with our country's conquests. It's the map and where it leads that we're interested in," spoke up another.

"Let's hear of it! And of the treasure," demanded a fourth man.

"No more!" shouted Mendivia, shoving Rome out of his memory.

OCEAN FLOOR, Present-day

She was no longer a fly on the wall and instantly found herself back at the bottom of the sea. The thought of her invading his memories angered Mendivia as he stared deep into her eyes before disappearing from sight. This was the first time she experienced a ghost entering his own memory to keep her from seeing more.

Glancing at her gauges, Rome was surprised to discover that what seemed like hours took less than a minute. Beat from the energy used to wander through Captain Mendivia's memories, she began her slow ascent toward the surface.

The sun was setting as Heath reached over the back of the boat to help her aboard. Seeing two silhouettes instead of one, Rome quickly pulled the mask from her face in the hopes that it was Jamie. But that was not the case. The man standing next to Heath was wearing cream-colored pants with a white, fitted jacket, laced down the front to a v-waist with accompanying ruffle. He was definitely not from our time.

Once aboard, Heath assisted Rome in removing her equipment while asking questions about her dive. Rome's attention, however, was focused on the spirit sitting on the side of the boat staring back at her.

Removing her wetsuit, Rome allowed her body to breath before pulling on a pair of shorts to cover the bottom half of her swimsuit.

"So does this mean you're not going back down," asked Heath, confused by her lack of response to his questions.

"Sit next to me. I need to show you something," responded Rome as she continued to stare at their ghostly visitor. Just as Heath sat down, Rome took his hand in hers, laid it comfortably across her thigh, then tilted her head toward their mystery guest. Glancing in the same direction, Heath flinched when he saw the ghost. "That never gets old. Maybe a little warning next time?"

"Sorry. I thought you'd be used to it by now."

"Are you used to it?"

"Not really."

"Did he just show up?" whispered Heath.

"He was on board when I surfaced."

"How long has he been here?"

"I don't know."

"What's he doing here?"

"Waiting for your return," interrupted the ghost.

"You know who I am?" asked Rome.

"You've come to find your friend."

"Word travels fast," commented Heath beneath his breath.

"Not fast enough," responded Rome. "Who are you?"

"Fernando Mendivia."

"I just met your relative."

"You did?" asked Heath in surprise.

"On the sea floor. I got a glimpse of him with a certain map," answered Rome.

"His actions betrayed the family name," added Fernando.

"By using the map to find the treasure?"

"That is only the beginning."

"Does he have anything to do with my missing friend?" asked Rome, hoping to learn of Jamie's whereabouts.

"To understand the present, you must search the past."

"Can you help us do that?"

"I can only speak of what I know and what I learned from my Aztec friend."

"I have a better idea," said Rome as she stretched out her arm. "Take hold of my hand."

"The violence will be too much for someone not acquainted with conquest and war," warned Fernando.

"I'll be fine," responded Rome with confidence. "I'm somewhat familiar with that part of history."

"Are you sure?" asked Heath, taking Fernando's warning seriously.

"I can handle it."

"Very well," said Fernando as he walked toward them. "Everything I know about the map I learned from my friend, Teno. He was a leader in the Aztec Emperor's royal guard and a good man.

During the eighteen years Teno served and protected Moctezuma, they developed a close friendship. He believed Moctezuma to be a great leader and warrior and it troubled Teno to see him reduced to nothing more than a glorified prisoner under Cortez's control," recalled Fernando as he sat down facing Heath and Rome before continuing.

"It all began at the temple massacre. I still remember it like it was yesterday. I was a distance from where the Festival of Toxcatl was being held. The pounding of the drums and the singing could be heard throughout the city... until it was replaced with bloodcurdling screams. I ran toward the temple to see what had happened and what I found was horrific."

Rome extended her hand toward him. "Showing me may be easier for you," but he stopped short of taking hold.

"It's one thing to learn history from a book. It's entirely different to see it with your own eyes. Are you certain?"

"Yes," replied Rome, "take my hand."

AZTEC EMPIRE'S Capita City of Tenochtitlan, 1520

Chaos reigned supreme as Fernando rushed through the rear gate into The Patio of the Gods. He stood in shock as he watched the Spaniards, his own people, use their swords to reap carnage on the unarmed Aztecs in attendance. He had seen battle between armies many times but never a slaughter like this. Hundreds of people were already dead, corpses heaped high upon each other. Men, women and children, all murdered in gruesome ways—proven by the number of mismatched limbs littering the floor. They were defenseless, and with the gates guarded, they had nowhere to run. Blood spatter coated the stone walls while puddles of blood covered the floor. He watched in horror as heads were severed with one swing of a Spaniard's heavy sword, while others were nearly sliced in half, their entrails falling to the floor before their bodies hit the ground.

Shocked, Fernando found himself unable to think or even move as he watched his own men gleefully rip the gold jewelry from the blood-covered corpses as though they were prizes at a festival. Searching the crowd, he saw his friend, Teno, fighting off the Spaniards in an attempt to save his people—a losing battle from Fernando's perspective.

CHARTERED BOAT, Present-day

Letting go of Fernando's hand, Rome found herself back on the boat where she quickly turned and threw her upper body over the side, vomiting into the water. Heath pulled her hair back as she continued to violently convulse. Staring at her reflection in the water, she saw the look of horror on her sickly-white face. She had chosen not to heed Fernando's warning, and by doing so, had paid a heavy price: a consequence that would remain with her for years to come. Once she finished, Heath grabbed a towel and helped her sit back down. He wrapped his arm around her shoulders for comfort as she wiped the remaining puke from her mouth.

For better or for worse, getting her own personal view of history was just one of the aftereffects Rome was learning to accept as part of her gift.

"Are you all right, Rome?"

"That was horrific. The screams. The smells. The violence."

"I tried to warn you," mentioned Fernando.

"Yes, you did."

"I will relate the rest of the story."

"No. Take me back. I know what to expect now," said Rome.

"I don't think that's a good idea," warned Heath.

"I need to do this... for Jamie."

Fernando looked to Heath, who cautiously nodded, giving the go-ahead. This time Fernando sat down next to Rome. "The worst is behind you," he said then he took hold of her hand.

AZTEC EMPIRE'S Capital City of Tenochtitlan, 1520

Coming to his senses, Fernando pulled his sword and began fighting his way toward his friend's position. Teno had received several wounds and Fernando fought the Spaniards off as he moved his friend to safety. The continuous arrival of Aztec warriors helped turn the attention of the Spaniards away from the two of them which allowed Fernando to help Teno out of the patio and into a nearby building where he could tend to his wounds.

After a quick examination, Fernando discovered that most of the cuts were superficial except for a deep gash through the back of his calf muscle. He did the best he could to clean the wound and wrap it, but knew it would take weeks to heal, and only if he were able to avoid infection.

"We must leave the city," said Teno.

"You can't travel in this condition."

"I can and I will."

"What about your wife and child?" asked Fernando.

"I sent them south four days ago. They will return to the village of my childhood. My family will welcome them."

"You will follow, no doubt?"

"After I fulfill a promise," responded Teno.

"Promise?"

"To my emperor. He has entrusted me with an important task. I must accomplish it before I can be reunited with my family."

"Not in this condition."

"I have a long journey ahead, but I am determined."

"What about the emperor? It's your job to protect him."

"He sees the mistake he made in welcoming Cortez. What Moctezuma has asked me to do is more important to him than his own life. I must succeed."

"You'll not succeed on your own."

"I must."

"Not with that wound. I'll go with you."

"I cannot ask that of you," replied Teno.

"I wouldn't expect you to. I'll gather supplies while you rest. It's best we leave during the night."

"You are a good friend, Fernando," said Teno as he laid his head back and closed his eyes.

The streets were active with chaos as Fernando left the building in search of provisions. Not knowing the promise Teno had made or the task ahead, he began to gather what he thought they might need. Using a blanket and hat to disguise himself, Fernando snuck through the recently-evacuated buildings. Most of the Spaniards were now holed up in the royal palace, using Moctezuma as their hostage, while the Aztec people plotted their revenge. The distraction was exactly what he needed.

Fernando's main objective was the Temple House, located next to the temple and the palace. It was home to the priests who served the emperor. He needed a remedy to help Teno with his pain and knew the priests concocted all sorts of potions.

Carefully, he skirted the palace unseen, hiding in the shadows as people passed. Reaching the rear of the Temple House, he entered and made his way to their medicinal room. Once inside, a light from the fire pit in the center of the floor allowed him to search through the remedies. Having been treated with the herbal medicine for his own pain shortly after they arrived, he quickly found it on the shelf.

Before he could escape the medicine room, he heard a door open. Slipping back into the dark part of the house, he waited for two priests to pass. While hiding in the shadows, he noticed several walking sticks leaning against the wall. Once the room was clear, he took two of the walking sticks and left the Temple House.

While Teno slept, he passed the time by fashioning a piece of wood into an arm rest. After cutting one of the walking sticks down to size, he screwed it into the carved-out hole on the bottom of the arm rest, forming a crude crutch to make travel easier for his friend.

Night had fallen, but there was still plenty of activity in the city. Fernando replaced the blood-soaked cloth bandage wrapped around Teno's leg then helped him to the floor. The crutch allowed Teno to take the weight off his damaged leg, and for that he was very grateful. Sneaking from building to building, they made their way through the great maze of Tenochtitlan until they reached the outskirts of the city. There they boarded an abandoned canoe and rowed across the shallow lake. They thought it best to avoid the causeways leading from the island city to the mainland.

DAWN CAME QUICKLY and Teno needed to rest for a moment. Fernando pulled a cloth from his bag and ripped off another piece to act as a bandage. He wrapped it securely around his calf, then rinsed the bloody one out in a stream and hung it from his pack to dry. He administered another dose of pain medicine mixed with water to Teno then sat beside him for a much needed drink of his own. Seeing the devotion of his friend, Teno knew the time had come to share the details of his promise. "I must destroy the only map leading to the sacred burial tomb of the emperors."

"Why?"

"To keep the Spaniards from desecrating their resting place," said Teno as he pulled a map from inside the waistband of his skirt.

"Why must you travel so far to destroy it?"

"It must be destroyed in a live volcano."

"Why not just build a fire right here and turn it to ash?"

"It is the will of the gods," responded Teno in complete belief.

"Your gods are far more demanding than mine," responded Fernando.

"The remains of eight great emperors lie in the tomb."

"Not to sound disrespectful, but I don't think Cortez would be interested in a pile of old bones."

"The tomb also contains the adornment of each of the eight emperors: their own personal headdress, jewelry and staff. When the gods return they will resurrect the emperors first, who will then adorn themselves properly to meet them."

"Surely, others know of the way to the burial sight. How else could they be entombed?"

"During the funeral, the fleshy remains of the dead emperor are consumed by fire atop the Great Temple, then the bones and skull are placed in a casket of sorts and carried to the sacred burial spot. Also taken are a few of the bones from those sacrificed during the funeral, as well as the bones of a large bird of prey. The funeral procession also required four men to carry a large, locked box containing the adornment."

"What keeps the men who know the way to the tomb from telling anyone?"

"Once they inter the bones in the cave, they sacrifice themselves, believing in the great blessings promised on the other side. Two of the men are selected to return the map to the emperor. Upon their arrival, they are honored with a banquet then sacrificed at dawn. It is a great honor for them as well as their families."

"Your customs are strange to my world," remarked Fernando.

"The greed I've seen in your people's hearts is strange to mine," responded Teno, giving them both pause for thought.

"How much further to the volcano?"

"Four days at the soonest."

"Then we better get at it," said Fernando as he grabbed Teno's hand to help him up.

"I see no sign of greed in your heart, my friend," said Teno before rising to his feet.

"Gold is not why I came to your land. I am merely an explorer."

Fernando helped Teno to his feet and they began their trek beneath the rising sun. The active volcano released lava and smoke often over the years, but the great increase in steam and smoke over the past several weeks had them worried that it could blow at any moment. Each day the tremors and small quakes grew more frequent the closer they came to the mountain. The forest was thick and the path to the volcano's top had not been traveled for many years. Tirelessly, Fernando used his machete to clear the path so Teno could pass more easily. The going was slow and Teno's need to rest occurred more often.

The wound looked worse each time Fernando attended to it. There was no stopping the infection growing within the open flesh, but Teno was determined to carry on. By the morning of the fourth day, his lower leg had turned gangrene, causing him to rely on Fernando's strength to begin the lengthy climb to the top of the volcano. It wasn't long before the increase in tremors caused the mountainside to crack open in random places, allowing the escape of steam and pungent gas. This new event made a straight course to the top impossible.

Halfway up the mountain, Teno could go no further. The fever had reached his mind and he began to lose lucidity. With his last clear thought, he entreated his friend to fulfill his promise and the Spaniard agreed. Before he left, Fernando helped him to the ground and made him as comfortable as possible, wiping the sweat from his face.

"Do not look at the map, Fernando," warned Teno. "It has a power about it."

"Rest, my friend, until I return."

Taking the map in his hand he continued toward the top as the earth rumbled violently beneath his feet. The terrain grew more steep and rocky but he continued undaunted until a mighty explosion blew from her peak, spewing rocks, ash and steam. The quakes that followed shook him from his feet several times. Getting up, he hurried as quickly as he could through the trees and down the side of the mountain until he reached Teno. The infection had claimed the life of his friend, and if Fernando didn't get off the mountain, the lava and ensuing mud slides would do the same for him. With a final goodbye, he bid him farewell and ran toward the bottom, losing his footing with each new tremor. Reaching the valley, he didn't stop running until the volcano was far behind him.

Finding a distant hilltop, Fernando sat down and stared at the volcano, her rumblings still felt in the ground beneath him. Although the explosion would be considered small in comparison to some, it was a magnificent sight. After a few minutes, curiosity got the best of him. Unrolling the map revealed a spectacular work of science and art. He became mesmerized by the colors and imagery. Time passed without recollection as he continued to survey every detail. The map became intoxicating as he traced the drawings with his finger.

Within his mind it seemed to take on a life of its own, complete with the sound of a beating heart and a whispering voice. It began calling to Fernando, tempting him to follow, luring him to the emperor's tomb of golden adornment, promising him wealth beyond his wildest dreams.

Quickly, Fernando turned the map over and slammed it to the ground, hiding it from his view. He could feel the obsession taking root and wanted nothing to do with it. Using his machete, he began frantically digging a hole. Once deep enough, he grabbed the map and shoved it into the bottom then covered it with dirt.

Standing up to get his bearings straight, he headed toward the ocean. But he didn't get far. He could hear it calling him, begging him to return. In a moment of weakness, he did just that. Digging up the map, he wiped off the dirt and tucked it into his bag.

All the way to the coast, Fernando looked for places to bury the map, but each time he tried he failed. He had no means of starting a fire to burn the map, and even if he had a piece of flint and a fire steel to strike it against, he would've had a difficult time finding any dry debris. It was rain forest, after all.

In a matter of days, it had become an enormous weight for him to carry. When he finally reached the beach, he was excited to see a ship preparing to leave. The time had come for him to make a decision about the map: leave it behind once and for all or take it with him to keep the tomb safe from his people. Teno had entrusted it to him and he had a decision to make. Hearing the last call from the ship, he decided to carry the map back to Spain until he found a way to destroy it. At least that's what he told himself.

CHARTERED BOAT, Present-day

Letting go of Rome's hand, Fernando stood up to clear his head. The story his memories told was compelling to say the least. A tale of two men from different worlds coming together to form a trusting friendship. The fact that Teno and Fernando's relationship survived the massacre was another example of how the goodness of humanity can triumph even in the darkest of times.

"How did you become such good friends with Teno?"

"A few days after we arrived in the city, I was attacked by a group of angry men. He fought them off and saved my life. Then he allowed me to heal in his home. His wife cared for me until I could return to my duties."

"So you owed him your life?" she asked.

"That's not why I did it."

"Then why?"

"He needed my help."

"Why take the map back to Spain?" asked Heath.

"I thought it was my decision, but in hindsight, it was the map who made the choice for me. I should have heeded Teno's warning and never looked at it."

"In order to keep it hidden, you were buried with it?" asked Rome.

"As a final request, I had my daughter bury a metal lockbox with me. It contained the map and my journal, but I was the only one who knew it. For nearly two centuries it lay in secret."

"Until it was dug up," commented Heath.

"In the end I failed to help Teno keep his promise."

"An impossible request, considering the circumstances," noted Rome.

"A failure is still a failure no matter how pretty you paint the picture," said Fernando, his final words before he disappeared from the boat.

"How are you holding up?" asked Heath.

"I'm all right. How about you?"

"I'm wondering what this has to do with Jamie."

"He did come to the Caribbean searching for sunken treasure."

"You think he found the map?"

"I don't know."

"He wouldn't know of its power," said Heath. "At least Fernando was warned."

"If I'd come with Jamie like we planned, I might have learned of the map in time to warn him," responded Rome expressing some of the guilt she was feeling for his disappearance.

"Now is not the time for 'what if,' Rome."

"Let's head back," she responded, slipping a tank top over her swimsuit then pulling a bottle of water out of the cooler.

Not knowing what to say, Heath stood up and walked toward the helm. Just as he started the engine, he felt Rome's hand slip around his waist. Raising his arm allowed her to complete the circle around his body and rest her head against his chest. "I need you so much right now."

"We'll find him, Rome," responded Heath as he steered the boat toward the island.

On the way back, Rome filled him in on her walk through Mendivia's memory at the bottom of the ocean. The sun had set by the time they reached shore and Heath paid the owners of the two businesses a generous compensation for waiting past closing time for the return of their boat and equipment, as well as a ride up the mountain.

THE FINAL CLIMB from the road to Jonah's house used up all the energy Rome had left. Their host was glad to hear them arrive and as promised had their evening meal ready and waiting. The inside of Jonah's kitchen was home to quite a collection of handcrafted items as well as colorful stories told over their "catch of the day" meal.

Carvings, clocks, bookends and artwork lined the shelves and walls, most made from the natural growth of the island as well as driftwood and sea shells. The collection made sense when he explained they were gifts and oftentimes payment from his patients over the years. With the exception of college and medical school, Jonah had spent his entire life on Providence. He knew just about everyone as well as the condition of their health, and when the loss of sight brought his medical career to a close, he made the transition back to his first love: mental health. Originally, Jonah had wanted to be a psychiatrist, but there was a bigger need for general practitioners on Providence, so he studied both.

"Is your office attached to your home?" enquired Rome,

yawning as they left the house and made their way to the lawn chairs surrounding the fire pit.

"You're sitting in it. The absence of walls on the outside leads to an absence of walls on the inside."

"So the setting itself is therapeutic," added Heath.

"Most people wear masks through life, facades that protect their image, their agenda or their secrets—a fact that most would never admit. Here the masks come off. Truth leads to freedom from all that ails."

"I've recently seen that proven," remarked Heath, sharing a wink with Rome as he thought of his own ancestors in Tasmania.

"Might I ask what you bring to the search for your friend?"

Heath looked to Rome for the answer as they both stayed silent in their response. "I hate to cut this evening short, but I'm about to fall asleep," said Rome in an attempt to avoid answering Jonah's question.

"Let's get you to bed," joined in Heath, helping Rome from the chair and leading her across the yard. "Thank you again for dinner, Jonah. It was delicious."

"Breakfast will be waiting in the morning," replied their host, somewhat curious about their visit to the island as he listened to their feet disappear down the trail. He felt a familiarity with Rome that he couldn't put his finger on, but he was confident that time would reveal all. In his experience... it usually did.

Chapter Five

The South'n Hunter

*T*wo hundred and ten feet from bow to stern, the South'n Hunter boasted a cruising speed of thirty knots. Originally designed for use as a ferry, the catamaran-style boat had a large deck on the bottom intended for parking vehicles and a top deck for passengers. It was found to be too small for the amount of water traffic, so the county auctioned it off to the highest bidder.

After its purchase by a private party, the catamaran was completely renovated. Much of the top deck was turned into the owner's home away from home and luxuriously furnished. The lower deck remained more utilitarian for the use of transporting goods. The opening at the front of the ship, once used as an exit for vehicles, was walled up, making it possible for the building of storage rooms and crew quarters in the front third of the lower deck. The traffic entrance had also been closed in, but with a large utility door for loading and unloading at the stern.

Jamie emerged between the two large hulls of the catamaran, his body weary from days of physical exertion. It'd been thirty-six hours since he witnessed the death of his diving partners and Jamie hadn't slept a wink since. The eight-foot distance between the water and the hatch would have been impossible to span without the cable hoisting him from the surface.

Once through the hatch of the lower deck, two men grabbed his arms and pulled him to the floor, helping him off with his scuba tanks. After removing his face mask and fins, Jamie followed one of the men to the stairs, motivated by two others with guns. Clinging to the handrails, he pulled himself toward the top deck of the catamaran, uncertain as to the mood of his captor, Jack Lazenby, one of the Caribbean's most notorious smugglers—a ruthless criminal who operated under the guise of a sea water exploration company and the man who had turned his vacation into a living hell.

As Jamie stepped from the last stair, he pulled back the hood of his wetsuit and ran all ten fingers through his thick, black head of hair, waiting for Lazenby to start the pointless questioning he had endured for days. Staring at the back of his perfectly-combed, platinum blonde hair, Jamie wanted nothing more than to wrap his arm around his neck and drop his lanky body to the ground. No one would miss him and the world would be better off without his brand of evil. But the timing wasn't right. And timing was everything.

"Well?" asked Lazenby in a deceivingly easy New Orleans accent while pouring himself a drink.

"You have a video feed of everything I'm doing down there. Why ask what you already know?"

Turning toward Jamie, he took a moment to let his prisoner's comment settle as he swirled the bourbon in his old-fashioned cocktail glass. "Get the boy."

Immediately, one of the guards turned toward the stairs.

"Wait! It won't happen again," yelled Jamie.

"Ya keep telling me that."

"I'm tired and on edge."

"Leave the boy... for now."

"We could avoid these little chats if you could find a new communications system," said Jamie.

"We're not leavin' this spot without what I came for and there's nothin' available on Providence."

"I rented a face mask with PTT."

"I'm not gonna have my diver wastin' time communicatin' with a push-to-talk. Ya need both hands to get the job done."

"Have your men tried to jury-rig the old system?"

"The base station receiver's been fried: wires, speakers and all. The electrical current that most likely killed my men blew the transmitter to pieces."

"Electrical current?" asked Jamie in confusion.

"What else could've done that kinda damage?"

"Having no way to communicate makes being down there by myself even more dangerous."

"The hand signals ya been showin' on video are workin' fine."

"What if I develop nitrogen narcosis and can't do hand signals? What then?"

"We'll deal with it."

"I'll be dead before you deal with it."

"It's not gonna happen, Webb!"

"Have you checked the dive shops on San Andres?"

"We're done talkin' about it!" screamed Lazenby. "Now tell me what I want to know."

Realizing he'd pushed Lazenby as far as he could without reaping the repercussions of his fierce temper, Jamie dropped the subject and gave him what he wanted. "No sign of it on the gun deck."

"Now we know," calmly responded Lazenby, taking a drink to wash down the bitter taste of disappointment.

"The treasure lies below the second deck if it even exists," added Jamie.

"It's there! And you'll keep searchin' till ya find it."

"I need to rest, Jack."

"You'll rest when ya done your job. A job that's not gettin' done fast enough."

"Do you know how difficult it is to move through an enclosed, underwater structure full of misplaced cannons, crates, furniture and sea life, wearing two tanks on your back and trying not to tear a hose or get pinned down if something I move causes a reaction?"

"We're anchored three miles north by northeast of Providence. At some point they're gonna get curious and wanna know what a ship this size is doin' out here. Especially since we're so close to their protected barrier reef. The last thing I want is the Marine Conservation Agency sendin' out the Columbian Coast Guard to have a look. So get the job done!"

"I can barely walk."

"Fine," conceded Lazenby after a few seconds of consideration. "You got a half hour."

"Half hour won't cut it."

"Feed him, and when his half hour's up, get him back in the water," he ordered his guards.

"When this is over…"

"Watch your tone, Webb. You know what's at stake," warned Lazenby, cutting him off mid-sentence. "There's still plenty of life left in the boy and I have no problem takin' more of it. After that, I'll start in on the girl."

"Half hour's enough," yielded Jamie.

"That's what I thought," he responded smugly, signaling the guard to take him away. As they reached the top of the stairs, Lazenby couldn't resist twisting the knife one more time by finishing Jamie's sentence. "When this is over, Webb… I'll be even more rich and you… well, that'll depend on how good a boy ya are."

A hard push against Jamie's shoulder was the signal to start down the stairs, but all he wanted to do was go at Lazenby like a pit bull—a message he sent by maintaining eye contact until he disappeared beneath the deck. They had years of history and Jamie was itching to close the book.

Watching from the top of the stairs, Lazenby reveled in the power he held over a worthy opponent and the pleasure he gleaned from tightening the links of his chains. Human beings were nothing more than tools of his trade, to be cast aside when no longer useful. Wiping the smile from his face, he turned his attention back to the detailed model of the sunken pirate ship, Maiden's Return, surrounded by plans, maps and charts.

Once the treasure was found and loaded onto his ship, there would be no announcement of his findings, no museum exhibit to view and no witnesses left to tell the tale. Finding the Aztec emperors' treasure was all about power and wealth rather than archeology or exploration. Without a drop of remorse, he swallowed the last of the bourbon, enjoying every second of the slow burn.

UNCERTAIN of what he might find, Jamie entered the overheated cabin being used as a jail cell. Not a whole lot had changed since he left them several hours earlier. As far as he was concerned, that was a good thing. The sight of his fellow captives was enough to break his heart as he found Leta holding her older brother in her arms. Gently wiping the sweat from his forehead, she was determined to make him as comfortable as possible.

"I'll be back with food," said one of the men, locking the door behind him.

"How's he doing?"

"Not much better, but no worse," quietly responded the twelve-year-old sister. "He's been sleeping since you left."

"We'll wake him when the food gets here. He needs to eat to regain his strength."

As usual, Leta nodded her head in agreement then continued to gently pat the rag against her brother's forehead.

Since their capture, Jamie had grown impressed with the young girl's strength and courage. She'd done everything he told her to do without a whimper or complaint, showing maturity beyond her years. Here's a kid who should have been playing with her friends on her day off from school, but chose to spend it at the family business, helping her older brother on the boat—a brother who only last week turned eighteen, but could easily pass for three years younger. Jamie thought of the worry and desperation their parents must be experiencing as they waited for word. He couldn't imagine being on that end of such a harrowing ordeal. In fact, his Navy experience made him more comfortable on this end. No matter what else happened, his personal mission was to return them safely to their home.

The latch on the door opened and one of the guards entered carrying a plate of sliced bread, cheese chunks and fruit, as well as a jug of water, while the other waited in the doorway, pointing a gun. "You got twenty minutes," he said coldly, then locked the door behind him.

"Let's get some water in him," said Jamie as he helped her sit him up. "Talin. Wake up. You need to drink."

Talin's eyes slowly opened as he looked around the room, trying to catch his bearings and find some comfort for the bruised muscles around his ribs. "We're still here?"

"Yes, we are," responded Jamie.

"How's the search going?"

"Slowly."

"That can't be making Mr. Lazenby happy," he responded, trying not to sound nervous. Hearing the fear in his voice, Jamie knew exactly what was going through Talin's mind. The black and blue bruises and bloody abrasions on his face and body were evidence of Lazenby's unhappiness with Jamie's results and overall 'bad' attitude. "We had a good talk. He knows I'm making progress."

"That's good, Mr. Webb."

"I'm heading down again. If it's there, I'll find it."

"And if it's not?" asked Leta.

"I'm working on that," replied Jamie with a reassuring wink. "Now eat up, both of you." Jamie handed the water jug to Talin who drank quite a bit, then passed it to Leta, who handed it back to Jamie. "You first. They'll come for you soon."

Jamie needed the hydration so he drank a good portion of the water then handed it back to Leta. The bread was stale, which made eating an exercise in survival, but no one complained. They ate in silence, staring at the walls, until Leta could no longer contain the question no one wanted to answer out loud. "What will they do with us when you find the treasure?"

"Leta, no," responded her brother, already sensing the obvious answer.

"It's all right, Talin." Jamie took a moment to find the best way to respond. "There may come a time when I ask you to do what you fear the most. Can you do that?"

"I trust you, Mr. Webb."

"Trust in me won't be enough. To have any shot at survival, you'll have to do what it takes."

"We come from a family of survivors. Right, Leta?" remarked Talin, trying to lighten the topic of conversation and reassure his kid sister that they would make it home safely. Leta wrapped her arms around her brother's neck and hugged him tightly, making it possible for Talin to exchange a sober look with Jamie behind her back. A whole lot can be said with a look.

"I can't wait to see what they're serving for dessert," joked Jamie, causing Leta to giggle as she sat back down and picked up a piece of pineapple. As much as he wanted to prepare them for what lay ahead, Talin was right to lighten the moment. Jamie's mind was trained to gather intel and use it to form a plan—exactly what he'd been doing since the moment they were captured. He already knew many of the strengths and weaknesses of the six armed guards aboard, except the two bodyguards who never left Lazenby's side. They were more like robots than men. He knew where the ship was vulnerable and the ways he could use that information. He'd mapped the layout of the ship and had already formed several escape routes. Truthfully, he would have used his skills to make a move by now, taking advantage of any moment of weakness, but he couldn't leave the siblings behind, nor would he risk Lazenby's wrath upon them if he failed.

Unexpectedly, the door opened, cutting Jamie's break time in half. What he didn't expect was to see so many guards. Two entered the room and walked toward Talin, while two more stood near the door, one inside and the other outside.

"What are you doing?" demanded Jamie.

"Mr. Lazenby wants the boy," said the guard as the two other men grabbed Talin by each arm and moved him toward the door.

"Don't take him!" cried Leta, grabbing onto his waist.

"It's okay, Leta," responded her brother, as one of the men pulled her away and threw her to the floor.

"Leave the kid alone!" yelled Jamie as he tried to impede the men's progress.

"You're coming as well," said the main guard, motioning with his gun. "Or maybe we take her instead and she can relay the message."

Jamie did his best to give a reassuring look to Leta then walked from the room. The door was latched behind them and they began the familiar walk toward the stairs. As Talin stepped on the first stair, he glanced back at Jamie, hoping for help. "Mr. Webb?"

"I'm right behind you, Talin," affirmed Jamie, uncertain as to how much more the kid could endure at the hands of someone so cruel.

Once they reached the top deck, Jamie tried to reason with Lazenby. "I've had enough rest. I'm ready to go. I'm ready to dive!"

"Of course you are. You have no choice."

"But you do, Jack. Don't hurt the kid."

"Who said I'm going to hurt him?" he asked rolling up the sleeves of his loose, white button-up shirt. "I thought he might enjoy seeing what you're doing down there."

"That's it?" asked Jamie, suspicious of his motives.

"For now."

Jamie watched as Lazenby picked up his glass from the end table then walked toward Talin. He took the kid's quivering jaw in his hand and rotated his head back and forth, admiring his handy work. "You probably don't know this, but Mr. Webb and I go way back. In fact, he's boarded my boat and the boats in my fleet many a time. When he was with the Navy he made doing business very difficult and expensive for me and enjoyed every minute of it," said Lazenby with disdain, then erratically threw his glass against a distant wall, smashing it to pieces. "Show the young captain to his chair."

One of his two bodyguards grabbed Talin by the arm and

planted him in a hard chair while the other guard tied his raw wrists tightly to the armrests.

After a moment, Lazenby continued his narration, directing his words at Talin but meaning them for Jamie. "I couldn't believe my ears when one of our divers returned from the island of Providence after fillin' tanks and said he saw Jamie Webb. Vacationing of all things. They served together for a brief time in the Navy. Jamie's got a reputation that proceeds him and one of those faces ya just don't forget. I know I haven't.

The timin' couldn't have been more perfect. I'd already lost four divers and needed someone to get the job done. Who popped into my mind but Jamie Webb, one of the best divers in the military and the man who spent years tryin' to arrest me for smugglin'. He came close. Had me in jail several times but could never close the deal. It's as though fate has brought us together for one last time. One last mission. But this time, I'm in charge. I'm callin' the shots."

"Then let me get to it," demanded Jamie, tired of listening to him.

"By all means. I'll walk ya down."

Before Jamie moved he glanced at Talin, sitting straight up in his chair, waiting for what he knew was coming. "I'll be back before you know it, Captain."

Talin attempted a smile but was unsuccessful before Jamie disappeared down the stairs.

Entering the lower deck, Jamie walked toward the hatch and began prepping for the dive. Lazenby sat down on the cleanest crate he could find in order to keep from getting dirt on his white linen pants, then stretched his legs out and crossed his sandal-wearing feet at the ankles. Confidently, he watched his two men help Jamie on with his scuba gear and accessories.

"I've spent a lot of years and money searching for the Maiden's Return and her treasure," began Lazenby.

"Many have."

"But failed... including yourself."

"My search was cut short."

"You were miles away."

"To start with," argued Jamie.

"She's been down there since 1725. That's a long time to set on the bottom of the ocean, undisturbed and undiscovered," shared Lazenby.

"Two hundred feet's not that deep in terms of exploration. If she had come to rest on the ocean floor at a hundred and seventy feet, instead of landing in that deep fissure, she would have been found years ago."

"She's been mine to find all along."

"Or maybe others have found her and not survived to tell the tale."

"Don't tell me ya grown superstitious?"

"The bodies of six of your divers are at the bottom of that abyss—if it has a bottom—all dead from supposed accidents. Something's down there... protecting it."

"Protecting what?"

"The ship. The treasure."

"Nonsense!"

"I'm only telling you what I've seen and felt."

"There's nothin' to prove it on the video feed."

"It's the truth, Jack. The deaths of your divers are proof."

"Two hundred feet is not for recreational divers."

"Most of them were ex-military with plenty of experience, wearing the highest tech available for deep dive and breathing the right mix of gases. This has nothing to do with diving depth."

"Then explain your success."

"I can't."

"Maybe you were meant to find her?"

"Now who's being superstitious?" asked Jamie as he stood up, dressed in full gear and ready to take the plunge.

"Need anything else down there?"

"I have what I need to do the job," he said, sliding a large knife into its sheath and sending an unspoken message to Lazenby.

"They probably stored the treasure in the bottom of the hull to keep it hidden."

"If it's down there, Jack, I'll find it," assured Jamie. "Don't hurt the kid while I'm gone."

"Make it a happy ending and I won't," threatened Lazenby as he pointed to the camera attached to his face mask. "Let the show begin."

Jamie put on his face mask, then grabbed onto the large cable attached to a winch, letting one of the guards lower him through the hatch and between the two large hulls of the South'n Hunter. Once he pierced the surface, he let go of the cable and disappeared into the ocean.

With a look of contempt, Lazenby bid Jamie goodbye then turned his thoughts toward the boy. Watching the grainy video feed of the exploration was interesting, but toying with the kid's emotions made the time between dives much more entertaining. With pleasure, he crossed the deck and bounced up the stairs to his home away from home.

Hearing the sound of footsteps ascending the metal staircase, Talin prepared himself as best he could for his oppressor's arrival. Keeping his eyes focused straight ahead, he could still see him approaching in his peripheral vision. The kid froze as he felt Lazenby's cold hand grip the back of his neck and squeeze tightly. He knew what was coming, so he closed his eyes and held his breath as though it would help lessen the blows.

"How's your sister holding up?"

Surprised by what appeared to be concern, Talin opened his eyes, uncertain as to how to respond.

"Your little sister, how's she doing?" he asked again, releasing his hold on the boy's neck.

"She... she's scared."

"One way or another, this ought to be over soon and ya can take her back home. Would you like that, son?"

"Yes," answered Talin, relaxing a bit in lieu of his supposed kindness.

"How about a drink?" asked Lazenby, then ordered his two bodyguards to untie one of his hands and get him a glass. "After all, what's a good movie without snacks and liquid refreshment?"

"I'm... I'm not thirsty," he stuttered, gripping the armrest in an attempt to steady his shaking as the man shoved a glass into his free hand.

"Who said anything about being thirsty? It'll calm your nerves. Drink it!" demanded Lazenby, lowering himself to the armrest of a nearby couch to better look the boy in the eye.

Recognizing the change of tone in his voice, Talin lifted the glass, but couldn't stop shaking enough to guide it to his mouth. Scared he was going to spill the contents, he lowered it back down, apologizing profusely until Lazenby demanded his silence. "When I tell someone to do somethin', boy, I expect it done."

"I'm... I'm sorry."

"Do you know why you're here?"

"Right now or... or in general?"

"Right now," laughed Lazenby, mocking his innocence. "I brought you up here to save a few glasses when I lose my temper. I'm starting to run low. Understand?"

"Why punish me?"

"To punish Webb. Now drink!"

More than anything, Talin wanted to return to Leta no worse for the wear, but he knew the odds were stacked against him. To Lazenby, he was nothing more than a punching bag, valued less than the glass he held in his hand. He knew what was coming, and yet for the first time in three days of captivity, he felt emboldened. Facing down his fear, Talin looked his torturer straight in the eye and made a choice to act rather than react. With new fortitude, he placed the drink on a nearby counter and without a stutter responded to his captor's threat. "I said I'm not thirsty."

Surprised by the kid's response, Lazenby backhanded him hard across the cheek, his gold, diamond-filled fleur de lis ring slicing through his skin. "You'll live to regret that, boy," he warned, then ordered one of his bodyguards to tie his wrist to the chair as he sat down on the couch and turned on the monitor.

Hiding a defiant smile behind his enemy's back, Talin felt a level of valiance he'd never known. In a matter of seconds he'd gone from boy to man, and age had nothing to do with it. Was a beat down imminent? Most likely. But Lazenby was wrong if he thought he would live to regret not cowering to his brutality.

SHIPWRECK of the Maiden's Return

With the skilled use of his fins, Jamie propelled himself toward the exploration site. In order to get the most time he could from each dive, he managed his physical exertion to control the need for heavy breathing. He needed the gases in his tanks to last as long as possible each trip.

This time he approached the ship from a different direction. He wanted to better examine the ornamentation on the front of the bow so he entered the chasm ahead of the ship and swam down the narrow canyon. As he approached the ship, his dive lights lit up the bowsprit and the beautiful figurehead of a mermaid beneath it. Slowly, he traced the lines of her face with the fingers of both hands in awe of the beautiful workmanship.

Carved from a piece of elm, the details were magnificent. She appeared lifelike with a wide-eyed, youthful expression surrounded by layers of wavy hair. Lowering himself beneath the figurehead, he found her arms extended, holding a queen conch shell with both hands, eager to show it to the world. Sliding his hands down her body, he examined the gold and silver scales that extended from her waist to her tail, then twisted up at the caudal fin. It was one of the most beautiful pieces of art Jamie had ever seen, and if he could take anything back from the Caribbean, it would be her.

All at once, he felt the same sensation as before move past him in every direction. He continued to hold tightly to the mermaid's waist as his body was bunted from every angle, swinging him back and forth. He'd been assaulted by the mysterious entity several times, and though it was terrifying, Jamie was learning how to better cope with it.

Eventually, the mysterious force disappeared, leaving him free to move toward the top deck where he turned on the lights attached to the broken mast. Instantly, the wreckage came to life. As far as Jamie knew, the Maiden's Return hadn't been disturbed for nearly three centuries until Lazenby's divers came aboard and started moving things around.

Most of the wood should have rotted away after nearly three hundred years, so the fact that she was still intact was a scientific phenomenon. For a moment, he wondered if the invisible force that kept attacking him had something to do with the preservation of the Maiden's Return—a question that may never be answered. Long story short, she was an unbelievable sight that belonged in a museum, and if this were his own discovery, he'd be enjoying every minute of the search.

According to Lazenby's model of the ship, the Maiden's Return had four decks: the top deck and three below. He'd already searched through the captain's quarters on the top deck, located at the stern, as well as the gun deck below, which also housed the kitchen and galley and doubled as crew quarters. This was no easy task when worried about ripping hoses and other equipment on cannons, chairs, jagged pieces of lumber and all manner of debris. Next came the third deck down which was home to the capstan, the winding machine used for lowering and raising the anchor. Anything could go wrong down there, including the collapse of the entire ship.

Jamie knew the lowest deck would be the most difficult. That's usually where the ship's store of food and cargo were located. He expected to find it full of cannon balls, barrels, piles of spare sail, rolls of heavy rope, nails to repair the wood, and extra lumber, not to mention the heavy rocks at the bottom of the bilge designed to keep the ship stable.

The last battle had done a number on the ship and the scars of the conflict were visible. What Jamie found strange was that it looked like the holes and splintered lumber had been roughly patched over the years. Examining the patchwork more closely, Jamie wondered why anyone would repair a sunken ship. More than that, he was curious to know who had done it.

Turning toward the companionway, he used his hands to walk himself down the stairs leading from the main deck to the gun deck beneath. Locating the opening to the lower deck, he pulled himself down the ladder and made his way into the darkness of the third deck.

As much as Jamie hated diving for Lazenby, he hated diving alone worse. It was risky. He had no one to watch his back and no one to come for him if something went wrong. And anything could go wrong. But that was the hand he was dealt and he would play it to the end.

Chapter Six

*R*ising at daybreak, Rome put on a pair of plaid board shorts and a tank top then picked up the white, linen shirt Heath had left behind and pressed it to her face. Breathing in the light scent of his cologne, she left her room and walked to his door. Stopping short of knocking, she decided to let him sleep instead, then headed up the trail toward Jonah's backyard.

The birds were busy greeting each other as Rome approached the edge of the cliff next to the patio. Although she was exhausted, worry had made it difficult to sleep and the absence of the spirit who approached her in Hawaii added to her concerns. "Maybe I'm too late," she said to herself. "What if that's why the spirit hasn't shown herself?"

She didn't expect the spirit with the long black hair to meet her at the airport, but she thought she'd see her sooner than this. "Where are you?" she asked loudly overlooking the island, "I need your help."

"I'm happy to help with whatever you need," responded Jonah from the deck above, surprising Rome with his presence. "But you weren't talking to me, were you?"

"Jonah! I didn't expect anyone to be up yet."

"I never miss feeling the sun rise each morning."

"Feeling?"

"On my face. That's how I know another glorious day has arrived. What brings you out so early?"

"I have a lot on my mind."

"More than most, I think."

"Why do you say that?"

"Just a feeling."

"Like the sun on your face?"

"Or a voice inside your head," said Jonah with a smile, indicating he knew more than he was letting on. "Come inside. Let us start the day together." Jonah stood up and disappeared from the deck as Rome put on Heath's shirt and walked toward the house.

Confused by his insinuation, she pondered his words as she stepped through the sliding door just as Jonah reached the bottom of the stairs.

"Normally, my guests don't roll out of bed at daybreak."

"If this were a vacation, I probably wouldn't either," responded Rome as she followed him through the house.

"Somehow I doubt that to be true."

"Based on what?"

"Your need to see the world around you."

"When I'm on assignment, maybe," countered Rome as they entered the kitchen.

"Did you pick your job or did your job pick you?"

"A bit of both, I suppose."

"One of the lucky ones."

"Lucky ones?"

"'Choose a job you love and you'll never have to work a day in your life,'" quoted Jonah, grabbing two glasses from the cupboard and placing them on the table.

"A student of Confucius."

"Truth is truth, no matter who coins the phrase."

"Then in the spirit of truth... you're right. I rarely sleep in."

"It's the sunriser special for you," announced Jonah, turning to the refrigerator and pulling out a pitcher of coconut milk. Rome watched as he poured the perfect amount into the blender then returned to the fridge for a dish of leftover fruit from last night's supper and emptied it in as well.

"What's the sunriser special?"

"The perfect way to fire up your engine," answered Jonah, peeling a couple of bananas and adding them to the mix. "Now for the special ingredients." Without missing a beat, he began opening lids to containers, smelling the contents, then choosing the right measurement of each. A pinch here, a squeeze there and a scoop or two of the good stuff.

"What are you putting in there?"

"The fire."

Placing the lid on the blender, he pushed the magic button and let her rip. Within seconds, Jonah filled the two glasses with a delicious breakfast pick-me-up and handed one to his guest.

In awe of what she'd witnessed, Rome was speechless as she took the glass from Jonah's hand. If she hadn't already known he was blind, she never would have believed it after watching him prepare his signature drink.

"To a new day. May you find the one you seek."

Clinking their glasses together, they drank to the toast.

"That's delicious. I've never tasted anything like it."

"Odds are, you never will again... except maybe tomorrow, and the next day. But only at sunrise."

"The perfect start to my day."

"You'll be in need of it."

"Why?"

"I hear they're close to calling off the search."

"How close?"

"Today or tomorrow."

"They can't do that!"

"It's a big ocean, Rome."

"They need to keep looking."

"Many be lost at sea and never found."

"I have to find him."

"Six months ago, I would have asked a good friend to come to your aide, but that's no longer an option."

"Why?"

"He suffered an ischemic stroke."

"I'm sorry to hear that."

"His daughter brings him up three times a week for physical therapy. We've made progress, but some paralysis remains."

"How could he have helped in the search?"

"Dr. Orlando Melgosa is a marine biologist who spent years studying the sea life in the Archipelago of Providencia, San Andres and Santa Catalina. Our reef is the third largest in the world. Eventually, he retired here instead of returning to Mexico City."

"He would have made a great resource."

"Not to mention all of his scientific equipment."

"Pretty advanced?" asked Rome as she took another drink.

"Top of the line."

"Has he helped in searches before?"

"Often. Hopefully he will again."

"You think highly of him."

"As both a man and a scientist. Orlando has a brilliant mind. I'm working to free it again, as well as his muscles."

"It's amazing what we do for those we care about."

"Like your missing friend."

"We will find him."

"It seems you know something the US and Columbian Navies don't."

"I know Jamie."

"Not much to go on."

"I have a few other tricks up my sleeve," claimed Rome as she finished off her drink.

"I suspect as much."

"Do you have a car I could borrow?"

"And what would a blind man be doing with a car?"

"Good point."

"I do have a motorcycle."

"I'll only be gone for an hour or so."

"Come with me," said Jonah as he put down his drink and walked out of the room. Rome followed him through the house and out to the carport on the other side, where he pulled a tarp off a brightly-colored, older-model motorcycle with an attached sidecar. "This was my means of making house calls when I practiced medicine. She knows the island well."

"She's very colorful."

"Like an ambulance. People will be seeing you coming."

"I'm sure they will, especially with this tall flagpole. A red cross insignia on the flag seems appropriate."

"Many times I was the ambulance. Have you driven one?"

"I had a scooter in college."

"Scooter, motorcycle... it's all good."

"If you say so."

"It's the island way."

"That seems to be the answer to everything."

"Only the things that matter. Let's push it to the top of the drive. You steer."

Rome grabbed onto the handlebars and steered it along. Once they reached the top of the hill, she straddled the bike while Jonah took a moment to brief her on the controls and unique quirks. He then pulled a bright green, opened-face, skull cap-style helmet from the side car and handed it to Rome.

"Break anything but the spine, neck and brain."

"Everything else can be fixed?" asked Rome rhetorically as she placed the helmet on her head and connected the chin strap.

"For the most part."

"I need to find a beach, Jonah."

"We're an island. You're surrounded by beach."

"A quiet one that I can find easily."

"Try Almond Beach. Stop when you see the octopus. Just stick to the road and look for the sign."

"Which road?"

"The only one that circles the island."

"Almond Beach. Sounds perfect. I hope I don't wake the entire island."

"I had a special noise reducing muffler put on her years ago."
"The island way?"
"It's not my right to take away other's peace and quiet."
"You're a good man, Jonah."
"I'll give you a push down the hill."
"Isn't there a starter?"
"Of course, but it no longer works."
"That's reassuring."
"Turn on the key, pull in the clutch and put it in second gear—less kick back than first. When you get about halfway down, let go of the clutch and be hanging on tight. Are you ready?"
"No, but let's do it."

Rome did as Jonah suggested and white-knuckled the grips as she began to roll down the steep drive. Both the speed of the bike and Rome's pulse increased rapidly, but she remained focused on Jonah's instructions. Nearing the end of the drive, she let out the clutch, which followed with a jerk and sound of the engine engaging. She quickly gained control of the bike and with a shout of excitement was off to destinations yet to be discovered. Her plan was to find a quiet beach and hope the mystery spirit would show up like in Hawaii.

Hearing the sound of the engine purr and Rome's subsequent cheer put Jonah's mind to rest as he returned to the house to continue his morning ritual. Just as he entered, a memory from his youth struck his mind. As a young man, he met a lady while playing on the beach. The woman's youthful appearance was striking with her black hair pulled back in a tight bun and a large pink flower tucked above her ear. She was visiting the neighboring island of San Andres and had travelled by boat to Providence in search of a particular person. Jonah knew of the elderly woman she sought, once a well-known figure on the island. But after her husband's accidental death she had shut herself away.

He remembered guiding her to the woman's home just up the beach from his location, then hiding behind a wall of the open-air room to eavesdrop. He listened as she spoke to the elderly widow with a beautiful Italian accent, telling the woman she was there to deliver a message from her husband. This piqued Jonah's interest even more than the strange feeling he had when she first approached him on the beach. Unfortunately, a neighbor lady caught him spying on the conversation and shooed him away from the house with her broom. After the elderly woman's encounter with the mysterious Italian, she returned to an active life on the island and no one ever knew what caused the change to take place.

Standing alone in the quiet of his kitchen, Jonah realized that the familiarity he felt with Rome was the same strange feeling he felt with the woman on the beach all those years ago. Even the voices seemed similar, minus the accent.

FEELING ONE WITH THE MOTORBIKE, Rome cruised down the mountain and rolled through town, Heath's white shirt flapping in the breeze like a cape. The morning air was refreshing as it blew past her face, clearing out enough worry to allow her to enjoy the drive. The roadsides were an alternate pairing of lush green trees and power poles, coupled with intermittent views of the ocean as she continued down Route 03, taking in the island as it slowly came to life.

Finally, she came upon the entrance to Almond Bay, guarded by the eight-legged octopus gazebo just as Jonah had described. After surveying the grade of the road, she decided there was enough of a slope to get her bike started once she returned from the beach, so she parked it and began to mosey down the trail. It was a beautiful walk off the beaten path, and although Rome tried to control the urge to run, she felt her speed increasing with every step. The thought of finding the spirit with the answer to Jamie's whereabouts meant more than enjoying a nice morning stroll. Soon her speed walking turned into a full-scale run, dashing down the rest of the trail and bursting onto the beach.

The view of the ocean took her breath away as she panned the horizon, eventually ending with a view of the smaller island of Santa Catalina to her right. The water was an inviting blend of turquoise blues and greens and Rome found herself wishing she was on vacation with snorkel, mask and fins in hand. But that was not what brought her to Almond Beach. Time moved slowly as she walked up and down the shore. With each passing minute she remained the sole visitor to the beach. An hour had passed and still no sign of the mystery spirit who visited her in Hawaii.

Knowing Heath would be waking soon, she decided to accept defeat and head back. But Rome hated defeat, so she allowed the hypnotic sound of the waves lapping the shore to convince her that a swim would be a suitable reward. After quickly removing her watch, white shirt and shoes, she ran into the water and began swimming against the surf. The energy required to power through the rolling water was just what she needed as a release for her frustrations. She continued to swim harder and faster, finding victory in each stroke. The therapy of pushing herself focused Rome to the point of losing track of the distance traveled. Reaching the peak of her endurance, Rome stopped swimming and turned back toward the shore. She was surprised to see how far she had gone, but looked forward to a leisurely return.

Without warning, the spirit she had been searching for appeared next to her in the water. "They're coming for you. Get to shore!"

"Who's coming for me?" Before Rome could get an answer, she felt something wrap around both of her ankles and begin pulling her down. Panic struck as she fought to keep her head above the water. She screamed for help, but there was no one to hear her cry. The only thing she could do was get as much air in her lungs as possible before being pulled beneath the surface.

Once submerged, she bent toward her feet, surprised to see the ghosts of two men pulling her toward the bottom. With the help of the female spirit, she fought to free herself from their clutches. Their grip was tight, but it was no match for the strength of human hands. Rome worked feverishly to escape their grasp as the air in her lungs had all but dissipated. Finally free, she swam to the top, bursting out of the water and filling her lungs with oxygen.

Rome worked to catch her breath as she began to swim to shore, but the ghosts below were not giving up that easily. Again, she felt their grip on her legs and this time around her waist, forcing her down. Once beneath, she saw more ghosts swimming in every direction, pulling her one way, then the other, causing her to briefly lose her frame of reference.

Again, she burst out of the water with only enough time to gasp for air, then back to the fight for her life. Although much of her strength had been drained, she continued her struggle for survival, each time finding it more difficult to reach the surface and uncertain as to how much longer she could last. No longer able to hold her breath, the mystery spirit pushed her to the surface just long enough to get a bit of air before being yanked below.

Growing limp from exhaustion and oxygen deprivation, Rome's objective started to change. She began to accept that she was fighting a losing battle from which there was no escape. Her need to rest, to close her eyes and float away in the warm waters of the Caribbean, chipped away at her stamina, until Rome did the unthinkable - she conceded defeat. Releasing the last bit of air from her lungs, she gave up the fight, allowing the ghosts to freely take hold of her body.

With Rome's last bit of consciousness, she felt someone take hold of her wrist, pulling against the direction of the ghosts. Before she knew it, her head was above the water.

"Breathe, Rome, breathe!"

Coughing up what felt like a bucket of water, Rome struggled to get air into her lungs as the man wrapped his arm around her chest and slowly pulled her back to shore. As they approached the beach, her rescuer helped Rome crawl out of the water until she collapse onto the sand. Feeling less disoriented, she recognized the man sitting next to her. It was Heath. He had come to her rescue and saved her from certain death. She half expected him to be lecturing her on the dangers of swimming in the ocean alone, but he just sat there, trying to catch his breath while staring at the ocean in silence.

"Heath?"

No response.

"How did you know I was here?"

"Jonah."

"How did you get here?"

"Bummed a ride with his neighbor," answered Heath abruptly as he stood up and extended his hand to Rome. "Can you walk?"

"I think so," responded Rome as she used Heath's strength to crawl to her feet, her legs weak from the battle.

"I'll see you back at Jonah's."

Rome watched as Heath walked away leaving her standing on the beach alone. She had survived a near-death experience and whatever Heath was experiencing could not compare to what she had gone through. Reaching down, she put on her shoes, shirt and wristwatch then slowly made her way to the trail. Thoughts of doing things differently played in hindsight as her mind continued to process. She could have left a note or shared her plan with Heath, but Rome wasn't used to having someone in tow when she travelled. She had her own schedule and ran each day according to her own plans.

The further she walked, the better her legs felt, and about halfway up the trail, she saw a much-needed sight, Heath pacing back and forth. Although happy to see him, she knew that look on his face. The lecture she had expected earlier was about to hit. What she got, however, was unexpected. Heath took her in his arm and held her tightly, whispering in her ear. "What if I hadn't come after you? What if I'd been a minute late… thirty-seconds late? I've already lost the two people I loved most in my life. I can't lose you, Rome. I can't go through that again."

Rome was silent as she digested why he left her alone on the beach. The fear of losing her was more than he could deal with at that moment. He needed space and she had to respect that. Softly she responded by wrapping her arms around his neck. "Thank you, Heath. Thank you for coming." Rome knew this moment belonged to Heath, so she waited until he was ready to let go.

Slowly he loosened his embrace and took hold of her hand. Together they started up the trail. "So what happened out there?"

"I was attacked by a group of ghosts."

"What?"

"I came to the beach this morning hoping to find the spirit that brought me here. I thought being alone would make a difference. When she didn't show up, I decided to take a quick swim before heading back."

"What did the ghosts want?"

"My life."

"Do you think the spirit you're looking for led you into a trap?"

"No. She warned me they were coming, but it was too late."

"So she did show up."

"She tried to help me fight them off, but there were too many."

"From now on... I'm not letting you out of my sight."

"Until we find Jamie, I may take you up on that."

"I'm serious, Rome."

"After nearly drowning, so am I."

"Let's get you back so you can rest."

"I'll rest after we find Jamie."

"You need to build your strength up."

"Jonah said they may call off the search today. They're giving up on him. We can't."

"So what's next?"

"Let's retrace his steps."

"Okay."

"But first a shower and something to eat. I'm starving."

"And she's back," said Heath with delight in his voice as they continued their stroll up the trail, making plans for the rest of the day.

In the recesses of her mind, however, Rome knew her experience in the ocean had changed her. She now understood a deeper fear and the horrors that accompany it. From now on, that level of fear would be the touchstone she would measure everything against.

Heath had a point. They were better together and Rome needed to convert to that way of thinking, not only for her safety, but for the sake of their relationship. She loved the freedom of traveling by herself for work, but this was life, a life with someone in it.

Reaching the road, Rome educated Heath on the motorcycle's starting procedure, and with his pushing strength, she fired right up. As Heath approached the bike, Rome pointed her thumb to the sidecar. "Looking for a ride, sailor?" Swallowing his manly pride, he squeezed his tall frame into the rig and away they went.

Following a late breakfast and a change of clothes, they were back at it. This time Rome generously let Heath drive, allowing her to navigate from the sidecar. Ross had told her where Jamie had been staying before his disappearance and she thought that might be a good place to start. Circling the circumference of the island, they eventually located Jamie's cabana. It was a beautiful location, within a stone's throw of the water and camouflaged by lush palm trees.

Jamie's room was easy to find due to the yellow caution tape stretched across the doorway. Twisting the door knob, she was surprised to find it unlocked which made entering the cabana easier than they thought. Bending over she swung herself beneath the tape and entered the room. Heath followed, leaving the door open behind him. As expected, Jamie's belongings had been confiscated as evidence, leaving the room empty. They wandered through the small cabana hoping to find the mystery spirit from the beach, but that was not the case.

Without warning, a boy's head popped around the corner of the wall, causing Rome to jump.

"When I saw the open door, I hoped to find Mr. Webb inside," spoke the scrawny young boy.

"That would be nice," responded Rome.

"Does he owe you money too?"

"No, we're friends. How do you know Mr. Webb?"

"I am his guide."

"Aren't you a little young to be employed as a guide?" asked Heath.

"My knowledge of the island makes up for lack of years."

"So you know the island well?" enquired Rome.

"Every foot of it, ma'am. No one knows it better."

"That's quite a statement to make for a ten year old," said Heath, skeptical of the boy's verbal resume.

"Good thing I'm twelve," responded Martin with a smile that stretched from ear to ear.

"Two years makes that much difference?"

"No, sir, but experience does."

"So why are you really here?"

"Hoping to get paid."

"Jamie hadn't paid you?" asked Rome, interrupting Heath's inquisition.

"He said he would make it worth my while if I worked hard for him."

"But then he disappeared," pointed out Rome.

"Mr. Webb was a good man."

"IS a good man."

"You believe he's alive as I do?"

"Yes."

"Then that doubles my hope of being paid."

"In the meantime, we could use a guide."

"I'm your boy, ma'am."

"Does our young guide have a name?"

"Martin."

"Well, Martin, when can you start?"

"Anytime. Day or night."

"You have no other responsibilities?"

"I have to check in on my aunt every now and then."

"We can make that work."

"Do you know where Jamie chartered his boat?"

"Yes, ma'am."

"I hope you had a good breakfast, 'cause you're in for a long day."

"My aunt was still asleep when I left this morning. I did not want to wake her."

"We'll grab something at the marina," said Heath.

"I never turn down free food, boss."

"That's one thing you two have in common," responded Heath with a wink at Rome. "Let's get out of here."

"Okay, ma'am."

Together they walked back through the cabana, bent under the caution tape and left the room as they found it. As Martin closed the door, his thoughts turned to his missing employer. Tourists came and went in Martin's life and he never formed attachments. But Jamie was different. The short time he spent as his guide was the best experience he'd had so far in his young career. Although disappointed that he was never compensated, Martin enjoyed being around Jamie and learning from his strange ways. He was full of advice, both practical and not, and Martin sucked up every bit, especially in the self-defense category.

He was on the doorstep of his cabana the minute Jamie opened the door to begin the day and said goodbye long after the sun set. He wanted to go on the boat with him, but both he and Jamie knew his aunt had to come first. Having never known his father, the boy had spent the first twelve years of life imagining what he would be like, or better yet, what he wanted him to be like. Jamie fit the bill perfectly. He was adventurous and smart, but most importantly, he treated the boy like a friend. And Martin felt the same in return.

Once they reached the motorcycle, Martin recognized the bike and knew just what to do. "I'll push."

"No, I'll push. Get in the side car and put on the helmet," ordered Rome.

"If you say so, ma'am."

"I'll be the one pushing. Get on the bike, Rome."

"Such a gentleman," she said as she walked around the back of the bike and straddled the seat.

"You know, we could just rent a car or even a motorbike with a starter," suggested Heath.

"Where would the fun be in that?"

"So now we're here to have fun?" countered Heath as he placed his hands on the back of the bike and began to easily push it down the hill.

"Don't mind Heath, Martin, it's been a rough start to the day," she said popping the clutch and driving a ways down the road before turning around and heading back up the hill. Heath straddled the back of the bike and wrapped his arms around Rome's waist.

"Definitely better than the sidecar," he whispered in her ear.

"Agreed."

FOLLOWING MARTIN'S DIRECTIONS, Rome drove to the harbor near the ferry terminal where Jamie last chartered a boat—the same boat he'd used for three days without incident. Upon arrival, they noticed a small U.S. Navy littoral combat ship anchored about a half mile off shore. Rome spun around looking for the helicopter and finally located it on the outskirts of town. Soon the door of a building opened and several military men exited, shook hands and went their separate ways. Half were U.S. Navy and the other half, Columbian military.

Without thinking of restarting the bike, Rome immediately parked on the side of the flat road and hurried toward the naval officer. Catching up with the U.S. captain, she introduced herself. "I'm Rome London and this is Heath Jones."

"An official from the State Department informed us of your arrival. I'm afraid there's nothing new in the search to report."

"Search and RESCUE," clarified Rome, testing the waters to see if they had given up on finding Jamie alive.

"Of course."

"I'm sure Ross... the State Department, informed you of how valuable I can be to this mission."

"With all due respect, Ms. London, whatever you think you have to offer, it could not possibly rival what the U.S. Navy has already tried."

"I have intimate knowledge of the missing man," she argued.

"We've combed these waters for the past several days, boarded boats of all kinds and have found no sign of Mr. Webb or the two others that went missing with him. The aircrew has been out all morning searching with the helicopter and still nothing. "

"Could we accompany you on your search today?" enquired Heath.

"You'd need special clearance and that's not possible at this late date," responded the Lieutenant.

"I could get it by tomorrow," negotiated Rome.

"We're not returning to Providencia tonight."

"Why not?"

"Our orders are to suspend the search at day's end."

"You can't just leave them out there!" exclaimed Rome.

"This is a joint search effort,"

"Search and rescue effort," countered Rome.

"The search and rescue effort being carried out by the Columbian National Navy from their naval base on the neighboring island of San Andres will continue. We'll stay in close contact with them," said the captain as the helicopter's engine started.

"Jamie's an American. You can't abandon him like this," yelled Rome.

"We have every confidence in the Columbian Navy's search efforts, ma'am, and your contact at the State Department will be made aware of any findings going forward," responded the Lieutenant loudly enough to be heard over the chopper, then he handed her his business card. "Here's my contact information if you do find anything." Without another word, the captain boarded the chopper and left the island. With no options left, Heath and Rome watched the helicopter fly to the distant naval ship and land on the helideck at the stern.

"What now, Rome?"

"I'm not sure. Without help from the spirit who brought us here, I'm useless to Jamie."

"So call her," suggested Heath.

"Call her?"

"You've done it before."

"Once. I don't even know the mystery spirit's name."

"She knows you're here, so there's got to be a reason she's not contacting you."

"Don't say it, Heath."

"Say what?"

"The same thing I've been thinking. That Jamie's dead and there's no point in contacting me now."

"She wouldn't bring you all the way to the Caribbean without telling you of Jamie's fate."

"Then what else is keeping her away?"

"Maybe she's in danger."

"How can a spirit be in danger?"

"I'm just throwing out possibilities."

"I know."

"I think your initial idea of meeting her alone on a beach was a good one."

"Really?"

"Just don't follow it up with a swim this time," advised Heath as he prepared to push the motorcycle.

"Good advice."

"Why don't we find a beach with a food shack on it? That way I can get the kid something to eat while I keep an eye on you."

"No argument here," she said approaching the motorbike.

"Any news on Mr. Webb?" asked Martin.

"Nothing so far. Why don't we find you something to eat?"

"Somewhere on the beach, off the beaten path," specified Heath.

"I know a place."

"Good. Let's find us a hill."

"Better yet, let's find a bike shop and get a starter installed," recommended Heath

"No time. Your turn to drive."

"After we get it started," insisted Heath. "It's going to take all three of us to get enough momentum."

Rome took hold of the handlebars, while Heath and Martin increased its speed with each step. Halfway down the street, she began to giggle at the irony of a billionaire pushing an old motorbike down the street when with the snap of a finger he could buy every bike on the island, new or used.

"What's so funny up there?" asked Heath from the rear.

"Just thinking of the things we do for love."

"Less thinking, more pushing. Right Martin?"

"If you say so, boss."

"Jump on!" yelled Heath as they continued to run at full force.

Rome leaped onto the bike and with a pop of the clutch they were back in action, their efforts applauded by some locals from the side of the street. Rome waved unassumingly as she brought the bike to a stop and waited for Heath and Martin to catch up. Sliding back, she let Heath straddle the driver's seat as Martin crawled into the sidecar and put on his helmet, happily continuing his wave to the crowd. Heath, on the other hand, wasted no time in getting out of town. Being a spectacle was not his thing.

Back on the road, Rome enjoyed watching Heath's wavy hair dance in the wind, while working to keep her own messy strands from disrupting her view. With the warmth of the sun on her back, Rome found herself in heaven as she wrapped her arms around Heath's waist and laid the side of her head against his back.

Watching the scenery go by, Rome felt a tinge of guilt over the pleasure she was experiencing. "If this road were only in Hawaii," she thought to herself. But she knew it wasn't. They'd been on the island for twenty-four hours and had made zero progress. Not one lead. She was useless to Jamie without the eyes and ears of the spirit who asked for her help. No wonder the Navy captain dismissed her so easily. He was right. She had nothing to offer the search. She was nothing more than a body. Pulling back from the negative thoughts, Rome breathed in the good air and let out the bad as she closed her eyes, letting the peace of the island wash over her.

Chapter Seven

Once again, Martin proved his ability as a first-rate guide by leading them to an out-of-the-way, brightly-painted rum shack on a secluded beach.

"Are you old enough to be in here?" asked Heath.

"In where? There are no walls."

"You know what I mean."

"Do not worry, boss, I come for the fish," said Martin as he walked through the mismatched tables and chairs scattered beneath the trees, greeting everyone like they were his best friends.

"Who is this kid?" asked Heath as he surveyed the seating area, locating the perfect spot. "That table will allow me to see down the length of the beach. I'll have eyes on you the entire time. Do not leave the beach."

"I feel safer already," responded Rome as she kissed him goodbye and started down the lengthy shore. Heath did as he promised and kept his eyes on her as he made his way to the table and sat down. He continued to watch as Rome moved further and further away, causing the confidence he had in his plan to waiver. The greater the distance between them grew, the more concerned he became, until he was forced to accept the fact that his hands were tied.

THE LONGER ROME walked the more discouraged she felt. It was daybreak all over again. "Hello. I'm here," she repeated for probably the fiftieth time, but still no response. "If you can hear me, I need to talk to you."

"I am here," came a voice from the thick grove next to the beach.

Rome stopped and looked deep into the trees, straining to find the source of the voice. Soon she saw the spirit's familiar face camouflaged in the greenery.

"Come into the forest," coaxed the spirit.

Rome knew better than to leave the beach, so she countered. "You come out."

"I can't. They'll see me."

"No one can see you but me."

"For your safety, you must come into the trees." Rome looked down the shoreline toward a distant Heath, hearing his final words ringing in her ears, "don't leave the beach." Chalking it up to 'the island way,' she knew what she had to do.

IT WASN'T LONG before Martin returned with what appeared to be a sampler plate full of seafood and fruit and placed it in the middle of the table. "I'll be back," he said, before running to the bar.

Even the delicious smell of the food couldn't distract Heath from his assignment as he watched Rome so far away. Quickly, Martin returned holding three hollowed-out coconut shells and set them carefully down on the table. "You're going to love these, boss."

Distracted from Rome, Heath watched him place the coconut

shells evenly spaced around the table. "They didn't sell you alcohol did they?"

"No, boss. Just a special blend of juice. No rum."

"Good."

"Try it."

Heath picked up the coconut and took a sip from the straw. "That's good." Taking another sip, his eyes returned to the beach. Unable to locate Rome, he dropped the coconut to the ground and jumped from his chair. "Stay here while I find Rome."

Martin pulled the tray of food toward him as he watched Heath burst from the table like a track star. Not understanding the urgency, Martin enjoyed his lunch, hoping his clients would return and not mysteriously disappear like the last one.

HOPING Heath would understand why she left the beach, Rome continued over and through the undergrowth. "I don't think we've been properly introduced. My name is Rome London."

"I know who you are."

"How?"

"Your friend, he called your name many times."

"You were with him?"

"Not that he knew. Or perhaps he did."

"What do you mean?"

"That is how I knew where to find you."

"Jamie told you I was on Kauai?"

"Not me particular. He just kept saying it out loud. He even knew the address of your beach house."

"Of course he did."

"He spoke much of you."

"Then you know more about me than I do you."

"People call me the mermaid."

"Mermaids don't exist."

"To superstitious pirates they do."

"Weren't all pirates superstitious?"

"All that I knew."

"So what's your real name?"

"Karukera. But I go by Kera."

"What does it mean?"

"It is Arawak for, 'Island of Beautiful Waters.' My father chose it. He said it reminded him of the island that saved his life after he washed ashore."

"It sounds like you were very close."

"We were," she said reaching out and taking hold of her hand, allowing Rome access to the deep recesses of her memory.

SMALL ISLAND IN THE CARIBBEAN, 1719.

Kera, as a child of thirteen years of age, burst out of the turquoise ocean, sucking in as much air as she could. She had dove deep searching for more keepsakes to add to her collection and wanted to examine one of her largest shells in the sunlight. Happy with her find, she returned the shell to the safety of the bag she wore around her neck, then stretched her body flat on the surface, allowing her long black hair to float in all directions. Not only was she diving for shells that afternoon, but she was waiting for her father to return from fishing with some of the men from their village.

Turning her head to the side, she saw them approaching from a distance and began to swim toward shore. She was a powerful swimmer for such a young age and beat them back with a couple of minutes to spare. As the boat rowed closer, she began jumping up and down, waving her arms as though they needed a guide to find their way back.

Reaching the shore, the men leaped into the shallow water and pulled the boat aground as Falcon Locke greeted his daughter with the hug she had waited for all day. "How's my little mermaid this afternoon?"

"Wonderful, Father. Look what I found," she responded excitedly showing him her prize conch shell.

"What a lovely treasure, but not as beautiful as you."

"You always say that."

"I only speak the truth."

"You always say that too." Wanting to help her father, she grabbed an armful of large fish from the boat and held them tightly next to her chest in an attempt to keep them from slipping through her arms. Falcon loved his daughter very much but never missed an opportunity to groom her in the ways of being a young lady.

"See how you're manhandling those fish."

"Yes, Father."

"How would a proper lady in England carry them?"

"I don't think a proper lady in England would touch a fish," responded Kera, causing her father to chuckle at her innocent candor.

"You've listened well over the years. Maybe a little too well," replied her father as they walked off the beach.

No father could be more proud of their daughter than Falcon Locke and Kera knew it. As a captain in the British Navy, he never planned to marry or raise a child, especially when traveling the globe for king and country. He accepted that fact when he was commissioned as captain and given his own ship to sail. Having lost his parents at a very young age, he was raised by his uncle, who had a stellar career in the Navy, which really meant he was raised by his uncle's servants. His life was mapped out for him the minute he arrived at his uncles's estate and he never strayed from the plan.

If he hadn't lost his ship in battle and washed ashore on the small island, he would never have known what it felt like to love so deeply or even at all. The years he'd spent stranded had taught him more about himself than any other time in his life and had changed him from a scrawny, pale-skinned sailor to a tanned and brawny islander. Although it was extremely primitive, he wouldn't trade it for anything merry-old England had to offer.

Once they reached the village and the fish were divided, Kera and her mother began preparing dinner over the fire. Falcon considered himself to be the luckiest man in the world as he watched his beautiful wife work her magic on a simple piece of fish, her long, black hair coiled in a knot at the base of her neck. All the other dinner items had been prepared previously and she'd been waiting for the main dish to arrive. Completely content, he picked up a well-worn copy of the only book on the island, a 1640 edition of William Shakespeare's sonnets. The pages were stained and warped from its time in seawater but had dried well enough after being rinsed in fresh water to read the print. It had been tucked in a bag of his most prized possessions that he hung around his neck before the ship sank.

His wife, Wanahani, who had become nearly fluent in her husband's language after thirteen years of marriage, asked him to read to her as she cooked. She loved to hear the words of poetry roll off his tongue and feel the sentiment they triggered in her heart. He promised her that one day they would visit England and he would show her all the places he had so colorfully described. Wanahani had a difficult time believing a world like London could ever exist, but the idea of experiencing such an adventure was the subject of many daydreams.

Dinner was delicious, and after helping to clean up, Kera crawled onto her mat where she secretly listened to the quiet conversation between her parents. Soon, the sound of their voices wafted away as they began their nightly stroll along the beach, and like usual, Kera wondered what they spent so much time talking about each evening. Her curiosity was quickly replaced by heavy eyelids and one last yawn as she drifted off to sleep.

The next day began the same as any other with breakfast and a verbal list of the chores her mother wanted her to accomplish before she could go swimming. Filling their drink containers with fresh water was the most important. Crossing her body with ropes made of vines holding hollowed-out coconuts, she made her way back and forth between the river of fresh water and her village. It was a monotonous chore, but her vivid imagination full of stories her father had told of life on the sea kept her entertained. He had gone into the forest with some other men to hunt for wild boars and she couldn't wait to hear all about it when they returned.

On her third trip back, she noticed many of the villagers looking out toward the ocean so she made her way toward the gathering crowd. Two large ships set anchored off their island as two rowboats from the first ship were making their way toward them. Uncertain of their intentions, some of the villagers chose to run to their homes while others waited to greet them. Wanahani's husband had told her many stories of the bad men who sail the seas and she tried to warn everyone before their arrival. Some listened to the Englishman's wife and disappeared into the forest, but most of them lingered out of curiosity.

"Track your father into the forest. Tell him we have visitors. No matter what happens, do not come back out until they are gone. Do you understand, Kera?" shouted her mother as she tucked her two cooking knifes into the back of the tie around her waist.

"Yes, Mother," she responded as she paused to take one last look at the boats nearing the shore.

"Run, Kera. Run!"

Quickly, she turned and disappeared into the forest, making her way down the trail her father and the other men had travelled. Suddenly, she was stopped in her tracks as she heard a series of loud bangs she'd never heard before, followed by distant screams. Fear for the safety of her mother caused her to turn and run back to the village. She was certain her father would have heard the loud noises as well, and would return on his own. Reaching the edge of the forest, Kera beheld the horrors of real pirates. A few women were being packed away as the men trying to defend them fell dead to the ground. Kera desperately searched for her mother as she made her way around the backside of the village. Just as she picked up a large stick to use as a weapon, she was grabbed from behind by arms too strong to escape.

Wanahani recognized the screams of her daughter and raced toward her to help, but before she could reach her she was knocked to the ground. With her daughter's safety paramount, she fought the large man off, and to his last great surprise, drove one of her knives into his chest. Retrieving the bloody knife, she continued undaunted toward her daughter. Finding Kera in the arms of her assailant, she thrust her knife into his back, causing him to release the girl and fall to the ground.

Losing all control, Wanahani picked up Kera's stick and began beating him as hard as she could. Once the life drained from his eyes, she turned back to her daughter, only to find a man holding a knife to her neck and several more surrounding her. Shaking from the adrenaline rushing through her veins, she dropped the club and pulled the second knife from her belt, pointing it at the men.

"Let her go or I will kill you."

The men burst into laughter mocking her ultimatum.

"Then take me instead," she insisted.

"Who be you to make demands of us?" asked the man holding the knife to Kera's throat.

"I am her mother and you will let go of my child," responded Wanahani with resolute courage.

"Release the girl!" shouted a man dressed in elaborate clothing from the top of his three-sided hat adorned with frills and feathers, to the bows on his shiny shoes. Wearing a large cross around his neck, he stood flanked by three more pirates, while the silk woven into his belted tunic glistened under the sun. His confident stance and impressive stature proved he was not a man to be trifled with.

"Aye, Capt'n," said the man, immediately releasing Kera who quickly ran to her mother's side.

"I'll deal with you later," he warned the small group, then turned to the woman who had just bested two of his men. "Where did you learn the English tongue?"

"My husband."

"Be it your husband who taught ye how t' wield a knife so exact?"

"Once he returns he will show you the answer firsthand."

"And where be your husband now?"

Before she could answer, their attention turned to a ruckus from across the village as the small hunting party returned to defend their loved ones.

"There's your answer," proudly exclaimed Wanahani.

The man watched as they fought the pirates with their knives and spears, attempting to free the women as they went. Focusing on the Englishman, the captain saw him kill one of his men with his own sword, then continue to fight with precision and great skill, taking the lives of three more of his crew. His loyalty to his people, even in the eye of defeat, impressed him greatly.

Seeing enough to know what he wanted, the man drew his flintlock pistol from the belt over his shoulder and shot into the air, bringing the fight to a halt. Ordering his men to subdue the islanders and the Englishman, he followed behind with the woman and child. Once he reached the men, now kneeling on the ground, he pulled his sword and pressed the point against Falcon's throat.

"To whom do I have the pleasure?"

"Falcon Locke," he answered staring at his wife and daughter in fear for their lives. "And who might you be?"

"Captain Bartholomew Roberts 'n I be the one askin' the questions."

"Then get on with it."

"What brings ye to this island paradise?" asked the pirate captain.

"My ship went down."

"To what reason was she lost?"

"Battle."

"I thought I smelt the British Navy kneeling at me feet. Name ye rank."

"Merely a mate. Nothing of consequence."

"Your educated tongue 'n prowess with the sword tells me otherwise."

"You are mistaken, sir."

"I think not. The evidence lies next t' you," he said alluding to the dead pirates.

"I will not apologize for their deaths."

"Nor would I be inclined t' ask for it, mate. They were to come ashore seeking fresh fruit 'n drinking water. They be knowin' the rules in regard to women and children and death be an appropriate punishment for breakin' 'em."

"Then you will leave us in peace?"

"To that I make no promise."

"Take what you want and leave. We will not stand in your way."

"Perchance I take her," said Captain Roberts grabbing Kera and pulling her to his side as one of his men restrained Wanahani. "She be likely t' fetch a fine amount in the slave trade."

Falcon attempted to lunge forward, but the captain quickly sliced down the side of his neck with the tip of his sword.

"I implore thee, Captain, do not take my daughter. She is innocent to the violence we have known," pleaded Falcon.

"Tell me what I want t' know 'n she remains by her mother's side."

Falcon looked at his beautiful daughter and wife, knowing what would happen to them if he didn't do what the captain demanded. He loved his family more than anything on earth and there was nothing he wouldn't do to keep them safe, even if it cost him his own freedom. With a reassuring wink to his daughter, he sealed his fate by giving Captain Bartholomew what he wanted. "I was a captain in the British Navy."

"And before that?"

"A sailing master."

"That be what I was hopin' to hear. A captain with a skill for navigation is hard t' come by 'n it just so happens I be needin' ya for me second ship."

"Why?" asked the current captain standing near him.

Captain Roberts nodded to his master gunner who pulled out his pistol and dropped the captain of his second ship to the ground. "He be no longer in command. The men will attest t' me fairness as captain of me fleet, so long as the rules are obeyed."

Wanahani let out a gasp as she realized what was happening between her husband and Bartholomew. Breaking free from the man's grip, she dropped to the ground beside Falcon and wrapped her arms around him. Kera tried to escape as well, but her strength was no match for her captor.

"What say ye, Captain Locke?" asked Bartholomew as he secured Kera tight to his body. "Who will I be takin' with me?"

Falcon raised his wife's head in his hands, staring deep into her eyes, then kissed her on the forehead for one last time before responding. "I accept the commission."

With the raise of the captain's sword, Falcon was immediately grabbed by two men and taken directly to the row boat, then Bartholomew turned back to Wanahani, shoving Kera toward her. "We'll take that water 'n food now."

Barely able to find the words, Wanahani spoke to her fellow villagers in her native tongue telling them to fill the men's boats with drinking water and fruit and they would leave them alone. Quickly, the islanders sprang to their feet and did as she asked, while Wanahani took her daughter's hand and hurried to a spot overlooking the ocean.

"Why are they taking father?" cried Kera hugging her mother's waist as they watched them push the boat into the water. "When is he coming back?"

Clinging to a palm tree, Wanahani dug her fingernails into the bark as she tried to find the words to answer her daughter's questions, her own heart aching within her chest. "I will explain later, Child."

"How long will he be gone?"

"I don't know."

"When will he return?"

"He may never return."

Hearing the unfathomable, Kera broke away from her mother and ran toward the ocean, calling for her father to return. Unyielding at the water's edge, she ran into the water and swam toward the boat. Falcon pleaded with the men to stop rowing and let him say goodbye to his daughter. Taking pity on him, they allowed him to jump over the side and wait for her to reach their location. Kera swam into her father's arms and wrapped her legs around his waist, determined to never let go.

"Don't go, Father."

"I have to go. Someday you'll understand why."

"No! Stay!"

Falcon knew he couldn't leave her this way, so he pressed her cheek next to his and whispered in her ear. "I will come back for you, my little mermaid, mark my words. Our family will be together again. Until then, you must be strong for your mother and for me."

"Do you promise to come back, Father?" asked his daughter, feeling a certain calm wash over her quivering body.

"I only speak the truth. Remember?"

Allowing enough time, the men in the boat pulled the girl away from their new captain and yanked him back into the boat.

As they rowed toward the ship, Falcon knew the odds of keeping his promise to his daughter were less than desirable, if not impossible. It was more likely he would die at sea or be hung for acts of piracy before he ever returned to his island home. Worse than that, after dealing with pirates during his time in the British Navy, he knew the type of life that awaited him and the crimes he would be forced to commit. But better his soul rot in hell than to see his daughter taken aboard, only to be sold to the first slave traders they encountered. He had made his decision and would live with it, come what may.

Kera refused to move as she and her father maintained eye contact until the distance between them grew too wide to see each other's faces. As she walked from the water to the beach, she was oblivious to all the pirates boarding their boats but one: the captain who stole her father away. Stopping Bartholomew in his tracks, she had something to say and no one was going to keep her from saying it. "My father is a better captain than you will ever be!"

"I'm countin' on it, lass. He'll make a fine pirate captain in the fleet I'm buildin'." Patting her on the head, he left her standing alone as he boarded his boat and made way toward his ship.

For the rest of the day, Kera sat on the beach, staring out at the ocean she once loved so much. The sea had always been kind and giving, but today it took her father from her and she would never be the same. The year was 1719 and she would count the days until his return.

FOREST NEAR BEACH, Present-day

Adjusting back to reality, Rome was worried that she'd been lost in Kera's memory for hours, leaving Heath to search aimlessly for her. Glancing at her watch showed it had only been a few minutes. "I'm sorry your father was taken from you as a child."

"He returned several years later... only to be taken from me again."

"What do you want from me, Kera?"

"You need my help to save your friend and I need yours to save my father."

"Assuming your father is already dead... my first priority has to be my friend."

"Rescuing him will prove difficult. There is much for you to know."

"I'm all ears," responded Rome as she straddled the trunk of a downed tree next to the mermaid.

"Your friend is alive for now, but his chance of survival lessens the longer he is down there."

"Down where?"

"At the bottom of the sea."

"Doing what?"

"On a quest for gold."

"Are you telling me that he's out there searching for treasure, while everyone else is looking for him?"

"Rome! Rome! Where are you? Rome!" came Heath's voice from down the shore.

"That's my friend. He told me not to leave the beach."

"The man who came to your rescue in the morning hour?"

"Yes."

"You must go."

"Wait, Kera. You're safe with him."

"He draws attention to you. I will find you again." With that said, Kera disappeared from Rome's sight.

"Rome! Where are you?" yelled Heath.

His voice growing closer signaled to Rome that it was time to go, so she fought her way back out of the forest, reaching the beach just as Heath arrived. The minute he saw her he grabbed the top of his head with both his hands in relief, then walked in circles trying to cool down from the long sprint through loose sand. "Where were you?"

"In the jungle talking with a mermaid."

"I asked you not to leave the beach," said Heath, barely able to speak and breathe at the same time. "Wait... you were what?"

"The spirit showed up, but she wouldn't come out of the trees. I had to go to her."

"Your ghost is a mermaid?"

"Walk me back and I'll tell you what I learned about Kera."

"You may have to carry me. I think I'm about to pass out."

Rome wrapped her arm around his waist as he rested his arm across her shoulders and together they began the long walk toward the rum shack. Rome's knight in shining armor had experienced a physically rough day, but he wasn't alone. She had too, and as Rome looked at her watch, she realized it was only noon.

REACHING THE RUM HUT, they both found much needed rest across the table from Martin. In their absence, he had devoured most of the platter of food and finished off his and Rome's drink. "Most people come to the island to relax, but not you two."

"Could you get us some water?"

"Right away, ma'am."

"We still don't have a lot to go on, but at least we know he's alive," concluded Heath once Martin was out of earshot.

"True. Now we wait for her to contact me again."

"You think she's hiding from someone?"

"Possibly," answered Rome as her attention turned to the man leaning up against a tree. She recognized him from the airstrip. Late twenties, still barefoot, wearing a loose white shirt with drawstring opening and tan pants. Rome now believed him to be a spirit.

"Rome?"

"Yeah."

"Are you feeling all right?"

"Uh-huh."

"Are you sure?"

"What?"

"You seem a little disoriented," observed Heath as he placed the palm of his hand against her forehead. With the touch of his hand, the ghost immediately popped into his sights and he reacted by quickly pulling his hand away. "There's a ghost by the tree."

"Yes, there is."

"Is he one of the ghosts that tried to drown you this morning?"

"I don't think so."

Heath touched her hand in order to see the spirit again, then continued whispering in her ear. "Does he know we can see him?"

"Aye," said the ghost as he instantly filled one of the chairs across from Rome and Heath, surprising them with his presence. "Ye be the one brought to the island by the hand of the mermaid."

"How does he know that?" whispered Heath

"Tis me business to know," responded the ghost.

"How do you know the mermaid?" enquired Rome.

"There be ties that bind."

"What kind of ties?"

"They that run deeper than the ocean's depth."

"You were there when we arrived on the island."

"He was?" asked Heath confused.

"I forgot to mention it."

"So you two know each other?"

"No, but we have a mutual acquaintance," surmised Rome.

"The mermaid never be far."

"From what?"

"Her captain."

"Of her ship?" she asked trying to piece the information she learned from Kera's memory and his story together.

"And her life."

"You mean her father?" asked Heath. "Was he a ship's captain as well?"

"Aye, but now he be lost to the sea."

"So she's trying to find him," clarified Rome.

"She be attempting to save him, but no one can."

"Why?"

"Falcon Locke's ship," said Rome. "It was sunk near the end of what historians call the golden age of piracy. Jamie and I planned our scuba diving trip around searching for the wreckage. Supposedly, it was carrying some Aztec treasure when she went down."

"What ship didn't have a bit of stolen loot aboard? But this treasure be cursed."

"I think you've seen one too many pirate movies," said Heath, finding it difficult to believe his story.

"Did you see the treasure?" asked Rome.

"I never looked upon it."

"You served aboard the Maiden's Return?"

"As helmsman."

"Were you aboard when she went down?"

"I witnessed it first hand."

"Then you know where she sank."

"Aye."

"Will you show us?"

"Find the mermaid. She be holding all the answers," responded the pirate ghost.

Suspecting he was about to disappear and end their conversation, Rome placed her hand over his and asked, "how do I find Kera again?"

"The Maiden's Return be doomed and all aboard doomed with her."

"Was the Maiden's Return her father's ship?" Heath asked.

"A beauty of a race-built galleon she was, and fast as can be. Modified to be such."

THE MAIDEN'S RETURN, 1724.

Immediately, she was transported to the bow of a beautiful, wooden ship. It was night and the moon was full as she found herself standing near the foremast. Looking around, she caught the silhouette of a mermaid figurehead protruding from the front of the ship.

From the description Jamie had told her, she knew she was standing on the Maiden's Return. Turning back she saw Kera running toward the man whose memory she invaded, her face beaming with enthusiasm. She fell into his arms and they kissed in the moonlight. Rome felt deeply the love he had for the girl he held so tightly.

BEACH HUT, Present-day

Quickly, the pirate pulled his hand away from Rome, ending her glimpse into his past as abruptly as it had began.

"You were in love with Kera."

"Did she speak of us?" asked the pirate with renewed hope.

"I saw your memory of her on the bow of the Maiden's Return. How did Kera end up on her father's ship?"

"Cap'n Bartholomew met his death in 1722, leavin' Cap'n Locke no longer obligated t' sail beneath his flag. We awayed t' the cap'n's island 'n brought his sixteen-year-old daughter aboard. She sailed with us 'til the ship be scuttled by cannon fire in 1725. The best years o' me life," said the pirate ghost, then he disappeared from the table, leaving Heath and Rome with more questions than answers.

"Water with lime slices," announced Martin proudly, sitting down in the chair recently vacated by the ghost while presenting two large water bottles containing fruit slices.

Frustrated by the ghosts disappearance, Heath responded before he processed Martin's words. "I hate that!"

"I can get lemon instead, boss. Whatever fruit you want."

"Lime's great," responded Rome.

"They have no sense of urgency," said Heath, still frustrated with not getting more information from their ghostly informant. "They just pop in and out whenever they choose."

"It's the island way," responded Martin as an excuse for taking so long.

"It's been almost three hundred years for them," said Rome.

Not getting a response, Martin tried again. "The lime helps with the thirst."

"Not to mention the flavor," responded Rome, trying to keep up with both conversations. "Thank you, Martin."

"All in a days work, ma'am."

"I think I've had enough beach time for a while," said Heath.

"Me too."

"Can we stop to check on my aunt?" asked the boy as they left the table carrying their water.

"Lead the way."

As Martin ran ahead, they followed in silence, trying to make sense of all they had learned from Kera and the mystery pirate who loved her. "At least we have some information we can use," said Heath.

"Which leads to more questions. How did Kera end up on her father's ship and where was Wanahani?"

"She probably came aboard too and he just didn't mention it. He was smitten by the beautiful mermaid."

"According to the dates, Kera sailed with her father for three years."

"Makes sense. You said they were close."

"Captain Locke had to have changed after three years of pillaging under the flag of Black Bart."

"What are you thinking?"

"I'm trying to figure out why he needs saving."

"The answer probably lies at the bottom of the ocean with the Maiden's Return."

"Let's ask around and see what we can find out about the ship's final resting place," recommended Rome as she glanced back to see the pirate walking alone down the beach. A slight chill ran down her back and she wasn't sure if it was from the cold drink or the short glimpse into his past. Wondering what was keeping him apart from Kera in the next life, she mentally added that to her list of questions to ask during her next ghostly encounter.

Chapter Eight

*L*eaving the main and only road around the island, Heath drove the motorcycle through a small neighborhood until Martin had him stop. "Would you mind if we met your aunt?" asked Rome as they dismounted the bike.

"Come on," replied Martin as he bounced toward the door of the small but well-kept home.

Once inside, Heath and Rome stopped in the main living area as Martin continued through. A wave of the young guide's hand signaled to Heath and Rome that it was okay to follow him into the room at the other end of the house. As they entered the aunt's bedroom, they were surprised to find a woman much older than expected. Sleeping on top of the bed covered with a sheet, she appeared to be dead or close to it. An old, very used walker set next to the bed and the only sound in the room was from the oscillating fan in the corner.

Martin pressed his finger to his lips as he carefully grabbed the empty glass from the nightstand and left the room. An onslaught of questions hit Rome's mind as she tried to understand how a woman who appeared to be in her nineties had the energy to care for a twelve-year-old boy. Her question was answered when Martin returned carrying a glass of water and a couple of bananas. They were taking care of each other.

He placed the items on the nightstand near her bed, adjusted the sheet, then motioned with his hand that it was time to leave. Heath and Rome quietly followed, not speaking a word to each other until they left the house. Martin walked straight to the motorcycle and took his place at the back of the side car, ready to push. Rome, on the other hand, needed some answers and that bike would stay put until she got them. "How old is your aunt, Martin?"

"Ninety-five this year."

"So she's your great-aunt?"

"Great, great."

"Where's your mom and dad?"

"Mom is dead and I've never met my father."

"I'm sorry to hear that."

"My aunt and I do fine, ma'am. I catch plenty of fish and the neighbors are always dropping by baskets of fresh fruit and bread. They also check on my aunt when I'm working."

"Do you attend school?"

"Not anymore, but I read a lot."

"How much does Mr. Webb owe you?" interrupted Heath.

"He never said," replied Martin.

Heath opened up his wallet and pulled out five thousand Columbian pesos, equalling a little over two hundred and fifty American dollars and handed them to Martin. "Mr. Webb would want to make sure you got paid. He can make up the rest when we find him."

"The rest?" responded Martin, surprised by the amount of money he held in his hand.

"If you were half the guide to Jamie as you've been to us, then you're well worth that and more," said Heath, patting him on the back. "Now, let's get this thing started."

As Rome straddled the bike, she couldn't help but smile at the relationship forming between Heath and Martin. It was one of the bright sides to their search for Jamie.

With their combined pushing efforts, the motorbike fired up once again and Rome steered her back toward the Santa Isabel Village aka 'Town' in the North. They spent the afternoon shopping as a cover for talking to people in the businesses and on the street, trying to find out as much as they could about the legend of the Maiden's Return and Captain Locke. The story of the ship's demise and location differed slightly depending on who they spoke with, but most people believed she went down somewhere near the island of San Andres rather than Providencia. By the end of the day, they had more questions than before.

"It's getting late. We should probably get Martin and his groceries home, then head back to Jonah's," suggested Heath.

"Are you game for another day as our guide, Martin?" asked Rome.

"Oh, yes, ma'am."

"Good. Then we'll see you in the morning."

Excited by the promise of another day's employment, Martin pushed with renewed strength, happy to return home and cook his aunt a wonderful dinner that didn't consist of fish and fruit.

The opposite was true of Rome and Heath, who were worn out from a day of physical exertion that started at the crack of dawn. They hadn't made much physical progress toward finding Jamie, but they had some new information to go on. Now they just needed the mermaid to show up and fill in the blanks, the biggest hole to fill being Jamie's location.

Finally reaching Jonah's home, they parked the bike and slowly got off. "Nothing like the Caribbean for a little relaxation," joked Heath as he and Rome walked stiffly toward the door.

"It could be worse."

"Don't say that."

"It's true."

"It may be true, but I'm hoping for a more productive day tomorrow."

"Here, here," responded Rome as she entered the house. "Jonah, we're home."

"Straight through to the back," hollered the doctor as he waited for them to reach the patio. "I was getting worried and that's not normal for me."

"Nothing to worry about," said Rome as she glanced at Heath rolling his eyes.

"So what do you think of our little island paradise?"

"Oh, it's definitely a paradise," remarked Heath with a touch of sarcasm, sinking into a chair near the fire pit with a sigh of relief.

Exhausted, Rome sat next to him while Jonah left his hammock and walked toward them.

As she watched him find his way toward a deck chair, she basked in the ambiance of the patio and its view of the island. "This is paradise," she thought to herself until a deeper examination of what she was experiencing caused her to reflect on the true meaning of the word.

This 'paradise' she was feeling was no different from what she felt at Heath's beach house on Kauai or his castle in Tasmania: all lovely settings but made heavenly by the people she surrounded herself with, both living and dead. The new friends she'd made over the past month were authentic, real people: the type who wear their hearts on their sleeves and let the chips fall where they may.

Somehow, Rome had become the student, fascinated by this new way of thinking and relating to others. She had no idea why her ability to listen to the dead had magnified at Port Arthur, but her choice to embrace it rather than run the other way had paid off, not only for the spirits who needed her help but for her own growth as well. Rome had spent most of her life viewing her inherited ability as an inconvenient burden rather than seeing it for what it truly was —a gift... a mistake she would never make again.

"A long day, my friends?" asked Jonah as he settled in to his favorite chair.

"A very long day," answered Rome.

"Did you find your way around well enough?"

"We hired a guide, a kid named Martin."

"You won't find a better guide on the island."

"He seems... capable," mentioned Heath, half asleep in the chair.

"That he is. We meet once a week to go fishing. He casts his line in the sea while I fish through his thoughts."

"For what?"

"What he wants his life to be."

"He's just a kid."

"His aunt is not long for this world."

"What will happen to him then?"

"The answer to that question is what I search for each week."

"Surely someone will take him in."

"There is no doubt his physical needs of shelter and food would be met by those of us who care for the boy and his aunt. But Martin is bright, very gifted."

"How long ago did his mother die?"

"She died giving birth. I was still practicing medicine, and by the time I arrived at their home, she was too far gone. I took the baby cesarean and his mother died not long after. His grandmother raised him until she passed away, then his great-aunt took over."

"Does anyone know who his father is?" asked Heath.

"Only by his pen name. He's a very popular but reclusive author who lives in England. He traveled to Providence thirteen years ago to do research for the book he was writing. Another ocean adventure. While on the island, he met a beautiful young woman who fell madly in love with him."

"Martin's mother," concluded Heath, intrigued by the new information.

"Before she was Martin's mother."

"Did he know she was pregnant?" asked Rome.

"She wrote him a letter when she found out but didn't have an address. About a month after she passed away, a pre-released copy of the published book he'd been working on arrived with a beautiful inscription. Martin's grandmother forwarded her daughter's prewritten letter to the publisher, but she never heard back."

"Does Martin know that?"

"Yes. He longs to meet his father but knows his life is here... for now at least."

"So you meet with him once a week to fish."

"The best pay I receive all week."

Rome laughed at Jonah's remarks, enjoying the comfort and ambience of her surroundings while trying not to fall asleep.

"Speaking of pen names... Is Rome London yours?"

"It's the real thing. My father's last name is London and he met my mother while stationed in Italy."

"Is your mother Italian?" asked Jonah, connecting the dots.

"Yes. I'm named after her grandmother."

"What a small world this earth can be."

"It can be," responded Rome, not sure what he was alluding to, but sharing in the sentiment.

"Did you come any closer to finding your friend today?"

"We got some leads. Hopefully tomorrow we'll have better luck," responded Rome.

"It will be difficult now that the search has been called off."

"I haven't given up hope."

"Especially when there are other ways to search."

"True," agreed Rome, recognizing he was doing a bit of fishing through her own mind. "I should probably get this guy to bed."

Using Heath's well-being as an excuse to end the conversation, she leaned over and picked up his hands. Heath allowed Rome to pull him from the chair and they disappeared from the courtyard.

Jonah listened to their footsteps fade as they walked down the path to their rooms. He enjoyed their company but was anxious to confirm his suspicions about Rome... a confirmation that would have to wait for another day.

Halfway down the trail, Heath stopped. "I'll be right back." Curiously, Rome watched him jog back down the trail until her need for sleep replaced her interest in what Heath forgot. Just as she reached her room, Heath returned, stopping her from opening the door by pulling her into his arms.

"Forget something back there?" asked Rome enjoying being held.

"Just a quick question about Martin's father."

"I've seen that look before."

"What look?"

"Jonah got the wheels turning in your head."

"I can't imagine growing up without a dad."

"Be careful, Heath. He's had plenty of time to respond to the letter."

"I'll keep it under the radar."

"You're a good man, Marshall Heath Jones Jr."

"Yeah? How good?" asked Heath taking advantage of the moment to steal a kiss.

Slowly pulling away, Rome attempted to say goodnight, but a second kiss silenced her words. Being held in his arms was a nice ending to a long day, but as much as Heath wanted to progress things forward, she had other thoughts on her mind, namely her ex-boyfriend's whereabouts. Stepping back, she bid him good night and opened the door.

"Don't forget to call your mom back."

"Thanks for the reminder," she said, entering her room. Before she closed the door, a wave of sweet introspection swept over her, causing her to turn back to the man she loved. "I'm glad you're here, Heath. Thanks for coming with me."

"There's nowhere else I'd rather be."

Closing the door behind her, she kicked off her sandals, determined to wear tennis shoes the next day, then collapsed on the bed. After a quick rest, she planned to brush her teeth, wash her face and call her mother. "I'm just going to rest for a few minutes," she whispered repeatedly until she drifted off to sleep.

Getting an unwanted second wind, Heath pulled out his phone and walked down the trail leading toward the driveway. It had been a couple days since he checked in with Sheldon and now was as good a time as any to do it. He also needed his butler's help. If anyone could find out the real name of Martin's father, it was Sheldon, even if all they had to go one was his nom de plume and London publishing company.

Chapter Nine

The South'n Hunter

Returning to the ship, one of Lazenby's men tied the tender snuggly to the tow bridle and waited for a fellow mercenary to lower the basket. Once it reached the boat, he loaded the recently-filled scuba tanks then stepped inside the basket and signaled he was done. He arrived inside the ship right after Jamie finished removing his gear and followed the prisoner and armed guards to the upper deck.

Angry at the sight of Talin's abuse, Jamie nearly lost control. "I'm doing exactly what you want me to do, Jack! Why hurt the kid?!"

"My ship, my rules."

"What are you talking about?"

"He's grown defiant. It seems ya rubbin' off on him, Webb."

"This is between you and me!"

"You keep talkin' and I'll keep him up here all night long."

"Is he conscious?"

"He clocked out about twenty minutes ago."

"His sister can't see him like that."

"Take him back," ordered Lazenby out of spite.

"Come on, Jack. Clean him up first."

"Ya lucky I'm feelin' generous. Take the kid to the lower deck and wait for Mr. Webb to clean him up."

Two of the guards untied Talin's hands and packed his limp body from the room, allowing Jamie to pivot toward Lazenby's desk, where he slid two paperclips into his hand.

"From the video, the third deck looks like a disaster," said Lazenby, getting back to the Maiden's Return. "How do ya propose to get the gold out once you find it?"

"The only way in or out is through the open hatches. If the treasure is in trunks, I'll have to remove it piece by piece."

"I've got plenty of canvas bags."

"Of course, you do," responded Heath, knowing the bags were used for smuggling.

"I'm assuming you were able to fill all the tanks?" asked Lazenby, redirecting his attention to the man who just returned to the ship.

"They're full."

"Did the Navy pull out as scheduled?"

"They're gone."

"Good. I've had enough of them snoopin' around my ship."

"We may have another problem."

"What kind of problem?"

"A man and woman are asking a lot of questions about the Maiden's Return."

"Locals?"

"Tourists."

"Get any names?"

"Yeah, but you're not going to like it. Heath Jones."

"Of Jones Shipping?"

"You know him?" enquired Jamie, his interest piqued at the mention of the man who stole his girlfriend.

"Jones Shippin' has cost me a lot of contraband over the years thanks to Marshall Jones' reward program for reporting suspicious activity. I sent a thank you card to his son when I heard he died."

"The woman's American. Most likely a girlfriend," continued the man. "Should I get rid of them?"

Jamie waited for Lazenby's decision, realizing that his friend Ross had done what he'd asked him to do several months earlier—contact Rome if anything happened to him.

"Make it look like an accident. A drownin' ought to be appropriate for someone in the shippin' industry."

"That's about the dumbest plan I ever heard," inserted Jamie. "You must be slipping, Jack."

"This is none of your business, Webb."

"Fine. Go for it... if you want investigators and reporters from all over the planet zeroing in on Providence and the death of billionaire shipping tycoon."

"My men are good. They'll never find the bodies."

"That won't stop them from launching a large-scale search and rescue mission. It'll make the search for me look like a boy scout activity."

"On second thought, get them off Providence. Make it look like they left on their own. I don't care where ya dump 'em, just make sure they're gone long enough to finish here."

"I'll need a bigger boat than the tender."

"I've got one making a run from Columbia tonight. Do you know where Jones is staying?"

"At the blind doctor's house."

"I'll contact the boat and send ya the coordinates. Go."

Watching the man quickly descend the stairs left Jamie feeling sick to his stomach. It was his fault Rome was on the island in the first place. She had come to find him, and now her life was in serious danger and there wasn't one thing he could do to help. He hated that feeling more than anything—the same feeling he was experiencing with Talin—but this was personal.

"Clean the kid up, then get back in the water," ordered Lazenby as he watched the guard push Jamie toward the stairs. "I expect results this time."

"I want this over just as fast, Jack," responded Jamie as he left the upper deck. Reaching the bottom of the stairs, he found Talin on the floor, somewhat conscious. "I need water, a towel and a clean shirt," ordered Jamie as he pulled Talin toward the wall and leaned him against it.

"I'm all right," said the boy, holding the side of his ribs as he coughed.

"I wasn't going to ask."

"I'm staying strong for Leta."

"Good. Let's get this bloody shirt off of you."

"This isn't your fault, Mr. Webb."

"I hear you got in his face."

"It was worth it," boasted Talin as he tried to smile.

"So I am rubbing off on you."

"In a good way."

Jamie's attention was split between his conversation with Talin and studying the men prepping for the abduction. Lazenby's entire crew were ex-military and could perform a simple mission like this blindfolded. Guns and knives were stuffed into bags then lowered through the hatch, followed by tarps, rope and several backpacks, no doubt containing the proper sedatives, restraints and night vision wear for a mission of this sort.

The guard returned with a bucket of warm water and a washcloth and Jamie began the process of cleaning the dried blood off the young captain's face and neck. "At least the bleeding's stopped."

It was painful for Talin to sit through, but he had to do it for Leta's sake. "Where are they going?"

"Who?"

"The men you've been watching," whispered Talin.

"Focus on Leta and leave them to me."

"He looks good enough," interrupted one of the guards. "Let's go."

"Stay strong," said Heath as they tossed a clean shirt at Talin's chest. Jamie stood up only to be pushed toward the hatch. He watched over his shoulder as they yanked Talin to his feet and forced him roughly down the hall. Reaching the dive staging area, the men helped him on with his equipment, then lowered him through the open hatch. His thoughts quickly switched from Talin to Rome as he watched the men in the boat disappear toward Providence.

PROVIDENCE FERRY TERMINAL

Dressed in black with their faces camouflaged, the three men pulled the boat up next to the ferry dock and tied her securely to the piling. One of the men climbed onto the dock and disappeared into town. Fortunately, everything shut down on the island by 10:00, so the odds of anyone disturbing their mission were slim. The other two men gathered the necessary equipment and left the dock in search of their leader. Seeing a small light flash three times down the street, they knew he had secured transportation. They quickly loaded their equipment and themselves into the minivan belonging to one of the businesses and headed down the road—lights off until they reached a safe distance.

Finding themselves at the target's house, they parked the van for a quick getaway. Putting on their night vision goggles, they split up in three directions and made their way into and around the house.

One of the men came upon Jonah, asleep in his chair. Knowing he was blind, the attacker concluded he would be no threat to the men's mission. It was better to keep him alive than add fuel to the fire by killing off such a prominent figure.

The two other men approached the outer rooms finding the first two empty. The opening of the third door revealed Rome, peacefully asleep on top of her bed. Hearing the sound of a floorboard squeak, she sat up, but before she could react, a man grabbed her from behind in a naked choke hold. Her outstretched hand reached desperately for the lamp to use as a weapon but knocked it from the stand instead. The sound of it smashing against the floor was not part of the abductor's plans, but they were no strangers to improvising.

Hearing a knock on the door to room three, two of the men hid in the shadows as Heath enquired. "Rome? Is everything all right?" Not getting a response, he opened the door and rushed toward Rome. Before making it halfway across the floor, one of the men in hiding grabbed him from behind in a chokehold and used his legs to drop Heath to his knees, while the other slapped a piece of duct tape across his mouth then left the room. It was the last thing Rome saw before losing consciousness.

Keeping an eye on the situation, the first man pulled out a kit from his backpack and opened it up. He pulled out a vial of liquid, a syringe and a rubber tourniquet, then prepared Rome for the sedative. A thump to the floor signaled that their main target was out for the count as he administered the narcotic into Rome's bloodstream.

The third man returned promptly with tarps and rope in hand and they began wrapping Rome's body while the man in charge administered a healthier dose of the same drug to Heath. Then the team leader made Rome's bed and collected the pieces of the broken lamp into a bag while his two partners wrapped Heath in a matching tarp and tied it snuggly. He also placed all her personal items and clothing back into her suitcase and hid it under the bed as the second man did the same thing in Heath's room. There would be no sign of a struggle by the time they left. Pulling out a note pad, the man doing the cleanup penned a message, alerting anyone curious that they decided to travel to San Andres for a day or so. Then he placed it on the bed and shut the door behind him.

Soon, both victims were in the car and the van was bound for the harbor. Reaching the dock, they unloaded the two body bags and lowered them into the tender while the van was returned to its original parking spot.

The boat slowly and quietly moved away from the harbor as one of the men examined the GPS. As in any mission, timing was everything, and reaching the right coordinates for the rendezvous with the larger boat was crucial. There they would unload Heath and Rome and wash their hands of it. Following their rendezvous, they would return to the South'n Hunter. Mission accomplished.

THE SOUTH'N Hunter

Returning to the ship some time later, the three-man abduction team's arrival synchronized perfectly with Jamie's resurfacing. As the guards switched out Jamie's tanks, he watched as Lazenby entered the lower deck and demanded a report. "How'd it go?"

"Like clockwork. We left a note saying they travelled to San Andres for a while."

"Where will they dump 'em?"

"Halfway up Nicaragua's Mosquito coast. They should reach shore just before dawn," answered the team leader.

"Lost in time with no way out," laughed another member of the abduction team.

"And no one who speaks English," added Lazenby, delighted with the choice.

"It'll take 'em a week or more to get outta there... if they survive."

"How were they when you left them?" asked Jamie inserting himself into the conversation.

"Who made you the interrogator?" asked Lazenby.

"Just curious."

"Sleeping off a drug-induced coma," answered one of the men.

"Do we have any contacts near the dumpin' site?"

"Bluefields would be the closest to the South and Puerto Cabezas to the North. I'll put the word out in case they make it to either of those locations."

"I want to know the minute Heath Jones finds his way back to civilization... if he ever does," demanded Lazenby laughing as he walked back toward the stairs leading to the upper deck.

Concerned for the life of his friend, Jamie sat on a crate unable to do a thing about it. His only hope was that Rome and Heath could stay alive long enough to find help for themselves. The environment, language barrier and the dengue fever epidemic currently raging throughout Central America would make surviving difficult for them, but Jamie was more concerned with the security risks along the Mosquito Coast: risks he was privy to through his current job with the State Department and his time in the Navy.

The fact that the Mosquito Coast is being used more and more as a corridor for cocaine trafficking was his biggest concern. That, coupled with reports of the Moskito people to the north of Nicaragua getting caught in the crossfire between Honduran/American commando raids and the drug traffickers, made it even worse. Factor in the Moskito dissidents, made up of veterans of the Contras, as well as developers who want to take the fertile land by force for their own agricultural use, and Heath and Rome have landed smack-dab in the middle of a dangerous situation. The worst part for Jamie was that he couldn't do a thing about it.

Rome was his last hope for being rescued, but that was the furthest thing from his mind. Now more than ever it was up to him to make it happen. Not only was he responsible for Talin and Leta's survival, but now Rome and Heath needed his help as well. He could feel the pressure of his 'to-do' list taking hold.

Standing up, he paced the deck to clear his mind. He had to remain calm, cool and collected or he would be of no use to anyone. "One thing at a time," he whispered to himself over and over again, refocusing himself on what he could control. Then he took a page from Rome London's book and began breathing in the good air and letting out the bad.

FOREST GATE CASTLE, Tasmania

Sheldon Burns, Heath's British butler and head of his household, placed his bag near the entranceway then walked back into the grand hall of the castle. Pacing back and forth, he dialed Heath's number again, but it went straight to voicemail. Sheldon had been trying for hours to reach Heath with no success. "I'm getting too old for this," he said as Beverly Hucker entered the hall.

"Fifty is the new forty, dear," she pointed out in an attempt to lighten the mood, but for Sheldon, just the sight of her was enough to brighten even his darkest hour.

Seeing the worry on her boyfriend's face, Bev knew it would take more than her gorgeous blonde hair and supermodel body to ease his concern. "Still no luck?" she asked rubbing her hand over the back of his shoulder.

"Heath never turns his phone off."

"Maybe the battery died."

"That's a possibility."

"You think something's wrong?"

"I know something's wrong. He was going to call me after he found out more information on the boy's father."

"The English author."

"Indeed."

"Maybe he hasn't found out anything."

"He planned to do it over breakfast."

"Our flight to England doesn't leave for a few hours. We have time."

"That's not what I'm concerned about."

"Do you think something's happened to him?"

"I have a bad feeling, Beverly."

"I'll ring Rome."

"I've already tried, several times. Same result."

"That's strange."

"We could stop over on our way to England," suggested Bev, growing concerned as well.

"The island is small and off the beaten path. It would take us too long. Heath wants us there as soon as possible."

"We're coming!" hollered Miss Lemmons, Heath's young maid with a big heart, as she and George rushed into the room.

"Sorry for being late," said George, the youthful groundskeeper turned butler in training.

"Have you already started?" asked Miss Lemmons.

"'Punctuality is the politeness of kings.' You'd both do well to remember that."

"Of course, sir."

"Yes, sir."

"While I'm gone, Gladys will be in charge. What she says is law. Understood?"

"Yes, sir."

"I'd love to go back to London," responded Miss Lemmons with a dreamy tone.

"How often have you been to the UK?" enquired Bev.

"My father lives there. He used to fly me out over school holidays."

"How familiar are you with London?"

"I navigate it well enough."

"Do you?" asked Bev, turning her attention to Sheldon with a twinkle in her eye.

"Completely out of the question," responded the butler.

"Completely?"

"Absolutely!"

"Someday, we need to discuss your love of 'intensifiers,'" responded Bev.

"'Intensifiers' are key to inspiring an orderly household," argued Sheldon.

"Until the day I showed up on your doorstep."

"You did bring a bit of disorder to the castle."

"And look at the results," said Bev as she wrapped her arm around his and whispered in his ear. "We can't be in two places at once. Either you and I split up or the four of us divide and conquer."

"Four?" responded Sheldon with disapproval.

"For safety purposes. Travel can be risky these days," replied Bev, playing to his soft spot.

After a moment of thought, Sheldon reconsidered his stance. "I suppose it could work."

"Do you hold a current passport, George?" asked Bev.

"I've yet to use it."

"And you, Miss Lemmons?"

"Mine's still current."

"What's this about?" asked George.

"We have a dilemma of sorts," answered Bev.

"I'm confused," noted Miss Lemmons. "Should I have been taking notes?"

"Oh, dear," expressed Sheldon as Bev tightened the grip around his arm for support while he continued, "it must be understood that this is business, not a paid vacation."

"Are you firing us?" asked George, equally confused.

"No. What Mr. Burns is trying to say... is that he needs you both to go on assignment to London for a few days."

"London? As in the UK? As in ten thousand miles away?"

"Yes. London, England."

"I've never even been on a plane," responded George with childlike anticipation.

"Don't plan on first class. It'll be coach the entire way," announced Sheldon.

"He means business class. After all, it is business," added Bev.

"Hmm."

"What about accommodations?" asked Miss Lemmons.

"I'm willing to allow you to stay with your father, so long as you remember..."

"It's business," said both George and Miss Lemmons in unison, about to explode from the excitement building inside of them.

"What's the assignment, sir?" asked George.

"We need the real name of a certain author as well as his personal contact information. All we have to go by is his pen name and publishing company."

"My father is a solicitor. I'm sure he'd love to help."

"Absolutely not! This has to be done under the radar and in no way be tied back to Heath or Jones Shipping. Discretion is of the utmost importance. Understood?"

"Like spies on a mission," blurted out George, his boyhood fantasies of international espionage coming to fruition.

"If I wanted spies, I'd employ the services of MI-6!"

"What Mr. Burns needs you to understand is that this is a very sensitive matter. The last thing Heath wants to do is hurt anyone involved," clarified Bev in a softer way.

"I couldn't have said it better myself," followed Sheldon.

"Thank you, dear. Continue."

"As far as your father's concerned, Miss Lemmons, you and your associate are in London doing research on Forest Gate."

"That's a great cover story," responded George. "We'll also need aliases and fake I.D.'s."

"You will require nothing of the sort!" demanded Sheldon, frustrated by their playful immaturity. "This was a bad idea. Let's forget the entire thing. Ms. Hucker will fly to London and I'll make arrangements to travel to the Caribbean. I'll be in the office if anyone needs me."

Shocked by his quick decision, the remaining three stood in silence, listening to the echo of the butler's footsteps striking the marble as he disappeared from the grand hall.

"Oh..." whined Miss Lemmons. "I wanted to go to London and see my father."

"Me too," agreed George. "Well, not the father part."

"You don't want to meet my father?" responded Miss Lemmons, shocked by his declaration.

"I didn't mean it that way."

"I can't believe you don't want to meet my father. We've been dating for almost a month."

"That long, ay?" asked George nervously. "Of course I want to meet your father."

"Good, 'cause I don't think I could go out with someone who doesn't want to meet my father."

"I definitely want to meet your father."

Relieved, Miss Lemmons smiled at George then quickly turned her attention to Bev. "Could you talk to him, Ms. Hucker? You have a way with Mr. Burns."

"Listen up, both of you. I'm done playing good cop to Mr. Burns's bad cop. This is a very serious matter and not to be taken lightly. At this point, I'm wondering why I recommended you both in the first place."

"We can do this," promised Miss Lemmons.

"We really can."

"So far, I've seen no sign of that. I'm inclined to side with

Sheldon and scratch the whole idea," said Bev, checking the time on her watch. "We have one hour before I check in at the airport. That means you have one hour to prove to Mr. Burns that you're mature enough to get the job done."

Without a word, Miss Lemmons and George ran up the stairs as Bev headed toward the office, patting herself on the back. "I've still got it."

Chapter Ten

The sound of birds screeching through the air mixed with the noise of waves hitting the shore, woke Rome from probably the deepest sleep of her life. Unable to open her eyes to the bright sunlight and blue sky, she sheltered her face with her hands as she tried to get her bearings. Her mind was in a fog, finding it difficult to focus her eyes as she turned her head to the right and then to the left. Several feet away she saw the blurry shape of a body on the beach. Squinting her eyes for better focus, she discovered it to be Heath.

With as much energy as she could muster, she rolled herself onto her belly and struggled to her hands and knees. Completely off-balance, she began to crawl toward him, steadying herself along the way until she reached his body. "Heath. Wake up. Wake up!" cried Rome, as she patted his face.

Slowly, he began to regain consciousness, groaning at the pain he felt when opening his eyes. Rome took hold of his hands and pulled him into a sitting position, securing him with her grip. He continued to open and close his eyes, trying to acclimate to his surroundings while dealing with the after effects of being drugged. "Where are we?"

"Looks like the beach."

"I'm really starting to hate the beach."

"What's the last thing you remember?"

"I heard a noise come from your room. I walked in. Someone grabbed me from behind."

"Same with me."

"They must have drugged us."

"That would explain why I feel like crap."

"Why go to all that trouble just to leave us on the beach?" said Heath as he struggled to get to his feet, staggering back and forth till he found his footing. Taking a few steps toward the water gave him more time to focus his eyes. "The ocean looks different, muddy."

Rome joined him on his feet and together they looked out to sea. "Maybe we're on a different side of the island."

Heath looked up and down the coast line as far as the eye could see. "I don't think we're on the island at all."

"What?" responded Rome, trying not to panic.

"The color of the ocean is wrong and this coastline looks more like a mainland shore."

"Then where are we?"

"The closest mainland would be Nicaragua."

"Or Costa Rica, Panama, Columbia... We could be anywhere," added Rome.

"Please don't let it be Columbia," said Heath, as he searched through the empty pockets of his shorts. "We have no phone, no money, no passport, which means no ID and no way to contact anyone."

"We're in serious trouble."

"More or less, depending on what country we're in. How's your Spanish?"

"I know enough to get around. I practice foreign languages in my downtime."

"Downtime?"

"When I'm traveling between destinations. I did a series on vacationing hot spots in Central America for the magazine a couple years ago, but I had a Spanish-speaking guide in every country."

"Does this look familiar?"

"Ocean and rainforest," said Rome looking at her surroundings. "We could be anywhere from Belize to Panama."

"Well, that narrows it down."

"Who would do this?"

"Probably the same people who have Jamie."

"We were getting close."

"Too close."

Rome sat back down on the beach and stared up at the sky. "The sun's straight up, so it must be around noon."

"Then we have about eight hours of daylight left to find help," responded Heath as he sat down next to her.

"Where do we start?"

"We could walk the beach until we run into a town."

"Up or down?"

"That's the gamble."

"We could stay here and wait for a boat to sail by," suggested Rome.

"I like the first plan better. At least we're moving."

"I'm so sorry, Heath," said Rome as she laid her head against his shoulder. "We're in this mess because of me."

"You didn't strand us here."

"You know what I mean."

"We're here because of Jamie. Let's blame it all on him," insisted Heath, trying to lighten the mood.

"You should have stayed in Hawaii."

"I'd rather be here with you than have you marooned by yourself."

"We really are stranded."

"Yes, we are."

"What are we going to do?"

"Figure it out."

"I like the sound of that."

"I came to help you find Jamie, but now it's personal."

"Agreed," said Rome as she lifted her head. "Let's get back to Providencia and finish what we started."

"That's the Rome London I adore," said Heath as he leaned his head sideways and kissed the top of her head.

"Sometimes I think you're too good to be true," said Rome tenderly.

"You have no idea how good you have it, sheila," joked Heath as he leaned her back, relaxing her to the ground. Suddenly, nothing else mattered as they found the security they needed in each other's arms. The panic of their situation was quickly replaced by the passion they felt, loving each other on the beach of an unknown land. Precious time passed with the lap of each wave against their feet, but that didn't seem to matter until the sound of an incoming airplane pulled them back to reality. "Do you hear that?" asked Heath, just as a small plane roared over them.

"There must be an airstrip around here," added Rome, as they both sprang to their feet.

"It was on descent. It could be nearby or twenty miles away."

"Through that," warned Rome, looking at the dense rainforest facing them.

"Looks like a jungle."

"I've hiked through rainforests in Costa Rica for the magazine, but that was on a trail. We're going to need a machete to get through there."

"And neither of us have shoes," he said eyeballing the rope and tarps left behind by their kidnappers. "If we can find something to cut with—a sharp rock or a broken sea shell—we could make a covering for our feet."

Rome quickly caught Heath's vision and they both went to work searching for sharp objects. Finding the first broken rock made Heath the designer as Rome continued to collect a few more sharp objects. Moving their operation to the edge of the forest provided driftwood as a base to cut against.

"While I cut pieces from the tarp, cut the half-inch cording in two-foot lengths."

Rome got right to it, using her broken seashells to cut the rope as Heath instructed. Soon, they had enough pieces to craft Rome a snazzy pair of boots. Making sure there were several layers on the bottom, Heath wrapped each foot with perfect precision and care, then tied pieces of rope strategically around her foot and up her calf. Satisfied with his handiwork, he waited for Rome to try them out.

"Practical, yet rainforest couture," quipped Rome, "look out, Paris... here we come."

Back to work they went until they had enough material cut for Heath's feet. Rome followed his persistent directions as she wrapped the tarp around his feet and tied the cording.

"Where's a camera when you need one," joked Heath as they smiled at each other before his tone turned serious. "Let's roll up what's left of the tarp and rope and take it with us. We may need it."

"How are we going to keep from getting lost in there?"

"Losing sight of the sun will be a problem."

"So will maintaining a straight path."

"The less detours the better."

"We only have about six hours of sun left. Let's hope the runway's close."

"And that it's not used for drug trafficking."

"Thanks for adding that to the mix."

"Stay close, Rome, and watch for snakes, high and low," reminded Heath as he entered the forest.

"I hate reptiles."

"Then you're going to hate this."

Entering the forest was like nothing they'd ever experienced. Walking involved more climbing, bending and surmounting than maintaining an actual stride. Any open ground they happened upon consisted of a muddy grass mix and Rome had lost count as to how many times she'd nearly been swallowed by the forest floor.

Most of the work fell to Heath who was clearing vines and bending branches while trying to maintain a straight course, north-northwest from the beach. Taking advantage of any opening in the tree canopy, they continued forward, hoping they were still on course. At one point, they came to an opening which allowed them to make up some time, as well as course correct according to the sun.

Other than swarming mosquitos, all the reptiles and monkeys seemed to leave them alone as they moved through their habitat. Frightened by the proposition of surviving a night in the rainforest, they pushed themselves hard to find civilization before they lost sunlight. Then something wonderful happened: they heard a noise not native to the forest. It sounded like children laughing.

Cutting through the last several feet of forest, they emerged into an opening and found their first sign of human life: a well-worn trail. "Is that what I think it is?"

"Looks like a footpath to me," replied Heath as he grabbed Rome and swung her around. Their excitement was short-lived as the concern of not knowing what they would find at the end of the trail registered on their faces. Heath lowered Rome to the ground and together they cautiously made their way down the trail. "It might be a good idea to keep our identities a secret."

"Identities? I just hope we can communicate. There's a lot of indigenous tribes that speak obscure languages in this part of the world."

"Great."

"We just spent hours fighting our way through a jungle. I think we can handle something as simple as a language barrier," said Rome as the end of their trail met with a well-worn dirt road leading into a village.

"I hope we're not getting into something worse than what we just went through," responded Heath as they slowly entered the town. The buildings were board houses with rusted tin roofs, many of which were built on stilts due to flooding.

Walking into the village felt familiar to Rome, and although the surroundings were foreign to her own lifestyle, she understood it was the way of a people who have called this land home for centuries. She had seen her fair share of third-world cultures and the impoverished conditions that accompany them, although it was usually from within the safety of a guided tour or through the window of a bus.

Heath, on the other hand, had never been exposed to this level of poverty and couldn't imagine how anyone still lived like this in a time when technology allows things to move and advance so quickly. It was as though time had come to a halt.

His pace slowed to a stop as he encountered his first sign of life, a group of children playing alongside the road. At first, he felt nothing but pity for the state of their existence. "What must their lives be like day after day?" he thought to himself. "What future could they possibly have in these conditions?" It was almost more than he could process until one of the children smiled at him, flashing the universal sign for 'hello.' In an instance, Heath's heart changed from sympathy to compassion as he smiled back, communicating beyond language, one human being to another.

Rome waited a few feet up the street as Heath stretched out his arm and shook the smiling boy's hand. She watched with great interest as one of the richest men in the world met one of the poorest and found common ground through a smile. It was genuine and sincere and exactly what Rome needed to see in Heath. Time stood still as she mentally captured a moment that she hoped would never fade from her memory.

The moment was short-lived as a teenage girl pointed to Rome, while informing the others of her find. Quickly, the group of children ran ahead, yelling words neither Rome nor Heath understood and alerting the community to their arrival.

"That didn't sound like Spanish to me."

"That's definitely not Spanish," confirmed Rome as they continued into town.

"Let's just hope the adults are friendly," mentioned Heath as residents began opening their doors and exiting their homes, curious at the sight of two strangers wearing very unusual boots.

"Where do we start?"

"We don't," responded Rome and they waited for someone to approach. It didn't take long for several males to meet them in the road and begin to question them in their native tongue. Rome did her best to respond in Spanish, hoping someone spoke enough to bridge the language barrier, but that was not the case. Quickly, one of the men called out to the rest of the onlookers and the message was relayed verbally throughout the village.

After a few minutes, a woman came running down the street and joined them. Rome was relieved when the kind woman greeted her in Spanish and opened up a line of dialogue. Rome was rusty, but the two of them worked at it until an understanding had been reached. Heath watched in amazement as Rome began a relationship with possibly the only person in the village who spoke Spanish. She told the woman of not knowing how they ended up on the beach or even where they were. Following their conversation, the linguist turned to the others and communicated Rome and Heath's situation.

Looks of confusion crossed the faces of all who were present, most likely from learning of the bizarre way the two strangers arrived in their land. Next, they appeared to consult with each other as Heath and Rome nervously awaited their decision.

Things only got stranger as the group of children returned waving a well-used magazine through the air. The teenage girl had it opened to a particular page and pointed back and forth between Rome and the magazine. The female translator showed the magazine to Rome, who stood in amazement to find an old issue of *Trekking the Globe* in such a remote village. Rome ran her finger along the byline located beneath her picture repeating, "Rome London," several times, as she pointed to herself.

"Rome London," said the woman from the village, then she introduced herself. "Bernicia."

Turning back to the men in the group, she proceeded to fill them in on the new information. With more questions in need of answers, Bernicia returned to her conversation with Rome and then back to the men in the group. This went on for several more minutes until one of the men turned to Rome and Heath, smiled and welcomed them to their village. The translator filled in the blanks and they all walked down the street together.

As the sun set, Heath and Rome were grateful to find refuge from the hoards of mosquitos who use the night to feed. Leaving their boots of tarp and rope outside the door, they entered the humble home of their translator and found respite from an afternoon of physical exertion. Quickly, Bernicia had her eldest of three fetch drinking water for her guests as she prepared a meal of leftover cold beans, mashed corn and a type of flatbread. The two younger children sat on the floor and stared at Rome and Heath, studying their every detail.

When the food was served, Heath had a hard time accepting her generosity without payment. Rome, on the other hand, thanked their host and began to eat, signaling to Heath that it was the right thing to do. After an entire day of no food or water, their meager meal felt like a banquet.

Following dinner, Bernicia brought out a small plate of fruit and they enjoyed the sweet follow-up to a hardy meal. As they sampled the local fruit, Rome and Bernicia settled into a conversation. She was of the Miskito people, an indigenous group some two hundred thousand strong, that live along the Mosquito Coast, from Honduras down through Nicaragua. The people in the village spoke Miskito, but she had been educated in Spanish by her mother who married into the Miskito culture.

She spoke proudly of her three children and the life they had carved out in their small village located on the banks of an important river. Her husband was no longer in the picture and Bernicia declined to say why. They had met when they were young in her home village located on Big Corn Island, a popular destination off the Southern Caribbean Coast of Nicaragua, near Bluefields. He had come to the island to work in the fishing industry, but the work was declining.

After their marriage, they moved north to her husband's village and began building a life. With him no longer part of the equation, she was hoping to return to her family home and find a job in the tourist industry, but it would take years before she could afford safe passage for all of them. Rome considered the irony of how with such ease she traveled the globe, yet here was a woman who lacked the means to travel a hundred miles south, a woman who was aged beyond her years but was beautiful in her own right.

Rome wanted to understand the geography of where they were

in order to formulate a plan for getting back to Providence, so Bernicia opened her children's writing tablet and drew a well-detailed picture of the coast of Nicaragua. Rome paused when she realized their location on the beach was only a few miles from the mouth of the river. If they'd gone with Heath's plan and walked the beach to the North, then followed the river inland, they would have eventually run into her village, avoiding the rainforest altogether.

As she turned to relay the new information, she found Heath asleep in the most uncomfortable position: shoulder to the wall, chin to chest and knees bent back to the side. Bernicia smiled as she shared with her new acquaintance the universal truth that men can fall asleep anywhere.

Together they stretched him out on the cot and hung an extra piece of mosquito netting above him. Rome joined Bernicia and her children on the floor bed in the corner of the room, also covered by mosquito netting. She drifted in thought as her head hit the well worn mattress, recognizing that things could have turned out so much worse. Together, she and Heath had survived another adventure after knowing each other for less than a month. The true test of their relationship may end up being how to deal with normalcy.

Although she was unable to see Heath through the darkness, she knew he was there and not just physically. He'd been there for her since they left Hawaii, repeatedly showing his love through commitment and support. But Rome realized she'd been so occupied with Jamie and his rescue over the past few days that she put Heath on the back burner. That was not the case tonight. Thoughts of him and their day together replayed like a movie in her mind as she stared into the darkness. Ironically, it took a hot and muddy slog through a rainforest to teach her the joy that can come from living in the moment. Being stuck in Nicaragua, she'd have no other choice but to continue in the present until their circumstances changed. Fortunately, the present consisted of only her and Heath as events of the world moved forward without them... a thought that brought a smile to her face as she drifted off to sleep.

Chapter Eleven

Morning brought with it a sore neck and back as Heath painfully sat up, accidentally wrapping himself in the mosquito netting. As he fought to find his way out, a long growl erupted from deep within his bowels causing a chain reaction. Grabbing his stomach, Heath knew he needed to find a bathroom fast, but there was no sign of a toilet in the two-room house. Quickly, he opened the door and stepped outside, desperately searching for a place to relieve himself. Rome glanced at Heath from the riverbank and recognized the urgency. Standing up, she used her finger to direct him to a communal outhouse around back. Moving as fast as he could, while tightening a certain sphincter muscle, he made it through the door of the small shack with no time to spare.

The children giggled as they heard a series of loud moans come from the outhouse. Rome laughed along with them, despite the fact that only two hours earlier she had made the same run: a fact Heath would never learn. Smiling with her new friends, she went back to helping Bernicia scrub laundry.

Meeting new people is part of her job description and in Rome's line of work she's always had a give-and-take relationship. They give their knowledge, goods and services and she happily takes them.

Although their time and services are paid for, it's always felt a bit one-sided. As she looked around at her new acquaintances, Rome's mind wandered to past opportunities she'd had to immerse herself in the culture of the different destinations she'd covered for *Trekking the Globe*. Unfortunately, it was a rare treat and only happened when circumstances allowed.

As a travel writer, most of her time is spent in locations and situations designed for tourism. Entering the muddy waters of a river with an indigenous people who didn't speak her language was a dream assignment. But this was life—real life—and they would eventually have to find their way back from the detour.

A half hour later Heath joined them at the water, keeping his distance as he waded in up to his waist. Rome allowed him to keep what was left of his dignity as she pretended not to see him secretly wash away any remaining evidence of last night's dinner downstream. Heath made his way back upstream and watched Bernicia and Rome take turns rubbing clothes against a type of washboard.

"How did you sleep?" asked Rome, kissing him on the cheek.

"Great, until I woke up."

"Would you like some breakfast?"

"Do not mention food."

"We're just finishing up the laundry. "

"You look like you know your way around that washboard."

"I've had a great teacher."

"Have you figured out where we are?"

"Upper part of the Nicaraguan coastline."

"Now we just need a phone."

"Bernicia said our best bet is to wait for the arrival of 'The Brit." He may be coming up the river today."

"Is 'The Brit' a man or a boat?"

"All I know is that he comes bearing gifts."

"That's our way out of Nicaragua."

"She thinks he may have a way to communicate."

"What time is he getting here?"

"They only know the day he usually comes and even that's weather dependent."

"It doesn't get much sunnier than this."

"Then let's hope he arrives."

"What do we do till then?"

"Look around you. When will you ever get to experience something like this again?"

"Hopefully never. I spend my time in offices and conference rooms doing business with other people who do business. Even when I sail, it's only to well-established ports."

"Then count yourself lucky," said Rome as she picked up the tub and washboard and followed Bernicia out of the water. Standing in the river, the lifeblood of this community, Heath took a moment to follow Rome's advice and look around. He watched as women washed their laundry in the river while others, including Rome, hung the clothes on lines to dry. Other women washed dishes and pans in the river and Heath wondered how they survived the lack of sanitation.

The sound of a child yelling turned his attention to some children in a long, shallow, wooden canoe carved out of a log, the same type of boat their distant ancestors most likely used hundreds of years ago. Heath watched as they pushed with long poles against the bottom of the river, propelling themselves forward. Many of the same type of canoes lay along the bank of the river, waiting to be used as a form of transportation.

Suddenly, the seriousness of he and Rome's situation hit him like a brick. Back on the beach they dealt with the unknown, making it easy to theorize and formulate plans. With the discovery of their location and given circumstances, their options had been whittled down to nil. Even if his pockets were full of money, this people had nothing to sell that could get them back to Providencia. They might be open to loaning them a dugout canoe, but the river would only take them further inland and to what? Not to mention, time was of the essence when it came to finding Jamie and canoeing through a rainforest could take weeks.

All at once, he was poked from behind. Turning around he saw a group of smiling children all trying to tell him something at the same time. After using hand motions to communicate, Heath figured out that they were egging him on to play a game of tag. He also understood that he was 'it' and his job was to tag out one of the kids. Trying to be quick, he moved his tall body through the water, but the kids were too fast at disappearing below and swimming to different locations. Heath was getting his butt whipped by a bunch of kids and Rome and the other women were enjoying the show. All at once, Heath adopted their strategy and disappeared beneath the water. The children looked around wondering where he would emerge, but there was no sign of him until he popped up behind one of the older boys and tapped him on the shoulder. "You're it."

The children busted out in laughter as Heath raised his arms in triumph. Of course, it wasn't long before Heath was declared 'it' again and the game continued for a good hour and a half until Heath could no longer keep up with the energy of youth. Making his way onto shore, he collapsed on the grass next to Rome, physically tired but on a mental high.

"Look at you all kid friendly," mentioned Rome with pleasure.

"It appears I have a knack for it."

"Not to mention some pretty impressive sign language skills."

"I'll add it to my resume."

"They're a beautiful people, aren't they?"

"Just yesterday I had no idea they even existed."

"Meeting new people is one of the things I love about my job."

"They're great, but I'm still not eating anything."

Rome laughed as she wrapped her arm around Heath and leaned her head against his shoulder. "I love you."

"Good, 'cause I'm running out of ways to impress you," joked Heath as they watched life on the river go on all around them until they heard the distant sound of a motor. They weren't the only ones excited as an instant commotion swept over the village.

"Is that what I think it is?" asked Rome as they watched the people rush toward the banks of the river.

Standing up they waited with the others till a white and red boat rounded the bend of the river and headed for their shore. From a distance it appeared to be an old-fashioned tugboat, but the closer she came, the more details they could see. Although it was shaped like a tug boat, it was longer in length and resembled more of a houseboat. The wheelhouse at the front was taller than the rest of the boat and had a British flag painted on the side beneath a series of small windows. The living quarters were connected to the back of the wheelhouse and ran the length of the boat to the stern. A deck lined the top of the housing quarters with a wooden railing surrounding it and a canvas canopy for shade.

The captain blew the horn as she neared the village, careful to stay in the middle of the river to avoid running aground. Heath and Rome watched as people jumped into canoes while others swam out to greet the boat. After shutting down the engine, the captain opened a door on the front of the wheelhouse and stepped out onto the pointed bow, standing directly above the boat's name: The Brit.

Since there was nowhere to moor the boat, he walked around the side and lowered an anchor into the water to secure her position. Although he towed a small rowboat behind for access to the shore, he would not need it today. He had his pick of rides as dugout canoes surrounded the boat.

Walking half way down the side of the boat, he rolled up a canvas curtain covering an opening in the side of the housing quarters, then began unloading supplies into the hands of eager recipients. Rome and Heath watched with great curiosity as bags, cans, boxes and baskets of unknown items were loaded into canoes and brought back to shore.

Eventually, the captain, fluent in the Miskito language, signaled an end to the supplies, then lowered himself down a short ladder into one of the canoes. Rome and Heath watched like flies on a wall as the villagers greeted him on the shore, then the adults gathered around the pile of supplies and began distributing them to those most in need. Rome made her way through the crowd in time to see hygiene kits, used clothing, canned foods, school supples, kitchen utensils and old books and magazines, all finding their way into the villagers' grateful hands.

Heath's attention fell on the captain as he pulled pieces of candy out of the many pockets of his cargo shorts and placed them in the outstretched hands of the children gathered around him. When the last hand received its candy, Heath made his way toward the captain who offered him a piece as well.

"It's a little early for Santa Claus to be handing out lollies," remarked Heath as he unwrapped the candy and popped it into his mouth.

"In this neck of the woods, it's never too early for Father Christmas," replied the captain in a British accent. "Oliver Hewitt, captain of the 'The Brit.'"

"Heath Jones."

"What brings an Aussie to this part of the world?"

"That's a good question."

"Is the answer a secret?"

"Not to the people who drugged us and dumped us on the beach."

"An intrigue," said the captain with excitement.

"We were kidnapped from the Isla de Providencia."

"Any thought to the reason?"

"We came to the island searching for a friend who disappeared close to a week ago."

"Sounds like you're in over your heads."

"Fortunately, we're both good swimmers."

"Will you return to the scene of the crime?"

"Yes."

"There's a small airstrip in a town up the river about 40 miles, but the flights are few and far between. Your best bet would be by ship."

"I can make that happen, but I need a phone."

"Then you're in luck. I have a ham radio, sat phone and cell phone on the boat."

"You are Santa Claus."

"Come on then. Row us out to the boat."

Heath caught Rome's attention and motioned to her that they were heading to the boat. Signaling she would stay behind, she watched as they boarded a canoe and used the sticks to push toward 'The Brit.' Rome returned her attention to the activity at hand, taking as many mental notes as possible—research for a future article of a personal nature.

Tying off the canoe, they boarded the boat and made their way down the side and into the living quarters. The inside resembled a tropical den with well-used furniture and a comfortable looking double bed, draped with plenty of mosquito netting. Books lined a small shelf near a drafting desk covered with maps, papers and notes. Near the front of the living quarters, next to the doorway to the wheelhouse, Heath found the communications hub.

"I recommend the sat phone," suggested Oliver as he found his way to a comfy chair, giving Heath a bit of privacy to dial the number of the one man he trusted most, his butler and friend, Sheldon. As the phone continued to ring, Heath prayed silently that he would answer. Finally, the sound of his voice brought with it great relief. "Hello, Sheldon. It's Heath. I'm calling from a satellite phone in Nicaragua." Heath paused as Sheldon shared his surprise at their being so off the beaten path. "Rome and I need a ride out of here. Can you send a rescue boat to the Mosquito Coast?" Sheldon asked for his coordinates and Heath turned to Oliver for help. Checking his GPS, Oliver showed Heath exactly where they were, allowing him to relay the latitude and longitude to his friend.

"We need to be picked up as quickly as possible, Sheldon. You have the means at your disposal. Make it happen." Ending the conversation by writing down Heath's number, Sheldon assured his boss that he would contact him with an ETA as soon as a ship was en route.

Heath sat the phone down and turned back to Oliver. "Thank you. You literally just saved our lives."

"And hopefully the life of your missing friend," encouraged Oliver as he noticed Heath eyeballing the large drink dispenser of water located on the counter near the hotplate. "Would you like a drink?"

"Desperately," answered Heath as he licked his lips watching Oliver fill a cup of purified drinking water. Trying not to guzzle the entire glass, Heath paced himself as Oliver filled a cup of his own. "Would you and your friend like to join me for tea tonight?"

"I hate to inconvenience you any more than I already have."

"Nonsense. Having a conversation in English will be a nice break from Miskito and Spanish."

"That would be great, especially since the local cuisine doesn't seem to agree with me," admitted Heath, much to the enjoyment of Oliver.

"I apologize for having fun at your expense... part and parcel of my current lifestyle. Shall we return to the village for the afternoon?"

"Do you mind if we take the sat phone?"

"Not at all."

Boarding the canoe, they pushed their way back across the river and pulled the boat ashore. Heath was excited to introduce Rome to his new friend and savior, who wasted no time in applauding her brilliance as a travel writer. Apparently, there was nowhere that Rome could hide from her celebrity status. Rome and Heath watched as Oliver engaged in conversations with individuals and families, assessing their ongoing needs. Many of the women in the village brought baskets of handmade crafts for him to sell to ecotourists whom he might encounter in his travels. Oliver compensated them with money in exchange and they received it with hugs and robust handshakes.

Separating herself from the other ladies, Bernicia counted the coins in her hand, calculating how much she could spare to set aside for their travel fund. It wasn't much, but it was more than she had when the week began and Rome couldn't help but be impressed by her tenacity. Catching sight of Heath out of the corner of her eye, she turned to see his attention fixed on Bernicia as well. His expression was more of concern than the smile Rome wore on her face and that made her smile even more.

Nearing the six o'clock hour, the three of them returned to 'The Brit.' Oliver checked the fuel in the covered generator at the rear of the boat before he entered his living quarters and closed the doors to the insects outside. Once inside, he accessed the front of the generator and started it up in order to heat the hot plate and give light to the room.

As the delicious aroma of food frying in a pan filled Heath's nostrils, his empty stomach began to growl in anticipation. With no room for a table, they balanced their plates on their laps and enjoyed a beautiful dinner. Following the cleanup, they settled in for a round of conversation.

"How are you so familiar with the Miskito culture?" asked Rome, curious to know the answer.

"I'm a sociocultural anthropologist," he replied. "I spent several years along the Mosquito coast while working toward my second doctorate degree. I was in my late twenties and it was all about the adventure. I returned to London and took a teaching position at my alma mater of Cambridge, where eventually I gained tenure."

"So what brought you back?"

"A desire to do more with my life. A legacy, I suppose."

"Teaching is a legacy in itself."

"I once believed that as well, until education lost the human element."

"How do you afford the supplies you bring to the villages?" asked Heath.

"Before I left, I set up a foundation in both the United Kingdom and the States, which accepts used and new items from donors, as well as money to pay for shipping. A good friend runs that end of it, while I see to the distribution. The only thing we don't accept is medical supplies. We leave that to the experts."

"Is it productive?"

"Like anything, it's hot and cold."

"So what do you do when you're not delivering goods?" enquired Rome.

"I teach Spanish to the children in the villages up and down the river. Communication can be key to resolving conflict, and with the ongoing violent struggle between the Miskito people and the mestizos—or settlers—moving onto their indigenous land, it can only help in the years to come."

The ringing of the sat phone brought a pause to the conversation as Heath quickly answered. "Yes, Sheldon." Grateful to hear his voice, Heath was all ears as his butler filled him in on the details of the plan. "I'll meet them at the mouth of the river. And Sheldon... make sure they bring some money, toothbrushes and paste." Before disconnecting the call, Heath listened to his friend's final thought then shared it with Rome. "Sheldon sends his regards."

"Ah, he does remember me," joked Rome, happy to know he was thinking of her as a yawn escaped her mouth. "We should get back to Bernicia's before it gets dark and leave you to your privacy."

"What time will they arrive?"

"They're coming from San Andres and should be here by daybreak."

"Take my watch. As tired as you look, you'll need an alarm."

"Thanks, Oliver."

"Wake me before you leave."

"We will," promised Heath as they shook hands. "Again, we can't thank you enough."

Rome said goodbye as well and they boarded the canoe, fighting off droves of mosquitos as they pushed their way to shore. Hurrying to the house, they entered after a quick knock, finding the small family preparing for bed. Bernicia and the children were excited to see their return and offered to prepare them a meal. Rome graciously declined, letting her know they had eaten with the captain. Bernicia wished them a good night, then she and her children crawled onto the mattress, leaving enough room on the edge for their guest.

Rome sat down next to Heath, quietly taking in her last night in the village, while Heath's mind was abuzz with thoughts of being rescued. Taking his hand in hers, she shared her thoughts about Bernicia and her children. "We have to make one stop before returning to Providence."

Heath took one look at Rome and knew exactly what she was thinking. "It's got to be her choice."

"I know."

"What about her home?"

"She rents, when she has enough money to pay."

"And her belongings?"

"I'll help her pack."

"We can't wait long."

"I get that."

"I want to help her as much as you do, Rome, but it's about the timing," he responded setting the alarm on Oliver's watch.

"For her as well."

"True. We can't do anything until daybreak. Let's see what tomorrow brings," suggested Heath as he weaved his fingers through hers and leaned his head back against the wall.

"Okay," agreed Rome, allowing silence to dictate the conversation. Once his eyes closed, Rome took the opportunity to study him as she'd never done before. She watched as a peaceful contentment washed over his face, no doubt brought on by the certainty of rescue. He had earned this moment and Rome couldn't help but wonder what thoughts of tomorrow were drifting through his mind.

"I love you, Rome," he whispered softly, drifting off to sleep.

The answer to her curiosity was sudden and unexpected. His thoughts were of her. She knew he loved her, but somehow the impact of those three words at that quiet moment was more than she could subdue. Rome's attempt to choke back the tears failed immediately, leaving her unable to respond. Trying not to call attention to herself, she covered her mouth and pressed her head against the wall to squelch the onset of sobbing. The only sound escaping were the rapid gasps of air being inhaled and exhaled through her fingers. There was no stopping the wave of emotional intensity. All she could do was let it come.

Pulling her trembling hand away from Heath's, she used it for backup as she moved to the corner and slid to the floor. Crying in the shadows of the dimly-lit room, she experienced a joy so powerful and profound that even as a writer she could never capture it in words. It was a personal confirmation, honest and real. A life altering moment she would never forget.

With the passing of time, the fervor began to lessen, leaving her alone with her thoughts. Before she fell in love with Heath, Rome had no idea what was missing from her life or her relationship with Jamie. It was a depth of love she'd never felt before. He completed her in a way she never thought possible and filled a space deep inside that she didn't realize was empty. She loved Jamie, but never on this level. They were happy with a relationship built around weekend activities and vacation planning. It was easy and fun. Would they have continued to be happy together? Most likely. But she would never have felt the true joy she found with Heath.

Rising to her feet, she wiped the remaining tears from her cheeks and gently encouraged Heath to lay down on the cot. After leaving him with a kiss on his cheek, she pulled the mosquito netting over his sleeping area and put out the light. Drained to the core from opening herself up so deeply, she crawled onto the mattress with Bernicia and the kids and stared into the darkness.

For the first time since they met, the need to test her relationship with Heath disappeared. Any doubts she had vanished as the beats of her heart slowed to a peaceful rhythm. There was no question left in her mind that Heath was the one for her. The great love of her life.

And it took being stranded together in a small village in Central America to help her see what was right in front of her the whole time.

Chapter Twelve

Shipwreck of the Maiden's Return

*S*earching through the lower hold of the Maiden's Return was an obstacle course that even the most experienced of divers would not attempt. Jamie had broken through barricades of loose lumber, originally stored for ship repairs, walls of floating canvas, intended for sail repair, and crates and boxes covered in what seemed like miles of heavy rope. Still he came up empty-handed. He lost count as to how many human bones and skulls he had come upon. These were the first he had found in the entire ship. He thought it strange that so many of the crew would have held up in the lowest part of the hull rather than abandon ship. He was also puzzled that the bones hadn't been eroded away by the warm sea water after so many years... but neither had the wood of the ship—just one more discovery he would chalk up to 'unexplainable.'

Continuing his search, he began to question whether there was any Aztec gold to be found. As much as he wanted the ordeal to be over, he hoped the legend of the Maiden's Return and her hidden treasure were true. Not only that, but the lives of his fellow captives depended on the search continuing. He needed time to come up with a plan and put it in motion.

With apprehension he continued to move objects from his path, wondering each time if it would be the straw that would break the camel's back, or in this case, send the ship to its final resting place at the bottom of the abyss. Jamie worked to control the anxiety created by such an impossible task, but the pressure was building and even the strongest of men have their breaking point. Clearing his mind of the possibility that he may be staring at the inside walls of his own coffin, he stopped to check the level of his tanks. Nearing the need for an exchange, he concluded there was time to open one last box.

With crowbar in hand, he brushed off the top of the next crate and discovered a wooden trunk sealed with a rusted padlock. Before he could bust the lock, the invisible force returned, invading the cramped quarters of the lower deck and forcefully bunting Jamie from all sides. He could do nothing to help himself but work to keep from panicking. He was nothing more than a human piñata, taking blows from all sides, until an opposing force filled the ship's hull from the other end, drawing the attention of his attacker. He had experienced the phenomenon before, but this was different. There now appeared to be two sides to the mysterious force, battling each other. Although he was still trapped, the battering of his body lessened thanks to the distraction of the second entity.

The claustrophobic feel of the crowded space was impacting him mentally as well, knowing his tanks could run dry before making it out of the ship. Jamie was caught in a perfect storm and all he could do was lie still, control his breathing, and let it rage around him.

After what seemed like an eternity, the mysterious attacker abruptly left the hull, chased away by the opposing force. With trepidation, Jamie checked his air and gas levels, finding just enough to get him back to the top. But instead of fleeing the ship, he allowed the curiosity surrounding the crate to overrule common sense.

Retrieving the hammer he left near the stairs, he used the pry bar to bust the latch from the crate, allowing him access to the contents of the trunk. As he opened the lid, a burst of air pushed the water past him, as though the trunk exhaled a mighty breath. A cold shiver ran from the top of his spine to the bottom, bringing with it a feeling of dread that Jamie felt to the bone—more fearsome than the physical force he had just experienced. Cautiously, he shined his light into the trunk, finding it to be full of gold jewelry. He had found the Aztec treasure stolen from the emperor's sacred burial grounds.

Jamie was stunned as he reached in with his gloved hand and pulled out several pieces. Many of the designs depicted angry faces, with jaws and eyes wide open and mouths full of teeth. Clearly, the gold pieces were designed to intimidate and show the power of the Aztec nation. Jamie placed them back in the trunk then continued to search through the rest, hooking a type of neck collar designed to wrap over the shoulders and across the upper chest. The heavy, gold neck piece was made of a series of thick rectangle-shaped, three inch long segments, engraved with a serpent's head on each one.

Although the discovery was exciting, he couldn't escape the darkness he felt while rifling through the contents of the trunk. To the Aztecs, gold was believed to have come from the sun and hold divine power. It was used to embellish monuments to their gods and adorn the earthly royalty who served them as kings and emperors. His thoughts turned to Aztecan history of mass human sacrifice and brutality of the innocent, mostly women and children. Human blood was given to the gods as a thanksgiving. They called it 'precious water' and gave it freely, all in the name of worship.

Closing the lid, he wanted to pretend he never found it, but he knew that Jack was watching. Everything he saw, Lazenby saw, through the lens of a camera. Almost everything. Jamie also knew the gold would find its way to the surface by his own hand and would be the means of making one of the worst men on earth even more powerful. Lazenby would worship the gold like the Aztecs worshipped their Gods... with disregard for human life.

It had been five days since he'd slept and his body was feeling it.

He'd gone that long during missions before, but combining the lack of sleep with the breathing of oxygen mixed with helium and nitrogen was taking a toll. He had heard of documented studies where people had gone up to eighteen days with no sleep, but that wasn't under such stressful conditions. For a brief moment, he contemplated releasing the air from his tank.

Shaking it off, he wondered how a thought of that nature had entered his mind. Even if he went through with it, Lazenby would just replace him. Worse than that, he'd take pleasure in eliminating Talin and Leta, and Jamie couldn't live with that, especially if he was dead and couldn't do anything about it. That would tick him off for eternity.

Hearing the alarm sound on his dive computer, he carefully left the hull of the Maiden's Return and swam through the open hatches of the top two decks. Leaving the wreck behind, he timed his rise to the surface, taking a break for decompression along the way. Eventually, he emerged from the ocean beneath the hulls of the catamaran. Accessing the surface air valve, he filled his lungs with the fresh air of daybreak as he watched the eastern sky light up in advance of the rising sun. Jamie needed a moment before facing Lazenby's egotistical narcissism. He knew he'd never hear the end of what he witnessed on video. Unfortunately, it didn't take long for him to be discovered. Jamie placed his foot in the hook and grabbed hold of the cable as he signaled to the man above to start the winch. As soon as his head cleared the South'n Hunter's hatch, he could hear the screaming and shouting. "We did it, Webb, we did it! We should have teamed up years ago!"

Jamie sat down on the crate, allowing the water to drip off his wetsuit while the men removed his scuba tank and face mask. Already irritated, he pulled his hood back and ran his fingers through his dark hair as Lazenby continued to hoot and holler.

"Come on, show it to me. Where is it?"

"I didn't bring anything up."

Disappointed, Lazenby sat down across the hatch from him. "Not even a gold earring or a bracelet?"

"I left it all down there."

"I'll hold it in my hands soon enough. I'm rich, Webb. Rich beyond my wildest dreams and I got you to thank for it!"

"I don't think you should bring it up, Jack."

"Have you lost your mind?"

"I got a bad feeling when I opened the crate."

"That gold is coming to the surface, bad feeling or not."

"I'm telling you... what I felt wasn't good."

"It's the gas. It's getting to your head."

"It wasn't the gas."

"Then you're hallucinating from lack of sleep. Now that we know the treasure's there, you can take a few hours to rest before we start the extraction process."

"I need to clean up first," responded Jamie as he stood up and unzipped the top of his wetsuit while one of the men helped him pull it down from the back.

"You'll sleep on that cot in the corner. I don't want you near the others," ordered Lazenby as he turned and walked toward the stairs. "And no more talk of what you felt down there!"

Before he could get far, a dark thought hit Jamie's mind. "Jack, can I have a word with you in private?"

"You've said enough."

"It's worth your while."

"Fine," responded Lazenby as he signaled for Jamie to catch up with him. Removing his fins as he walked, Jamie waited to speak until he felt they were at a safe distance from everyone else. "How well do you trust your men?"

"I don't trust anyone."

"What if they demand a bigger take?"

"No one makes demands of me. You of all people should know that."

"How do you know they won't turn on you once they see the gold?"

"They'll be well paid."

"Will that be enough to keep them from popping both of us and dumping our bodies overboard once they see all that gold? Just something to consider as you're making plans," whispered Jamie, planting a seed of doubt and conspiracy in Lazenby's mind.

"What are you thinkin'?"

"The gold won't be nearly as powerful if they don't see it," suggested Jamie as several guards walked by packing arms full of canvas bags.

"Does this have to do with what you felt down there?"

"I'm just trying to avoid resurfacing during a civil war."

"So tie the top of the bags before sending them up."

"Ties can be undone and bags can be cut."

"Then how do we keep them from seeing it?"

"Do you have any metal trunks aboard?" responded Jamie.

"Water won't drain from a trunk."

"It will if I drill several small holes in the bottom of each trunk then secure them with a lock before your guys pull them up with the winch."

"I suppose it'd be good way to control the inventory."

"And I get to avoid a gun battle."

"First I need a sample."

"Done. This would go a lot faster if I had some help."

"Tell that to my six dead divers."

As Lazenby disappeared up the stairs, Jamie grabbed a t-shirt and a clean pair of swim trunks from a pile and walked across the deck to the shower room.

No longer in sight of the guards or cameras, Jamie snuck down the hall toward a room that had caught his attention. He needed to know what was behind the gray, metal door, especially if the contents could help facilitate their escape. Two days earlier, he saw a guard enter the room empty-handed then exit with an assault rifle. Since then he'd waited for the right moment to investigate. Reaching the door, he found it necessary to utilize his lock-picking skill. Pulling out the two large, heavy-duty paper clips he'd borrowed from Lazenby's desk during one of their arduous meetings, he straightened both of them. He then bent the last eighth of the first clip to a twenty-degree angle for the pick and the second clip into an L shape to use as his tension wrench. Working his magic, he had the door open within seconds, entered the room and closed the door quietly behind him.

As he flipped on the light, he took a quick one-eighty of the very organized storage room full of shelves lined with food and supplies. Ropes, chains and cables of all kinds hung on the wall with a bucket of padlocks setting on the shelf next to them. Several plastic tubs, metal trunks and heavy duty canvas bags took up the space on the floor beneath them. He noted the number of trunks and hoped it would be enough to hold everything, then he took two padlocks with their inserted keys out of the bucket and rolled them into his clean shirt.

Zeroing in on an open box of candy, Jamie helped himself to a chocolate bar as he continued to surveil the room. Near the back he found what he was searching for: a stack of crates full of knives and guns. He quickly examined the selection of pistols and rifles, removing their clips to make sure they were loaded, then replaced them with perfect precision. With time running out, he chose to open one last crate next to the weapons. To his surprise, the wooden box was full of composition 4, otherwise known as C4, an explosive he was very familiar with. He knew the detonators and blasting caps had to be nearby so he searched through a couple more crates full of ammunition and gun accessories until he found them.

This new discovery gave Jamie exactly what he'd been looking for: a better option for planning a successful escape. Grabbing a couple more candy bars, he used a marker to write a message on the wrapper, "Still alive. See you soon. J," then left the storage area the way he found it. As he approached the door to Talin and Leta's room, he quickly slid the candy under their door, then slipped into the shower room.

Once inside, he peeled the wetsuit from his body and tossed it out the door. Stepping into the shower, the pulsating water helped to relieve a portion of the tension ranging from his neck to the lower back. Finding it hard to stay awake, he turned off the shower, dried himself, then brushed his teeth and left the bathroom. Walking across the deck, the only thing in his sights was the cot near the wall. On his mind, however, was the weight of the world in the form of Talin, Leta, Rome and Heath. He shouldered much of the responsibility for their current circumstances, especially with Rome's abduction. Fortunately, his military experience taught him to shut down his mind in order to sleep. A few hours wasn't much, but he'd take anything he could get.

ONE OF LAZENBY'S bodyguards reached the top of the stairs, interrupting his boss spying on Jamie as he crawled onto the cot. "Circumstances have changed with Jones."

"How?"

"A yacht was chartered out of San Andres last night. They'll be picking up Jones off the Nicaragua coast at daybreak."

"Do I own the captain of the yacht?"

"Just the chief mate. The captain has no idea we use his boat to smuggle."

"We can't let them reach the island."

"What do you want done?"

"Send a boat to intercept them. The chief mate can keep us updated on their location."

"You got it," said the bodyguard as he left the upper deck.

Glancing at the clock on the wall, he checked the time while rubbing his eyes. Jamie wasn't the only one being deprived of sleep, but Lazenby's self-induced insomnia came from his obsession with finding the treasure and the anxiety it produced. Walking back to his chair, he switched from the camera feed on the lower deck to the grainy video of Jamie and the treasure. The discovery of the gold had taken the edge off his compulsion, causing him to relax for the first time in a week. He watched again as Jamie reached into the trunk, hooking a gold neck piece and bringing it into the light.

All at once, an idea struck that would solve more problems than just one. Lazenby called his bodyguard back and gave him orders in regard to Heath Jones, then turned his attention back to the monitor. He could feel lust for the treasure growing inside him as he continued to replay Jamie's discovery, but the physical need for rest demanded more attention. Unable to keep his eyes open, his remote control dropped from his hand and he surrendered to his body's need for sleep.

Chapter Thirteen

Heath woke to the beeping of his watch and quickly silenced the alarm. Normally he was an early riser, but his body wasn't reacting too well to the physical nature of their recent circumstances. Crawling across the floor and lifting the mosquito netting, he nudged Rome's shoulder to wake her enough to share his plans. "I'll be back when the boat arrives." Then he kissed her cheek and left the house.

Rome followed suit by reaching over and nudging Bernicia's shoulder, then motioned for her to move away from the children so they could speak. She wanted to give her as much time as possible if she chose to leave. Walking into the cooking area, Rome informed Bernicia of their imminent departure, then offered her a boat ride down the coastline to her island hometown. Bernicia burst into tears and jumped at the prospect of returning home. Rome offered help in packing and she happily accepted with an enormous hug.

Soon, the sleepy children entered the room, awakened by the voice of their mother. She took them into her arms and related the good news. Rome watched as the excitement spread from Bernicia to the children and they hurried off to find makeshift bags to hold their few earthly belongings. If anything good had come from the nightmare Heath and Rome found themselves in just two days earlier, it was this. With nothing to give but kindness, Bernicia had given them all she had and now it was their chance to return the favor.

REACHING THE RIVER, Heath pushed himself in a canoe toward 'The Brit' and boarded the boat. Oliver was already awake and greeted him with two cups in hand. Grateful for the morning pick-me-up, Heath exchanged the watch for the cup then asked to borrow his tender. Oliver walked to the back and untied the tow knot securing the dinghy, then pulled it around the opposite side of the boat for Heath to access from the ladder. Heath crawled into the dinghy, started the small outboard motor then steered her toward the mouth of the river. Rounding the bend, he saw one of the most beautiful sights he'd ever seen... a large boat anchored about a half mile off shore.

Heath pulled the flagpole from the back of the dingy and waved the British flag at the rescue party. They signaled back by blinking their lights. Contact had been made. He watched as a tender left the boat and traveled across the waves toward the mouth of the river. Heath turned his dinghy and headed back up the river, tying off the tender and boarding Oliver's boat. They waited on the bow for the rescue party to make its way around the curve of the river, then Heath waved his hands and guided it toward 'The Brit.'

Coming into view, Heath was surprised to see his old friend, Sheldon Burns, captaining the vessel, with Beverly Hucker as his first mate. "How did you get here from Australia so fast?"

"That's the beauty of it... we had just arrived on San Andres," responded Mr. Burns.

"We were waiting for the ferry to takes us to the Isla de Providencia when you called," added Bev.

"It was perfect timing. We were able to rent the yacht then start west."

"What are you doing in the Caribbean?" asked Heath.

"When you didn't call back, I grew nervous."

"So we came to help."

"Who's taking care of the castle?"

"Gladys and her husband," replied Mr. Burns.

"I'm so glad you stopped over on your way to England," said Heath.

"About that...," started Bev.

"We sent Miss Lemmons and George to England in our place," responded Sheldon.

"With your credit card," added Bev.

"I'm not sure which is more scary... two young adults in London with unlimited access to my bank card or that you're finishing each other's sentences."

"The first, but it had to be done. Now where's Rome?" asked Bev.

"She'll be down in a minute. We may have to make one stop south of here."

"The yacht's fueled up so that shouldn't be a problem."

"Speaking of the yacht, how much is that costing me?"

"Ten thousand a day."

"Which is good, considering you almost had to buy one," shared Bev.

"She's all that was available at the last minute."

"It's great. Thank you. Both of you," responded Heath as he stepped from Oliver's boat back into the dugout canoe and pushed his way back to shore, securing it on the bank. Just as he started toward Bernicia's house, he saw them all walking toward him. Once he saw the smiles on Bernicia and her children's faces, he knew that taking the time to go out of their way would be well spent. Sheldon motored his boat toward the shore, and Heath and Bev helped everyone and their belongings into the boat, then Heath boarded himself.

Rome and her Aussie friend greeted each other with a hug as she introduced their fellow passengers, while Heath pulled his butler aside and whispered in his ear. Sheldon pulled a wad of pesos from his pocket and handed it to Heath, then steered the boat toward

'The Brit.' Oliver watched as they came about, then kneeled down and took hold of Heath's extended hand. Surprised to find a clip of money exchanged during the shake, Oliver nodded his head in gratitude.

"For Santa," called out Heath as they headed toward the ocean. "Expect more from where that came from."

As Bev used her guide skills to make everyone comfortable, Rome visually bid farewell to the little village that took them in when they were lost. She would always remember them fondly in her heart and possibly in a future article. Turning to face the boat in the distance, she immediately switched gears back to locating Jamie. She was determined to find Kera, or 'the mermaid' as the pirate ghost called her, and this time she would get the answers she needs. Glancing at Heath, she found him staring back at her with the same look of determination on his face. They had already lost two crucial days in the search for Jamie and neither of them were sure if he was still alive.

Boarding the yacht, Heath introduced himself to the captain and his two-man crew and let them know they would be taking a detour to Big Corn Island on their way back. The captain informed him that it was about one hundred and forty miles from their current location back to the Isla de Providencia and about the same distance between Big Corn Island and Providence. Traveling south would add an extra eighty or so miles to their return trip. Heath thanked him for the itinerary and asked him to get under way.

Pulling anchor, the boat headed south as Bev and Rome helped Bernicia and her children find breakfast and settle in the lounge. Fortunately, Bev had grown familiar with many languages during her years as a guide and was able to communicate the basics in Spanish. Rome looked to Heath, busy on the phone catching up on shipping business, while Sheldon played the dutiful assistant. With everyone settled into their own routines, she decided to take some time for herself. So she picked up a croissant, wrapped a light blanket around her shoulders, then walked out to the deck located at the stern of the ship. Finding a comfortable chair, she nestled herself into the cushions and used the blanket to protect her from the cool morning air blowing past at thirty knots. Although she appreciated the perspective she gained during her time with the Miskito people, she was glad to be back to civilization and the amenities of her life.

"He has found it," declared the mermaid, surprising Rome by sitting down next to her.

"Who's found what, Kera?"

"Your friend. He has discovered the treasure."

"Jamie found the sunken treasure?" Rome thought for a moment as she attempted to make sense of their kidnapping. "Did Jamie have something to do with our abduction?"

"It was his idea not to kill you both."

"Who wanted to kill us?"

"A man named Lazenby."

"Why is that name familiar?"

"Your friend seems to know him."

"Is Jamie working with this man?"

"He works for him."

"I don't believe this," shouted Rome outraged by Jamie's apparent actions.

"You misunderstand. Your friend's death will come soon."

"It'll come soon all right... as soon as I get my hands around his neck!"

"Not by your hands."

"What?"

"His death will come at the hand of the man who owns him."

"Owns him?"

"His taskmaster."

"So he's being held against his will?"

"Forced to dive for the treasure."

"And now that he's found it, he's expendable."

"Yes."

"What's this Lazenby like?"

"From what I've witnessed, a very evil man. I once knew someone just like him."

"No one fights evil better than Jamie."

"Do not take this man lightly," she warned Rome, grabbing onto her hand and accidentally opening a window to a past memory.

THE MAIDEN'S RETURN, 1724

A seventeen-year-old Kera rushed from her quarters, weaving in and out of the crewmen preparing to board the two rowboats. It was a beautiful morning and the Maiden's Return had just arrived near what was left of the harbor of Port Royal, a coastal town located on the British island of Jamaica. The late seventeenth-century earthquake and tsunami had sent two-thirds of the popular port town into the ocean, and an early eighteenth-century fire destroyed much of the rest, as well as anything they rebuilt. Thousands had lost their lives to the natural disasters as well as the diseases that followed.

Jamaica, once home to Henry Morgan and a safe haven for pirates and buccaneers, was no longer a friendly center of pirate trade thanks to the passing of anti-piracy laws. But the Maiden's Return needed supplies, so the captain and crew lowered their flag and dressed like merchant sailors to hide their true identities. The agricultural town of Kingston, located on the other side of the harbor, had replaced Port Royal as the center of trade in Jamaica and that's where they were headed. But before the Captain could leave the ship, he was stopped by his daughter.

"Can I go ashore, Father? I've heard so many stories of Port Royal."

"That's no place for a lady. It wasn't then and it's not now."

"I want to see it."

"There's nothing left to see, only a prison for pirates and the gallows known for hanging them."

"But it's right there, across the harbor."

"You'll stay with Henry and the others until we return from Kingston."

"Father, please."

"It's too dangerous, Kera!" responded Captain Locke, pointing across the harbor. "With those British warships anchored nearby, we're all in danger." Kissing her on the forehead, he bid her farewell and let himself over the side into one of the two rowboats.

Kera watched them row toward shore, disappointed to be trapped on the boat. Running to the opposite side of the ship, she picked up Henry's spyglass along the way and looked across the harbor at Port Royal.

Feeling a familiar set of arms wrap around her waist, she lowered the telescope and let out an enormous sigh.

"You know he be right," Henry whispered in her ear.

"He's a pirate, Henry, but you wouldn't know it by all the rules."

"Tis your father first."

"Why must you always take his side?" she asked.

"He be me captain."

Raising the spyglass again to her eye, she scanned the port town. "I just want to see what's left of it."

Moving her long black hair aside, Henry pressed his lips to her neck. "There be better ways to pass the time."

Closing the spyglass, she turned in Henry's arms to face him. "What do ya have in mind?" Allowing him to pull her close, she wrapped her arms around his neck and let him show her what he had planned. The kiss was perfect and Kera began to forget all about Port Royal.

The opposite was true for Henry. Pulling away from her, he remembered what he wished he could forget. "I'm supposed to be cleaning the hull with the men. Captain wants it ready for the new supplies."

"How long is that going to take?"

"Oh, I be making it quick, lass," he said, kissing her goodbye and running toward the companionway.

Discontented, Kera extended the spyglass and turned back toward Port Royal. Scanning the sites, she came upon a man with a spyglass staring in her direction. He looked to be an officer in the British Navy, and in her innocence, she treated it like nothing more than a coincidence.

Closing her telescope, she glanced at one of the rowboats,

wondering if she could make it there and back by the time Henry finished cleaning and mopping the lower deck. There was little wind to speak of and the water was calm, which meant easy rowing. She also wondered what the punishment would be if her father found out. Then again, what could he say? She was the daughter of a pirate, after all.

Resolved to give it a try, she quickly lowered the rowboat, let herself down and set the oars to the water. Pulling evenly, she watched the Maiden's Return get farther away as she rotated her head back and forth to avoid running into the many ships anchored in the harbor. She was confident her spur-of-the-moment plan would go exactly as expected.

Returning to the upper deck to fill a bucket with water, Henry expected to see Kera, but she was nowhere in sight. Noticing his spyglass on the deck where he had left her, he glanced at the rowboats. One was missing. Dropping the bucket, he ran to the side of the ship, scooped up the telescope and began searching for her. Not far from shore, he caught her in his sites. "No, Kera. Kera!" he yelled out loud as he rushed to the last rowboat and let it down to the water. Grabbing two swords and a pouch of gunpowder, he threw a belt containing a flintlock pistol over his shoulder and lowered himself into the boat. With all his strength, he began to row like his life depended on it.

Kera reached the shore and tied her boat to a piling beneath the dock. Climbing barefoot up the side of a hill, she found herself standing in Port Royal. She knew her time was limited so she made a beeline for the main street. She was wearing the casual style of clothing she wore each day on the ship: a wide-necked, white chemise, normally worn by women as an undergarment, belted at the waist, hanging over a cotton, slip-style skirt that ended just below the knee. Unaware that her wardrobe was less than formal for a British port, she made her way down the street, garnering strange looks from all who passed.

Kera saw evidence of the earthquake, fires and hurricanes that had plagued the town over the past twenty or so years, but she was also intrigued by the amount of rebuilding going on all around her.

Little did she realize the buildings being built were for the British Navy. She was surrounded by the enemy and had no idea the danger she was in until she came upon the gallows where two pirates hung by their necks. Stopping in her tracks, she slowly started to back away.

"It's a shame really," came a low voice from behind. "To die so young at the end of a rope."

Kera tried to run but the man caught her by the upper arm and pulled her back.

"I must be going, sir," she said, trying to pull away from his grip.

"Actually, it's Admiral. Admiral Cross. Why don't we take a walk instead?"

"Please, let me go."

"Why the hurry? Your ship remains anchored and your captain has yet to return."

Surprised by all he knew, she realized he was the man behind the spyglass. Forcefully, she began to fight for her freedom. "Let go of my arm!"

Pulling her toward the gallows instead, he began his questioning. "Under what captain's name do you sail?"

"Let go!"

"Answer my question and I will consider it," said the admiral stopping next to the gallows.

Standing in silence, they watched as several British soldiers removed the pirates' bodies and laid them in the back of a cart. She had seen death in her short life, more than she wanted to, but never feared losing her own life until that moment.

"You sail aboard the Maiden's Return, do you not?"

Pulling hard, she freed herself from the admiral only to run into the two naval soldiers standing behind her. Surprised by their presence, she fought to get away, but they flanked her on both sides. No matter how hard she fought, there was no escaping their hold. She was trapped.

Intrigued by her unique beauty, the admiral stepped toward her, removed his glove and ran his fingers down her silky, long black hair. "You're the mermaid that brings luck to her captain."

"No, I am not," implored Kera. "That's a myth. There is no mermaid."

"Of course there is. She stands before me."

"It's not true!"

"I heard of your existence before I left London and now I have you within my grasp."

"Sir, you must believe me!"

"Enough!" Returning his hand to the glove, he turned from Kera and looked to the ocean. "See my warships just off the harbor?"

Kera looked to the same ships her father had pointed to as reason not to come to Port Royal. She now understood her captain's resolve, a decision she so easily dismissed as 'too protective' just an hour ago.

"I've already alerted my fleet to the presence of the Maiden's Return. When Captain Locke and his crew return, I will give the order to take them prisoner and it will be their necks that stretch from these gallows."

"No, please," Kera pleaded with her captor. "They mean you no harm."

"Pirates are a scourge to the New World. Soon they'll all meet their end."

"My captain is different."

Turning back to Kera, he asked the question whose answer he sought the most. "You're a creature of the sea. Why do you stay aboard the Maiden's Return with Falcon Locke?"

"I love him."

"A mermaid in love with a ship's captain."

"Not in that way."

"It's the young sailor you were with earlier. He holds the key to your heart."

"He does," admitted Kera.

"The New World is strange indeed, but not without its charms."

"Please allow my ship to sail away unharmed."

"Admit to being a mermaid and I will."

"I cannot," responded Kera.

"Or will not." Again, the admiral turned away from his prize, taking a moment to rethink his strategy. "I'll allow your crew their freedom on one condition: you choose to remain here, by my side, bringing me the same luck as your Captain Locke."

"I would rather hang from the gallows," she said resolute.

"Next to the man you love," he responded, taking her chin gently in his hands and raising her face to him. "Knowing you could have saved him and your precious captain?"

Pulling her chin from his hand, Kera stood in silence, trying to wrap her head around the decision she was forced to make. She held the freedom and the lives of her father, Henry and the crew in her hand and all she had to do was agree to his terms. The terms of an evil man.

A young soldier, barely old enough to be in uniform, quickly approached and stood at attention. "The captain and crew have returned to their ship. They're loading the supplies. What are your orders?"

"What are my orders?" he asked her, knowing she was about to break. "Will you save your captain and crew or watch them hang?"

Before she could answer, a rock smashed into the side of the admiral's head, dropping him unconscious to the ground. Rushing toward them, Henry pulled his sword and took on the messenger who recently joined them. Surprised by the attack on their admiral, the two soldiers let go of Kera and went after Henry with their swords. "Run, Kera!" he yelled taking on the three men by himself.

"Give me a sword!" she yelled.

"No! Get to the ship!"

"I'm not leaving you!"

"Do what your told!"

"Lend me a sword!"

No longer able to split his focus between the three soldiers and his argument with Kera, he tossed her his extra sword.

Separating the young soldier from Henry, she used her adequate sword fighting skills to distract him while Henry took on the other two.

Fighting to protect more than his own life, Henry quickly

dispatched one of the soldiers, leaving one to go. His sword fighting prowess was far better than both soldiers and it didn't take him long to end the second soldier's life. Turning back to take on the third soldier, he found him trembling, kneeling at the tip of Kera's sword, his own weapon several feet away.

"I see your lessons be paying off," observed Henry, impressed with what he saw.

Unable to end the young man's life, Kera looked to Henry for help. "I can't do it."

Lifting his bloody sword, Henry chose to strike the young man in the back of the head with its heavy grip. Kera breathed a sigh of relief as the soldier fell to the ground, then she took Henry's hand and together they snuck through the buildings on their way back to the dock.

Both in one boat, they rowed as hard as they could toward the Maiden's Return. The wind had picked up against them, making the water choppy and the pull of each stroke more difficult.

The crew was still storing supplies when they saw them coming. The Captain ordered the crew to drop everything and ready the ship for sail. His men went to work, raising the anchor and releasing the sails.

Once Kera and Henry reached the ship, several crew members helped them aboard and stowed their boat just as the sails opened and caught the wind. Without a cannon shot from Port Royal's fort or any of the British warships nearby, the Maiden's Return sailed from Jamaica, fully stocked with supplies and with their ship and crew intact.

THE RESCUE YACHT, Present-day

Kera pulled her hand away from her new friend, ending Rome's view of the mermaids's past. "After our escape, I never thought I would see Admiral Cross again, but I was wrong."

"He was an evil man."

"No different than Jack Lazenby."

"I do know that name. Jamie once told me his only regret was not bringing him to justice. He's practically untouchable."

"If Lazenby doesn't kill your friend, the treasure will. He cannot escape the darkness much longer or those protecting it," warned Kera, then she disappeared from the yacht, leaving Rome with a deeper insight into her past. She was grateful for the update on Jamie as well. Quickly leaving her chair, she hurried toward Heath, interrupting his business call. "I need to talk to you."

"Hold on a minute," responded Heath, muting his phone and turning his attention to Rome. "What is it?"

"Jamie needs our help... now."

"How do you know that?"

"Kera just told me."

"Now she shows up?"

"We don't have much time."

"There's nothing I can do to get us there any faster."

"The man who abducted him is going to kill him."

"Most likely the same man who stranded us in Nicaragua," responded Heath.

"Jack Lazenby."

"The drug and weapons smuggler?"

"You've heard of him?"

"Anyone in the shipping industry knows that name. This just went from bad to worse. I've heard horror stories about that guy."

"He'll stop at nothing."

"Do you have that Navy Lieutenant's business card?"

"Back at Jonah's, but we have no proof."

"So we're back to square one."

"And running out of time."

"We'd get back a lot faster if we weren't taking Bernicia home."

"That ship's already sailed. Excuse the pun."

"That's it."

"What's it?"

"Come on," said Heath as he ended the phone conversation. Rome followed, anxious to know what he was planning. Entering the bridge, they ran into the captain as well as Sheldon. "We need to borrow your yacht tender so we can get back to Providence."

"Borrow?"

"Rent."

"The sea's choppy today. It'll be a rough ride back," warned the captain.

"We'll be fine."

"All right," he agreed then ordered his helmsman to bring the ship to a stop and the chief mate to unload the tender.

Designed for waterskiing and carving out surf waves, the water-sport would be a bumpy ride back at the speed Heath wanted to travel, but comfort had to take a back seat to time. As the chief mate used the crane to unload the tender from the ship's bow, the captain assured them that it had enough fuel to make it to Providencia. That was all Heath needed to know as he settled in behind the wheel with Rome at his side, packing several water bottles for the trip.

Waving goodbye to their friends, Heath charted a course using the GPS system, then he started the engine and throttled it up. Immediately, the boat raced forward, jolting Rome backwards and causing her to buckle her seatbelt for safety. At forty-seven miles per hour, the boat bounced over the waves at roughly forty knots. If they could maintain their speed, Heath estimated it would take them four and a half hours to reach Providencia... four and a half very rough hours.

Chapter Fourteen

With the wind at their back, Heath raced the boat across the choppy water. They had made good time but at a cost to Rome's physical well-being. No longer able to ignore the nausea, she signaled for Heath to stop the boat from pounding over the waves. Barely making it to the side before releasing the contents of her stomach, she experienced her first bout with seasickness. Heath dug into the first aid kit and found some wet wipes for Rome's face and some medicine for motion sickness. "Sorry. I'm trying to get us back as quick as possible."

As she sat back down, he opened a bottle of water then handed it to her with a couple of pills. "They should kick in pretty quick."

"How much longer?" she asked after rinsing her mouth with the water and spitting over the side.

"We're close."

"Looks like we're not alone," said Rome noticing a larger boat coming from the East.

"It's the first boat we've seen all morning."

"It's early in the day."

"If I were vacationing in the Caribbean, I'd still be in bed too," admitted Heath as they continued to watch the boat get closer.

Sea to See

"Do you think they sees us?"

"Not sure. It looks like she's coming right for us," responded Heath as he started the engine and moved out of the boat's path.

"They just changed course," noted Rome as she buckled herself into the seat.

Again, Heath changed course only to find the approaching boat adjusting their direction to intercept. "They are coming for us," said Heath as he pulled back the throttle and sped away.

As the boat corrected course, two small motorboats pulled out from behind the large one and surprised Rome and Heath by circling ahead, causing them to switch directions. Heath continued to try and outmaneuver them, but they were relentless in their pursuit. Suddenly, automatic weapon fire from the surrounding boats gave Heath no place to go, so he throttled her down as the enemy closed in for the kill. Within seconds, Heath and Rome were surrounded by men pointing a pretty impressive array of guns, then the captain of the large boat barked out the orders. "Just Jones."

Heath attempted to grab the flare gun, but before he could use it, two men jumped onto the back of their tender and pulled him from his seat. He did his best to fight them off but couldn't escape their hold. Rome attempted to come to his defense, but another man threw her back into the seat and restrained her with a piece of rope. They were taking Heath from her and there was nothing she could do to stop them.

Rome screamed for Heath as he fought back while being loaded onto the deck of the large boat. Within seconds of removing Heath, a man jumped into the driver's seat of Rome's tender and started the engine while two others climbed into the back with a folded canvas tarp and an armful of rope. Pulling away, she watched as several men beat Heath into submission then dragged his limp body into the cabin of the large boat. "Breathe in the good air, let out the bad," she whispered to herself trying to keep from hyperventilating.

It was their second kidnapping in less than three days and this time they were both on their own. With no idea of her fate, she worked to keep herself from a full meltdown while thoughts of the rope and canvas tarp in the back led to imaginings of her own burial at sea. No one would ever find her, nor would they know what happened. She had come to the Caribbean to save her friend and now she was helpless to save herself. Her disappearance would end up being the topic of cable and network shows alike, bent on speculation and hearsay. That's not how she pictured her legacy.

After about ten minutes with her mind in panic mode, the man driving the tender turned off the engine while the one behind untied her from the seat. As they pulled her kicking and screaming into the back seat, she saw the third man unfold the canvas and lay it flat, then unhook the boat anchor and set it nearby. Her fear of being buried at sea was being realized. Coming to the aid of the man attempting to restrain her, both men held her tightly while she watched the third man pull out a rubber tourniquet, syringe and vial of liquid.

Rome's panic heightened as she realized they were drugging her again, most likely to keep her from fighting for her life once they threw her over the side. She kicked the man several times with her legs to interrupt the prepping of her arm, but all that did was earn her a series of slaps across the face. The poke of the needle brought tears to her eyes as she helplessly faced what she believed were her last coherent moments of life.

Once the heroine hit her brain and converted back to morphine she felt nothing but pleasure as they picked her up and laid her flat on the tarp in the back of the boat. Unable to fight back, Rome squinted as she stared at the blurry sun until the folding of the canvas shut out the light.

THE SOUTH'N Hunter

The boat that kidnapped Heath pulled alongside the stern of Lazenby's ship and unloaded him. His abductors received a bag of cash as payment before they pushed away. The transfer was quick and polished. He'd had it rough, but was able to walk on his own as his new captors pushed him forward toward the stairs. Arriving on the top deck, Heath came face to face with the man whose name he'd only heard mentioned in disgust by his father and in infamous terms throughout the shipping industry.

"Well, if it isn't the ever-impressive Heath Jones. Born with a silver spoon in his mouth and a trust fund at his disposal," said Lazenby delighting in his pain.

"The name's Jack Lazenby. Welcome to the South'n Hunter."

"Where did they take Rome?"

"Who?"

"The woman I was with. Where is she?"

"That's no longer your concern."

"What have you done with her, Lazenby?" demanded Heath.

"Women are a dime a dozen to a billionaire."

"If you've hurt her I will..."

"What? Have me arrested? Or worse yet, kill me? Take a look around ya, Mr. Jones, you're surrounded by professional killers. I don't think ya understand the gravity of your situation."

"What do you want?"

"Why the interest in the Maiden's Return?"

"Pirate lore is a hobby of mine."

"So that's what brings ya to Providence?"

"That and Henry Morgan's buried loot."

"A billionaire digging for buried treasure?"

"Takes money to make money."

"That we can both agree on."

"Is it money you want?" asked Heath, hoping to find a way to negotiate.

"In a way. Do you dive, Mr. Jones?"

"Why?"

"I asked you a question."

"And I asked you why." With a glance from Lazenby to his bodyguard, Heath quickly found himself doubled over from a hard punch to the gut.

"Do you dive?" asked Lazenby forcefully, this time expecting an answer.

Straightening up, Heath was determined to get what he wanted. "Not until you tell me where to find Rome." Again, the bodyguard punched him in the stomach, this time dropping him to one knee.

Lazenby walked toward Heath and leaned down toward his ear, whispering the answer he feared the most. "Probably at the bottom of the ocean by now." Heath lunged forward and grabbed Lazenby around the waist, taking him to the floor. Before his men could get him off, he got in a couple good swings. It took everything the bodyguards had to restrain Heath as Lazenby crawled backwards to escape his rage.

"Why?" screamed Heath.

"She was of no use to me!"

"You didn't have to kill her!"

"If it makes any difference, she felt nothin'."

"He's back," noted one of the bodyguards as he pointed to the monitor.

"I believe introductions are in order."

Yanking Heath from the floor, they forced him down the stairs a safe distance behind Lazenby.

As promised, Jamie had returned with the sample gold piece Lazenby requested tucked inside a pouch hanging from his waist. The last thing he wanted to do was surface with some of the treasure, but he knew he couldn't put him off any longer.

"Do I have a surprise for you," boasted Lazenby as he walked toward Jamie still waiting for the men to finish removing his equipment.

"That makes two of us," responded Jamie, his head bent down as he worked his feet out of his fins. Standing up, he saw what he least expected: Rome's boyfriend standing in front of him between the two bodyguards. With a burst of anger at his apparent involvement, Heath broke free of the men and took a swing at Jamie who dodged his fist.

Instantly, Heath became a puppet in his skilled hands as he turned his body and wrapped his arm around his neck. Jamie knew he had to keep Heath from shooting off his mouth so he applied enough pressure to his air pipe to render him unconscious, then dropped him to his knees.

"You ask for help then knock the guy out," responded Lazenby enjoying the moment more than he anticipated.

"Force of habit."

"Get me some smelling salts!" ordered Lazenby.

"Who is he?"

"Heath Jones."

"The shipping guy you were talking about?" enquired Jamie, playing along to keep Lazenby in the dark about their relationship. "I thought he was lost on the Mosquito Coast."

"So did I."

"What about the woman?"

"Why's everyone so interested in the girl?"

One of the guards returned with the smelling salts and Jamie reached out his hand. "I'm the one who put him out."

Lazenby signaled to the guard to let Jamie have the box who then opened it and pulled out an ampule. He had years of experience using the chemical compound to wake others and had been revived by them countless times himself.

Kneeling down next to Heath, he snapped the ampule, instantly allowing the chemicals to mix and release the ammonia stimulant. Heath shook his head as the pungent smell entered his nostrils and began the physical process that led to an oxygen rush to his brain. Before Heath could form any words other than the guttural groans from the putrescent smell, Jamie whispered loud enough for him to hear. "We don't know each other. Understand?"

Heath nodded his head enough to satisfy Jamie who stood up and allowed two of the guards to pull Heath to his feet. Staggering back and forth, the guards steadied him until he could stand on his own.

"Ya picked the wrong person to take a swing at, Jones. Meet ya diving partner, Jamie Webb."

To keep the game going, Jamie extended his hand. After a brief hesitation, Heath grabbed on and shook. "Let him get his head on straight then get him in a wetsuit."

"Does he dive?" asked Jamie.

"We're about to find out. Upstairs with me, Webb."

Jamie glanced back at Heath as he followed Lazenby to the stairs. He appeared to be a shell of the man he met at the castle only a couple of weeks ago and the defeated look on his face caused Jamie to worry that his worst fear about Rome had come to fruition.

Reaching the top deck, Lazenby held out his hand leading Jamie to unzip the pouch that hung from his waist. Reaching in, he pulled out a gold arm band, large enough to be worn around and a man's bicep then tossed it to Lazenby. Catching it in his grasp, he turned his back to his bodyguards to examine the detail. Instantly drawn to its magnificence, Lazenby studied the large opals embedded in the gold base. The opal's blue flashes of light flickered like fire as he rotated it back and forth. He'd never seen such large stones or such exquisite gold. He couldn't take his eyes off the royal piece of jewelry or stop his mind from dreaming of the wealth it would bring to his life.

"You never said how Jones made it onto your ship," mentioned Jamie, receiving no response as he waited for an answer. "Jack?"

"Ya ruinin' the moment, Webb."

"Just wondering how Jones got here."

"How's that any of your business?"

"I'm the one doing your business."

Lazenby placed the arm band in a drawer, then turned back to Webb. "He found a way out of Nicaragua quicker than he should've. I had some men intercept him before he reached Providence."

"Was he alone?"

"He is now," answered Lazenby, then he ordered his men to take him below and get him some water before sending him down again.

"What if Jones doesn't dive?"

"He better or he's no use to me."

"I'll need some time with him either way."

"It's called on the job training, Webb."

"If you want this done right, let me do it my way."

"And how much time will 'your way' take?"

"Two hours."

"Two hours?"

"Now that I've located all the gold, I've approximated how many trunks I need. I'll have to drill holes in a couple more for drainage."

"Two hours. No more," ordered Lazenby. "Now, get out of here."

Alone on the upper deck, Lazenby opened the drawer and pulled out the arm band. There was a life to the gold and he felt its pulse as he slid it over his hand, allowing it to dangle from his forearm. Running his finger across the patterns laid in the gold, indiscernible voices from ages past began to penetrate his hearing. Its value on the open market became less important as a trance-like intoxication took hold.

Refusing to take his eyes off it for more than a split second at a time, he slowly pushed each button on the safe's electronic keypad then opened the door. Sliding the arm cuff toward his wrist, he stopped short of removing it from his arm. Slamming the safe door, he put the band into his pocket. An obsession had taken root and he would never allow himself to be separated from it again.

On the deck below, Lazenby's personal guard ordered one of the other guards to get two more metal trunks from the storage room and the drill for Jamie. As the guards went their separate ways, Jamie returned to Heath and sat down on the crate next to him. Lowering his voice, he asked the question he did not want answered. "Where's Rome?"

No response.

"I said where's Rome?"

"I can't."

"You can't what?"

"Say it."

"Is she dead or alive?"

"Please don't make me, Jamie."

"Dead or alive, Jones?"

"Dead. She's dead."

Before he could continue, Jamie had to control his reaction. Although he was trained to receive tragic news, the reality of losing Rome pushed his control measures to the extreme. He knew he had to maintain his composure or Lazenby would know of their connection, but knowing and doing were suddenly at odds. Finding a morsel of strength, he returned his attention to the conversation. "How?"

"I don't know."

"Didn't you see them do it?"

"They loaded me onto a bigger boat."

"How many were left with her?"

"Three."

"Were they professionals?"

"Not like these guys."

"Drug runners most likely."

"With guns."

"What makes you think she's dead?"

"Lazenby all but said it."

"Did he show you proof?"

"No."

"Then there's hope," responded Jamie, switching gears for Heath's sake.

"Hope for what?"

"That she's still alive."

"It would take a miracle, Jamie."

"I saw a few of those in my old line of work."

"Do you think Lazenby's lying?"

"He doesn't know what truth is."

"So there's a chance she could still be alive?" asked Heath with renewed hope.

"I've known Rome a long time. She's smart, she's strong and she's skilled. Until we have proof otherwise, my money's on her," responded Jamie with as much confidence as he could muster.

Based on the circumstances, Jamie knew the likelihood of Rome surviving was next to zero and behind his confident persona he could feel his heart crumbling into his guts. More than anything he wanted to believe the lie, but fairytales had never been his thing. For practical purposes, he needed Heath in better shape than he found him and the best place to start was his mind. If there was any hope of saving him and the siblings, he needed to sell hope like rain in a drought, even if it meant lying through his teeth.

On a personal level, plans of retribution were building inside him—a good way to counter the pain of losing his best friend. Rome's supposed death fanned the fires of vengeance and nothing would stop him from exacting the type of justice that would rid the world of Jack Lazenby once and for all.

Despite the rage in Jamie's heart, he naturally slipped into planning mode, quizzing Heath on his diving experience and technique, then proceeded to instruct.

"Conserve as much air and gas as possible down there."

"Breathing is not optional, Webb, even for a superhero."

"The slower your breathing, the less air you need to breathe. Use as little energy as possible."

"I can do that."

"Do you scare easily?"

"Not since meeting Rome," responded Heath. "I mean… we've been through some scary stuff over the last few weeks. I'm kind of getting used to it."

Purposefully ignoring Heath's reference to his time with Rome, Jamie continued. "Panicking is not an option. I need you focused no matter what you see or feel."

"Just for conversation's sake… what will I see?"

"I wish I had an answer for that."

"Dead bodies?"

"No. They were taken to the bottom of the abyss."

"By who?"

"The better question is, 'By what?'"

"How many have died?"

"Six."

"Who were they?"

"Divers."

"Not as good as you?"

"Military trained and experienced."

"How did they die?"

"They panicked."

"Over what?"

"I wish I had answer for that. The only thing that matters is not becoming number seven."

"How deep are we going?"

"Two hundred feet, give or take."

"That's deep."

"Dive depth is the least of your concern. We'll be working inside the hull of a three hundred- year-old ship, wedged between the walls of what appears to be a bottomless crevasse. At any moment, the Maiden's Return could break apart and fall into the abyss, taking both of us with her. Anything could set it off: the shifting of weight, movement of the chasm's walls, the random snapping of a rotten plank."

"And I'm not supposed to panic?"

"If you want to live through this."

"Do you want me to live through this?" asked Heath, testing the waters.

"Why wouldn't I?"

"Rome."

"I'm trained to take lives and save lives. I prefer the latter."

"Even if my death could give you back the life you want with Rome?"

"When I left the Navy after more than a decade of service, I had a hard time assimilating to civilian life at the State Department. I went from living and fighting in the shadows to being in the public eye. It was rough. Then I met Rome. She helped me through the transition period. She literally saved my life. She means more to me than anyone on this earth."

"You didn't answer my question," said Heath.

"I know what losing you would do to her. I'd go down with the Maiden's Return before I'd see her in that kind of pain. She chose you, Jones. Now prove she was right."

"You are a superhero," responded Heath in complete sincerity.

"I'm just a guy trying to save two kids and my ex's boyfriend, while stopping a madman from gaining even more power."

Speechless, Heath sat in awe as he watched Jamie stand up to get the attention of the guards. Any jealousy or rivalry that he once felt for him was instantly replaced by a powerful respect. He had this sudden urge to follow him anywhere, even into battle... or the hull of a ship that may become his coffin.

"I need to see Talin and Leta," said Jamie.

"Not without Lazenby's okay."

"Open the door, so I can see they're all right."

"You don't give the orders around here."

"I'm not leaving this ship until I've checked on them. You want to be responsible for the hold up? Go for it. Lazenby's a reasonable guy."

"They're scheduled for a bathroom break. You can see them from over there. Now sit down!"

Jamie sat back down next to Heath and watched as three guards walked down the hall toward the siblings' room. They opened the door and roughly pulled the younger sister into the hall. Talin tried to come to her aid but was shoved against the wall and threatened by the guard. "You want to walk or crawl, kid?"

Jamie reacted by rising to his feet, but no matter how much he wanted to save them, the timing wasn't right. He also knew the guards were determined to show who was in control as they pushed Leta into the bathroom and again pressed her older brother against the wall. The young captain appeared no stronger than when he last saw him and Jamie wondered if they were even being fed.

Talin's eyes caught Jamie's stare from across the deck and found relief in his presence. Jamie nodded his head to reassure him that he was working toward a solution, which caused Talin to stand a bit taller. The door opened and Leta walked out and waited by the wall for Talin to take his turn. Jamie whistled at his young friend and caught her attention. Instantly, a smile washed over her face, then she yelled two words that only Jamie would understand. "I'm willing!"

Jamie knew she was referring to their earlier conversation about being willing to do what it takes at the very moment you need to do it. He nodded his head in response, impressed by her courage. Once Talin exited the bathroom, they were pushed back down the hallway to their room. Jamie sat back down, content for the moment that they were still alive.

"What kind of monster frightens a young girl like that?" asked Heath.

"Someone who sold his soul a long time ago."

"So what's the plan?"

"I'll pull the gold pieces from the hull, transport them through the upper two decks, then you'll take them up to the sea floor and place them in the trunks."

"That's your plan?"

"The official one."

"And unofficially?"

"Sleight of hand," responded Jamie, scooping a beer cap from the floor then enclosing it in his fist, while moving his other hand around it.

"You're a magician as well?"

"No," answered Jamie, showing him his empty hands. "But my uncle was."

"That's impressive. You get many dates that way?"

"A few."

"Is there anything else I need to know before we get down there?"

"Hand signals, so we can communicate."

"Why not take a dive slate to write back and forth on?"

"The difference is a whisper verses a billboard when it comes to video."

"So we need a secret code."

"Or just hand signals," noted Jamie as he began to teach him. "We have two hours. I'll re-teach you how to dive as well."

"Here's your trunks and drill," yelled one of the guards.

"Come on," said Jamie, leading him across the deck.

"You never answered my question," said Heath as they walked toward the trunks. "What panicked the dead divers?"

"You wouldn't believe me if I told you."

"You'd be surprised what I believe these days."

"Then you'll be more likely to remain calm when you feel it for yourself."

"Feel it?"

"Yeah." Feeling relatively confident in Heath's safety and success, Jamie picked up the drill and began sharing his plan with Heath in more detail. The teaching of hand signals came next.

Eventually Jamie switched face masks with Heath knowing the video was grainy coming from the bottom. Lazenby wouldn't be able to differentiate between them—a factor that would allow Jamie to do what he needed to do without being observed.

Chapter Fifteen

Rome woke slowly from a deep sleep, trying to focus on her surroundings. Her grogginess had an air of familiarity as she continued to open and close her eyes. Elements of a hospital setting led her to believe she was in some kind of observation area. The room was small with just enough space between the surrounding curtain and the bed for the equipment and professionals to do their job. The only thing she recognized was her ghostly acquaintance sitting on the side of the bed holding her hand.

"Am I dead or alive, Kera?"

"Alive and safe."

"How did I get here?"

"You were found drifting about a mile off shore."

"I don't understand. I should be anchored at the bottom of the ocean."

"You're alive and that's all that matters for now."

"What about Heath? Is he all right?"

"He's alive as well," responded Kera, standing up and walking toward the foot of the bed.

"But?"

Suddenly, the curtain parted and Jonah entered the makeshift room. "Are you awake, Rome."

"Barely."

"I thought I heard a voice. You had us all worried."

"Where's Heath?"

"Rest for now. We can talk about that later?"

"How did I get here?"

"For the past twenty-four hours, I've had everyone on the island looking for the two of you. A fishermen found you this morning."

"Was there anyone else on the boat?"

"Three men. They're currently being held at the police station. You were all unconscious when the fishing boat found you, so they removed the weapons from the boat, hooked onto your towline and pulled you back to the ferry terminal. The doctor diagnosed the three men with sunstroke due to the state of confusion they were in when they woke up. They were babbling all sorts of nonsense. A background revealed they've all done time for one crime or another. The police are waiting for a statement from you to find out what really happened."

"I don't know what happened."

"Do you remember how you ended up on the boat?"

"Not that I can recall," answered Rome deceitfully. She hated to lie to Jonah but didn't want to put his life in danger as well.

"Martin made his way up the mountain and found the note you left. He also found a piece of my lamp on the floor beneath your bed as well as your suitcase. For two days, I made phone calls all over the island and to San Andres. There was no evidence of you chartering a boat, taking the ferry or booking a flight to the island. With Martin's help I called every hotel on San Andres and nothing. That's when I organized the search."

"Thank you, Jonah."

"Enough about that. You need to rest. Doctor's orders."

"I have to get out of here," said Rome as she attempted to sit.

"You nearly overdosed. They administered an opioid receptor antagonist to reverse the effects."

"Sounds like I'm good to go," responded Rome, sliding herself to the edge of the bed and planting her feet on the floor. Carefully, she pushed herself off the bed but lacked the strength to stand, causing her to hit the floor.

"We need some help in here!" yelled Jonah as he fumbled in the dark trying to help her up. A nurse and her assistant rushed through the curtains and helped her back into bed. Rome's strength had been spent with one attempt at standing, causing her to fall back to sleep once her head hit the pillow.

AGAIN, Rome opened her eyes, but this time she found herself staring at the frigate bird clock next to the bed. She was in her room at Jonah's home and the familiarity felt good. Turning over, she saw Bev asleep in a chair with her long legs stretched across the bottom of the bed. Quietly, she moved to the edge and removed the IV line from her arm. Applying pressure to the needle wound, she noticed how much stronger and hydrated she felt. Attempting to get up, she put her feet on the floor and lifted herself with no problem, then rummaged through her suitcase for some clothes to wear.

Grabbing her cell phone from exactly where she left it the night of her kidnapping, she tip-toed to the door and left the room. As she scrolled through her phone, she saw several more missed calls from her mother as well as voicemails. She still hadn't found time to call her back. To Rome's surprise, Sheldon exited Heath's room and nearly bumped into her.

"It's good to see you up."

"It's good to be up. Please tell me you were checking on Heath."

"I wish I could. I was actually unpacking his bag."

"We haven't had a whole lot of time to settle in since we got here."

"By the sound of it, it's been a rough few days."

"Yes, it has," agreed Rome, then without hesitation she wrapped her arms around his neck and held on tightly. "Thank you for coming."

"There's no place I'd rather be."

"I have to find him, Sheldon."

"WE have to find him," responded the butler. "You're not alone in this, Rome."

"I'm the reason he's in this mess in the first place."

"Heath's a big boy who makes his own decisions."

"He's in real trouble, Sheldon."

"That's what the police are for. Speaking of which, they're due in an hour to take your statement. Jonah bought you as much time as he could."

"I need a few minutes to myself. I think I'll take a walk."

"Don't be long," he responded as he watched her walk away, finding himself completely unequipped to help.

Following a well-worn trail, Rome walked around the house and into the trees. Within minutes, Kera was by her side as they made their way deeper into the forest.

"Where is he, Kera? Where's Heath?"

"With your friend."

"Is that good or bad?"

"From what I've seen... good. Somehow your friend has avoided the curse of the treasure and the dangerous circumstances created by the hands of the crew."

"Circumstances?" enquired Rome.

"Accidents that can lead to death. As proven with the six divers who came before your friend."

"How long ago was that?"

"Days."

"Were they part of Lazenby's crew?"

"Yes. Your friend now dives alone."

"Why do they want the divers dead?"

"They're attached to the gold."

"Attached?"

"Obsessed."

"Are they the ghosts who tried to drown me?"

"That would be a different crew."

"So not only is there an ancient curse in play, but there's more than one gang of obsessed spirits who can't let go of their loot?"

"Mendivia and his men."

"That makes sense."

"Captain Locke's crew protects the gold but does not kill for it," said a voice from the trees.

"Henry?"

"Good day, Kera."

"Why have you come?"

"The time be at hand to end it," said the pirate ghost as he walked toward them.

"You're the one Heath and I spoke to on the beach," said Rome, intrigued by their reunion.

"My name be Henry."

"He was the helmsman aboard my father's ship."

"I be more than that or have ye forgotten?"

"We haven't time to visit the past."

"Time be irrelevant, Kera," reminded Henry, hoping she would take the time to talk with him.

"Why come to me now?"

"Ye have found a way to right the wrong," Henry said with hope.

"What makes you think that?"

"Hold it!" said Rome. "This is no time for 'he said, she said.'"

"What?" responded both Henry and Kera.

"No time for arguing. We have loved ones that need our help and the only way to be successful is to work together. Agreed?"

"Yes," replied the two ghosts.

"We only had one argument," said Henry turning to Kera with fondness.

"The night you gave your life for mine," responded Kera with a heavy heart.

"Were you being attacked?" asked Rome.

"Nay. Early on, the crew gave birth to a superstition that spread like a storm. After the captain brought his daughter aboard, our fortunes changed. The crew claimed the reasoning to be that of 'the mermaid' who now sailed aboard the Maiden's Return. Word spread through pirate ports and beyond."

"It didn't help that my father still called me his mermaid."

"Or that he be stopping the ship by night for ya to swim in the ocean."

"Even the crew believed me to be a mermaid," said Kera. "I never thought anything bad would come of it."

"Bad?" enquired Rome.

"Exaggerations of Kera holding mermaid powers spread from ship to ship, as well as stories of her beauty. Those be no lie," said Henry staring deep into her eyes. "Before we knew it, a legend be born of the Maiden's Return and her captain's mermaid."

"So there's a bit of truth to the legend," said Rome.

"Twas amusing till Admiral Cross of the British Navy made Kera the object of his obsession."

"He meant to take me home to England as a pet for his King George."

"But as his obsession grew, so be his desire to keep her for himself. We crossed paths with the Admiral's warship many a time, but the Maiden's Return, she be light. We could outrun him. There'd be no beating a ship of that size in battle."

"The British Admiral also put out a bounty for my capture, turning others against us and making it hard to maneuver between ports," added Kera.

"One night, we lowered our sails and anchored near the last port the Spaniards be using for fresh water and food before heading back to Spain. We be desperate for supplies and knew the pickings would be ripe. Twas a risk, but one we had to take for survival. The crew, including Captain Locke, boarded the rowboats and made way to the abandoned Spanish ships anchored closer to port. They knew the Spaniards could be returning at any moment, so they needed to be quick in their plundering. The Captain thought nothing of leaving Kera aboard the Maiden's Return under my protection."

"A choice neither of us argued with," added Kera.

Taking advantage of their moment of reflection, Rome reached out and gently took hold of both their hands, allowing her access to one of the most painful moments of their young lives.

THE MAIDEN'S Return - 1722

Leaning his back against a pile of canvas stacked near the stairs, Henry held Kera in his arms. His primary concern was to keep her safe and out of sight, so staying below the bulwark or sides of the ship allowed them to remain on the top deck, rather than hide out in the hull, a place Kera rarely went. She'd venture as far as the galley to get her meals but ate them all up top surrounded by fresh air rather than the smells of rarely-bathed men and the sounds of poor manners.

Side by side, their legs outstretched on the deck, they engaged in one of their favorite pastimes: staring at the beauty of the night sky. Kera's joy was obvious as she listened to Henry tell his latest mythical story of a distant star or constellation he had gathered from his travels.

"Do you use that star in your navigation?" asked Kera.

"Only to woo young maidens caught in me arms," replied Henry as they kissed beneath the canopy of stars.

"I'm scared, Henry," said Kera as she broke away, bending her knees to her chest and wrapping her arms around them.

"No harm will come to ya. That I promise."

"I'm scared for us all. It's my fault the British admiral pursues us."

"That burden be not yours to carry. Tis the admiral's madness that be to blame."

"And what if we do escape? What lies beyond the great ocean?"

"A new life."

"I'm frightened to leave everything I know behind."

"Don't be, Kera. I'll be with ya every step of the way."

"Do you promise, Henry?" pleaded Kera as she lay back down next to him, wrapping her arm around his chest.

"They'd have to drag me from you, kicking and screaming," he responded, kissing her on the top of the head.

As he leaned back to begin another story, he heard something in the quiet of his pause. Sitting up, Henry looked about the ship.

"What is it?" asked Kera.

"Listen," whispered Henry. "That be the sound of oars moving the water."

"They can't be back already."

"Shh," responded Henry placing his index finger over his lips. "Stay here."

Henry crawled to the side of the deck and slowly lifted his forehead above the bulwark. Finding it difficult to see in the dark, he continued to crawl along the side of the ship, peering over every few feet, until his worst fear was realized: a rowboat full of men a few feet off the ship's stern. Henry looked to the ropes hanging over the aft side, but before he could get to them, they began to climb. He only had seconds to prepare. Bent over, he ran toward Kera.

"We've got to get ya off the ship!" he whispered forcefully.

"Is it the British?"

"Merchant sailors, collecting ya for bounty."

"There's no boats left for our escape."

"You've got to swim. They won't be finding ya in the dark."

"I'm not leaving without you."

"It won't be for long," said Henry pulling out his sword as he grabbed onto her arm. "Come along."

"Wait. I know the sword. I'll stay and fight."

"They are not many. I'll dispatch them in no time," assured Henry as he moved her to the opposite side of the ship.

"Then there be no harm in letting me stay aboard," argued Kera.

"The captain made me your protector. Do as I be telling ya."

"I can't let you fight alone!"

Henry's attention turned to the stern of the boat as a sailor crawled over the wall, followed by another. "Jump, Kera, before they catch sight of ya."

"I will not leave you, Henry!"

"Then you be leaving me no choice," he responded, sheathing his sword and picking her up in his arms. "I love you, Kera. I always will." Then he kissed her one last time and tossed her over the other side of the ship.

Turning toward his attackers, it was clear he was severely outnumbered as they continued to pour onto the ship. He lied to Kera to give her hope but knew his survival was unlikely. They'd never find her in the water. She was too good a swimmer. Running across the deck, Henry met them head on, taking out three of them before being subdued.

FOREST NEAR JONAH'S HOUSE, Present-day

Kera broke free of Rome's grip and turned her back to Henry. "Because of me, he ended up in servitude to the British Navy."

"It was my own choice to stay and I be doing it again if need be," responded Henry.

"What happened next?" asked Rome.

"I waited near the hull until the merchant sailors gave up the search. I watched as they loaded Henry captive onto their boat and rowed away, then I climbed back onto the ship. After the crew returned and heard the story, my father saw how desperate the situation had become."

"And that's when he went after the treasure," asked Rome.

"The Admiral's large bounty for my capture was irresistible to those sailing the same waters."

"As well as in the ports," added Henry.

"I tried to stop my father, to change his mind about making the deal with Mendivia, but he felt it was the only way to save me, as well as his crew. They had sworn to protect me which put their lives in peril. Wealth from the treasure would buy us the freedom we needed."

"Leaving their captain no other choice," added Rome.

"After sealing the deal with the Spaniard Mendivia and bringing the treasure aboard, bad luck began to befall the ship. Accidents were abundant. Sails would come unattached for no reason. The food went rancid and the water became undrinkable. Eventually, the ship's rudder system broke, leaving us dead in the water. Not a good place to be when you're a pirate ship being hunted by the British and Spanish Navies. Due to the mental sickness of the crew brought on by the cursed treasure, it fell to my father to fix the rudder."

"How was he able to avoid the curse?" asked Rome.

"Of that I am not sure. Father hadn't slept for days, working tirelessly to get the Maiden's Return back to sailing order. I helped with all my strength while mourning the loss of Henry in silence. I had no one to turn to for comfort."

"You thought me dead," said Henry, taking hold of her hand.

"What else could I believe?" she responded, turning and looking deep into his eyes. "The moon was full that night but tucked behind the passing clouds. I dove off the ship for a quick swim to clear my head and calm my nerves. Before long, I'd left a lengthy distance between me and the ship. Just as I was about to return, I felt a rush of air, then a great movement in the water as a large wooden wall, not five feet from my position, slowly moved past. It was the hull of another ship: a British warship. I knew the crew didn't stand a chance in their current state."

Rome reached out and took hold of both their hands, more for support than anything else. Instantly, she was allowed access to that fateful night through the viewpoint of Kera. The ending was all too familiar to Rome. She had experienced it several times during her nightmares in Hawaii and now she would see it play out from the beginning.

OFF THE COAST of Old Providence, 1725

Kera continued to tread water near the British warship uncertain as to what to do as a voice hailed from the British ship. "Give us the mermaid and you will not be harmed!"

All remained silent until the silhouette of Captain Locke stepped into sight just as the moon broke free of the clouds. "You will find no mermaid aboard this ship!"

"Don't be foolish, Captain Locke. She will be mine! Save yourself and your crew!" he hollered across the water.

"Never!" replied the captain as he signaled to one of his men.

Slowly, the doors to the only three of the gun ports along the side of the Maiden's Return opened and the cannons were inched into view, one after the other.

"I propose a trade," yelled Admiral Cross. "I have something that may be of value to you." Signaling to his men, the sailors shoved Henry beneath the glow of the lanterns, bound and weary from days of abuse.

Kera gasped loudly at the sight of the man she loved, drawing the attention of one of the British sailors. "Down there! The mermaid's in the water!" he yelled causing everyone to look.

Quickly, Kera submerged herself beneath the surface and swam to the hull of the warship, pressing herself up against it and out of sight. But it was too late. They had caught a glimpse of her.

"You speak the truth, Captain!" yelled the Admiral as he signaled his men to open the gun ports and prepare for battle. "She is not aboard your ship. Then let us end it!"

The warship's cannons quickly moved into place, easily outnumbering the fire power of the Maiden's Return. In perfect rhythm they began to fire.

Kera felt the power of each round shake the hull of the ship as the explosions filled the sky with smoke. There was nothing she could do but watch in horror as the ship she had called home for three and a half years began to list and eventually sail to her watery grave. She had no idea if her father had survived the explosions or not, but she had to do something.

Diving below the surface, she pulled herself deeper and deeper toward the sinking ship, encountering the occasional dead crew member along the way. But it was no use. The darkness of the water and shortness of breath made any kind of rescue attempt impossible. For a brief moment she thought of releasing the remaining air from her lungs and joining them, but her survival instincts kicked in, helping her reach the surface.

In the meantime, the admiral turned his attention to the mermaid, ordering his crew to capture his prize. Kera knew she had a chance at making it to Old Providence, once a Captain Morgan strong hold, so she began to swim as the boats were being lowered from the ship. With all her force she cut through the water, widening the distance between herself and the sailors chasing their tails, searching the dark waters for a mermaid that didn't exist.

Using the stars as her compass when the clouds would permit, she pressed forward, stroke after stroke. By daylight, the island was within view, but the grief of losing everyone she loved had taken its toll. The guilt she felt for their loss was manifest by the amount of tears she left in her wake. Using the last of her energy to crawl onto the beach, Kera passed out from physical and emotional exhaustion. She was parched but lacked the energy and motivation to search for fresh water. She had no reason left to live and no one left to live for. Death came to her as she slept.

FOREST NEAR JONAH'S HOME, Present-day

Rome let go of Kera's hands and wiped a tear from her eye. The pain she felt while watching her memory was overwhelming and she needed a moment to pull herself together.

"I remember that night, be it as yesterday," said Henry.

"It was my fault they lost their lives," quietly uttered Kera.

"No!"

"You lost your freedom because of me as well."

"It be given freely for you."

"But what you had to endure."

"Tis the risk ya take when choosing the life of a pirate."

"And what of you, Henry?" said Rome.

"Memories I wish not to relive, nor anyone to see."

"She needs to know."

Henry paused for a moment to collect his thoughts before he felt comfortable enough to continue. "Following the sinking of the Maiden's Return, I endured weeks of brutality and punishment until I abandoned me self-restraint and admitted to me station as helmsman. Choosing not to transport me to Jamaica or England for trial, the captain served as me judge and jury, pronouncing me guilty and handing me a sentence: fourteen years of servitude to the

Royal Navy. The sailor, whose post I replaced, died of a sickness and it became me duty to spell the ship's two helmsmen when they be requiring sleep.

The captain and his officers kept a tight reign on the crew to ward off plans of mutiny. The punishments were cruel and attendance required by all. I be the subject of many a public beating. But the worst punishment be to never again plant me feet on the shore, no matter what port we anchored near. The ship became me cell and the open sea me prison. I be no more than a stick being whittled to a pile of shavings, severing more of me self with each slice of the knife. Eventually, there be nothing left to be cut away.

One calm night, the ship be barely moving from a lack of wind to her sails. The air was thick and muggy, wrapping itself around the guard like a blanket, causing him to fall into a slumber. It be a moonlit night which meant I be thinking of you and wondering what had become of ye life. I had to believe ye survived. That it all be not for nothing. The hope of seeing ye again, kept me going, year after year, until I could go no more.

I left the wheel and walked to the side of the boat. The water be calm, reflecting me shadow on the surface. Like so many lonely nights before, ye seem to appear in the water, tempting me to come for a swim—delusions brought on by me own madness. I be wanting to join me captain and crew at the bottom of the sea for so long that I abandoned the wheel. Leaving me uniform on the deck, I hoisted me self to the top of the bulwark and dove into the deep. It be the first time in years I felt the welcoming embrace of the water and its merciful relief."

"It wasn't the water's embrace you felt," quietly interrupted Kera as she wrapped her arms around him from behind.

"Be it your arms that held me close as life drifted from me body?" asked Henry astonished by the revelation.

"Yes. I was there on the ship that night as I had been so many times before. I watched you make the decision to jump. Then I followed."

"Why not join me once me spirit left me body?"

"I could not ask more of you than I already had. You earned

your freedom. It became my duty and mine alone to fight for my father's freedom."

"Then ye be knowing me story all along?"

"Painfully so. I am sorry, Henry."

"No more than I be for you."

"You needn't. I felt no pain in passing from life."

"But ye have for centuries as spirit, seeking penance."

"Have you watched me as I watched you aboard the ship all those years?"

"Aye. Trying to free your father."

"And you've been near all this time?"

"Where else would I be?"

Rome watched as Kera and Henry passionately embraced each other. Wanting to allow them some privacy at the climax of their beautiful reunion, Rome turned her back and wiped away more tears. After several minutes of silence, she began to wonder if they were still present. Glancing over her shoulder, she found them romantically engaged. Clearing her throat, Rome attempted to be nonchalant about breaking up their magic moment... and it worked. Time was of the essence and they had eternity for that. "So who do I thank for ending up in the clinic and not the bottom of the ocean?"

"Be it the superstition of the Caribbean people. They be easily bewitched."

"Sounds like you scared the bad guys nearly to death."

"It be the only way to keep them from drowning ya. Kera awayed to the South'n Hunter to check on your friends, leaving the rescue to me."

"I'm sad I missed the show."

"Ye be the show's main player," remarked Henry before telling of the rescue: a story Rome paid close attention to so she could relay the details to Heath once they were reunited.

THE TENDER, Hours Earlier

Henry knew he couldn't save Rome by himself, so he called in a favor from the spirits of two pirates he once sailed with. There's not much call for commandeering boats in the next life, so they were gung ho to put their skills back in action. They approached the tender just in time, finding Rome wrapped tightly in the tarp and one of the men about to wind the rope/chain anchor rode around her body. Needing to act fast, they put their plan in motion.

Their first move was to extract the key from the ignition, stranding them with no way to get to shore. The removal of the key caught the attention of one of the kidnappers who continued to watch it float past his head. After several attempts to grab the key from midair, he closed his eyes then reopened them to take a second look. Concluding that he wasn't hallucinating, he alerted the others to the strange occurrence. All three of them froze in place and watched as the key floated beyond their reach.

Next, Henry and the other spirit pulled the cell phones from the men's pockets and tossed them overboard. Angry at losing their only way to communicate, one of the men picked up his semi-automatic rifle and began spraying the air with bullets. Like sheep, the two others followed suit until they'd spent every bullet in their clips. Still pointing their guns toward the sky, they waited in silence to see if they had rid themselves of their invisible assailants. Letting out a cheer, they raised their rifles above their heads, only to have them plucked from their hands by the spirits. Then the real fear set in.

Henry and his ghostly friends delighted in showing them how dangerous guns can be even without bullets. Using them as prods and bats, they jabbed the kidnappers all over their bodies, moving so quickly the men could not anticipate what direction the next stab or hit would originate. Tripping over the seats and each other, they were frantic to find shelter from the animated weapons.

Having had enough fun, the spirits dropped the guns and prepared for the finale. The look on the criminals' faces was priceless as Henry and his two friends slowly raised Rome from the boat, her floating body turning in mid-air. Slowly the body bag moved toward her attackers, the best part being the unscripted moaning by Rome. Cowering below the seat backs, the three highjackers began crying and pleading for help, until their extreme fear caused two of them to pass out one after the other. The third man would not go so easily so Henry picked up a rifle and knocked him over the head, leaving him down for the count.

Gently, they laid Rome back down and unwrapped her head and upper body so she could better breathe. In the distance, they could see a fishing vessel moving toward them. Rome's rescue was imminent, as well as their departure. Leaving the key on the driver's seat, the three ghosts bid Rome farewell and returned to shore.

FOREST NEAR JONAH'S Home

The story of her rescue was the perfect respite from the worry and stress she was dealing with. "Thank you, Henry," she said, grateful for being alive and the opportunity to laugh for a moment.

"If Kera has faith in ya, then I be believing as well."

"Let's start with the curse. How do we break it?" asked Rome getting back to business.

"My father may know, but he will not allow me near the Maiden's Return."

"Then it be left to me," responded Henry.

"He may let you approach," said Kera.

"Can we get him to the island?"

"Only one thing be powerful enough to bring him up from the Maiden's Return," suggested Henry.

"What's that?" asked Rome.

"His daughter's lack of well-bein'."

"What will you say, Henry?" asked Kera.

"Leave it to me. Be ye at the Northwest tip of Santa Catalina in one hour," responded Henry, then he disappeared from view.

"That should give me enough time to meet with the police."

"Will you employ their help?"

"This is beyond their help, but I do plan to fabricate a wonderful story for them to pursue."

"You'll need a boat."

"The police should be done gathering evidence off the tender we borrowed. Hopefully, I can get it out of impound."

"I will join you there," said the captain's daughter.

"Stay away from the island, Kera. I need information and he won't stay if he realizes we tricked him into coming."

"How do you know that?"

"Experience."

"But I long to see my father, to talk with him. Tis his own guilt that keeps me at bay."

"Sounds like you're two peas in a pod."

"I don't know how to feel anything else."

"Soon you will, Kera. I promise."

"You'll speak of my desire to see him?"

"You brought me here to help. Let me do it my way."

"I trust you, Rome London. Just as your friend, Jamie, trusts you," said Kera before she disappeared from sight.

Rome left the woods and returned to the house. The police would be arriving soon and she needed to be convincing in her story. She also needed to fill Sheldon and Bev in on the truth about Jamie, Heath and a horrible man named Jack Lazenby. She was glad they were there and would utilize their help as soon as she finalized her plan.

Chapter Sixteen

Santa Catalina Island

*R*ome drove the tender around the West side of the small island of Santa Catalina, watching for signs of her ghostly friends. She was glad the watersport had been impounded as evidence, forcing the captain of the yacht who rescued them to return to San Andres without his tender. She and Heath would make it right as soon as they found Jamie.

Just as she rounded the northern top of the island, she saw where the point headed east. Slowly steering her boat toward shore, she carefully found a place to anchor, then leaped over the side and walked to the island in waist-high water. Henry greeted her at the shore with a confident look that told Rome all she needed to know as she followed him into the trees. There she came face to face with the legendary captain. "Thank you for coming, Captain Locke," began Rome. "It's an honor to meet you."

"There is no honor in meeting me."

"I've met some people who would disagree with that."

"What of Kera?"

"She misses you dearly."

"What grave danger befalls her?"

"The worst kind. Eternal heartache."

"She must let go of the past and join her mother. I have told her that," responded Captain Locke, dismissing the situation as routine.

"She wants the same thing for you."

"That is not possible."

"You've come this far, just keep walking."

"It was my promise of untold wealth that put the Maiden's Return in harm's way and delivered her to the bottom of the sea. It was my decision as captain to forge a deal with Mendivia that took the life of my daughter and any promise of eternal rest for my crew."

"Why are you not affected by the gold's curse?"

"I'm not sure I ever was."

"Then what's keeping you down there?"

"My crew was loyal to me for many years. Henry will attest to that fact."

"Aye, and our captain be just as loyal to us."

"I will not abandon them."

"What if we can break the curse?"

"'Tis impossible."

"Why?"

"There is no breaking of the curse."

"What if the gold is returned?"

"Returned where?"

"To where it was stolen from."

"Captain Mendivia will never tell the location of the Aztec burial tomb."

"Why strike a deal with a man so evil? There had to be another way."

"You could never understand."

"Try me," said Rome, reaching out her hand and taking hold of Captain Locke's.

"When Captain Roberts was killed in February of 1722, I returned to the island to reunite with my family..."

THE MAIDEN'S RETURN, 1722

Captain Falcon Locke stood on the bow of the Maiden's Return, staring at the horizon through a spyglass. Although he could not see the island in the distance, he knew they were close. It'd been three long years since he saw his family and he could only imagine the beautiful young woman his daughter had become. More than that was the need to hold his wife, to wrap his arms around her and never let go. Years of piracy had changed him, but he hoped the husband and father inside would surface as soon as he made contact with those he loved.

"Land ho," yelled one of the crew from atop the crows nest. "The captain's island lay ahead!"

Quickly, Falcon pulled his spyglass from the case as he leaped to the highest part of the bow and extended it toward the East. His home was in sight. He was finally returning to the life he left behind, the life he loved so dearly. Condensing his telescope, he placed it in the leather case hanging from his waist, then bent toward the railing. He needed a private moment to experience what he'd been dreaming of for more than three years. With his eyes closed, he imagined sinking his feet into the warm, white sands of the beach as his family welcomed him with open arms.

Wiping a tear from his rugged, tanned cheek, he turned to his crew and began making plans for going ashore. The crew celebrated as they went about the job of preparing to anchor. Falcon wanted everything to be just right. A quick wash and a change of clothes was in order and he bid his crew to do the same. He'd told them of the great feast they would have of fresh fruit and seafood, wild hog cooked in a pit and the sweetest desserts ever to be found. They were salivating just thinking of a home-cooked meal, rather than the three revolving meals fixed by the ship's cook.

As they came within sight of the island, however, the mood of the crew changed dramatically. Trees were snapped in half, some bent to the ground, while others were completely uprooted. The devastation was shocking. It was clear that a mighty storm had hit the island with full force. Falcon's beautiful paradise had been nearly destroyed by nature.

Once they cast anchor, a small boat was lowered and Falcon and three of his most trusted crew, including Henry, rowed quickly to shore. They found a man-made trail through the debris which told the captain there were survivors, but the questions of who and how many plagued his mind as he hurried toward the village. Reaching the site of the village, Falcon stopped in his tracks. There was nothing left to see. The homes of his friends and family had been literally wiped from existence. Remnants of their lives could be found scattered about as Falcon reached down and picked up a brightly-colored piece of cloth, but there was no sign of life. Splitting up, the crew searched for clues that would lead them to human life.

"Over here," yelled Henry pointing to another trail through the debris.

Everyone responded by following their helmsman down the trail, eventually coming to a spring near a cave. Signs of life surrounded the entrance to the cave in the form of fire pits and baskets full of fish and fruit. Slowly, the villagers made their way out of the cave, nervous at first to face the unknown pirates. Falcon took off his hat and yelled, "Wanahani!" Soon, a beautiful teenage girl squeezed through the crowd of men near the end of the cave and ran toward the captain. "Father. You've come back," cried his daughter as she wrapped her arms around Falcon's neck.

"Kera?" asked the captain, shocked by her maturity.

"Yes, it's me. Your little mermaid."

"Last I held you, you were little indeed."

"I am a woman now, father."

"You're sixteen. Let's not get ahead of ourselves. Where's your mother?"

Kera withdrew her arms and stepped back. Falcon's greatest fear was realized by the expression of grief on his daughter's face.

Unable to stand beneath the weight of his loss, he dropped to both knees and lowered his head to the ground. Kera immediately came to his side, wrapping her arms around him as she relayed the story of her mother's death. "The wind came quickly in the night with no warning. We grabbed as much as we could and rushed toward the cave, but mother forgot something. She told me to keep going, so I did. Once we reached the cave, the storm hit with full force. Many of our friends never made it. I wanted to search for mother, but they would not let me go. The next morning I found her beneath a tree. She was holding this." Kera pulled out his copy of Shakespeare's sonnets and handed it to her father. "It was all she had left of you, Father."

"When did the storm hit?"

"Five nights past."

"The day of Captain Robert's death," quietly mentioned Henry from behind.

"He took from me in life and in death."

"I miss her too, Father," said Kera as she tightened her arms around him.

Henry motioned to the other two crewmen to give them some space as they backed away and began dipping from the spring of fresh drinking water.

"There's nothing left for you here, Kera."

"Plans have been made to rebuild."

"You cannot stay alone."

"I won't be. You're here now."

"We will leave this island together."

"This is my home, our home."

"This will never be home without your mother," said Falcon as he rose to his feet, leaving Kera kneeling on the ground. "We will camp for the night."

As he turned to leave, Kera stopped him in his tracks. "We can still be happy here, Father."

"We leave at dawn. Do what you must to prepare," ordered the captain as though she were a member of his crew, then he disappeared back down the trail. Reaching the site of the village, he walked to where his home once stood. Memories flooded his mind as he sat down on a toppled tree and relived the happiest time of his life. Suddenly, more than three years of bottled emotion burst from inside as he allowed himself to freely feel the pain of losing his wife.

The next morning he woke to the motion of Kera shaking his shoulder. He had fallen asleep on the ground where his home once stood. Sitting up, the first thing he saw was his daughter holding all her worldly possessions in her arms. She had taken the night to prepare as her father had asked her to do. Looking up at his mermaid, Falcon saw more than the great beauty that she had become. He saw a courageous young woman, willing to leave the only home she'd ever known. He had no idea if it was the right choice, but she was his child and he was solely responsible for her now.

Rising to his feet, he placed his hands on her upper arms and looked deeply into her eyes. "We can always return to the island, but for now, all I know is captaining my ship. I have a crew to look after as well."

"Home is where my family is and if that's the open sea, then so be it."

"I'll gather my men and meet you at the beach," he said, then kissed her forehead and walked away.

Finding his men asleep near the cave, he woke them up and motioned for them to follow. Before they reached the beach, he stopped to discuss a situation he had on his mind. "Having my daughter aboard may pose some problems."

"Tis rare to find a lady aboard a pirate ship, Captain," commented one of his crew, the rest agreeing.

"Thus, my concern."

"With the crew, sir?" whispered Henry as he moved Falcon away from the other two mates.

"I trust my crew. I'm more concerned with whom we'll encounter on our journeys."

"If I might say, Captain, she be a beauty beyond description."

"You may not! That's my daughter you're talking about!"

"I be meaning no disrespect."

"Nevertheless, you see my difficulty."

"Not to worry, Captain, we shall keep your mermaid safe at all costs," vowed Henry as the other two men, eavesdropping on the conversation, shook their heads in agreement.

"Today the Maiden's Return begins a new chapter and I know not what lies ahead."

"The best of times, sir," answered Henry with a smile on his face. "We be free of Captain Roberts' command."

"Tis the best of times," agreed the others.

Falcon slapped Henry robustly on the back of the shoulder and they headed toward the beach. Although his men had alleviated some of his concern, he still worried about their fate as they boarded the rowboat and left the island behind.

SANTA CATALINA ISLAND, Present-day

Pulling away from Rome's hand, Captain Locke ended his walk through the past. "Those memories are difficult to relive."

"Was it the best of times?"

"For the first two years it be," agreed Henry. "We only stole from the Spaniards, provin' that two wrongs be makin' a right."

"What do you mean?"

"They conquered an entire civilization and enslaved many of them to mine for gold and silver," said the captain.

"Stealing from the Spaniards didn't change anything for the people they conquered," argued Rome.

"No, but we became a thorn in their side. We would creep aboard at night while their ships were anchored and steal cacao, vanilla, tobacco, as well as silver and gold, then pass it along to those in need on the islands," said Captain Locke.

"Making you the 'Robin Hood' of the Caribbean."

"Who?"

"Sorry, wrong century."

"We used our ill-gotten skills to relieve the Spaniards of everything and anything and did it all during a time of great upheaval.

Pirates in large number were either dying at sea with the sinking of their ships or captured and transported back to England for trial."

"Is that why you struck a deal with Captain Mendivia?"

"It was the only option I had left to save my daughter."

"Because of the bounty on Kera's head," concluded Rome.

"I could not let her fall into the hands of such a sick man, even if he was an admiral."

"Yet you welcomed a man like Mendivia aboard your ship."

"If only I had known. After hearing of my ability to elude capture, he sought me out. His ship had run aground and he needed another ship to transport himself and his treasure to the south of Spain. The idea of settling somewhere along the Mediterranean had crossed my mind, so it felt like a bargain worth pursuing. The plan, once we reached the Mediterranean, was to take my daughter ashore and relinquish control of the Maiden's Return to my crew, allowing them the freedom to sail wherever they chose."

"What about Henry?"

"My fate be sealed," responded Henry.

"We had no way of knowing if he was even still alive."

"So what went wrong?" asked Rome as she reached out and took hold of his wrist.

"Everything."

THE MAIDEN'S RETURN, 1725

Under the dark of night with only half a moon to work beneath, the Maiden's Return lowered her sails as she moved toward the wreckage site of Mendivia's Spanish ship. The wrath of the curse was strongest against the men who originally stole it from the tomb, Mendivia and his crew. Their close proximity to the gold while transporting it to the ship had taken its toll. Captain Locke had no idea what had become of Mendivia's crew, leaving him alone to sail a large merchant ship.

Tilted on its side in shallow water, the Spanish ship had a haunted feel to her that silenced the crew of the Maiden's Return.

In order to avoid getting too close to the sandbar that grounded the Spaniard's stolen ship, they anchored and lowered their rowboats.

Carefully, several of Captain Locke's crew followed Mendivia aboard the shipwreck, loaded the chests onto the rowboats and made their way back to the Maiden's Return. Although the plan was progressing without a hitch, Captain Locke felt an uneasiness in his bones as dark clouds immediately covered the sky, hiding the light of the moon. It was as though a dark shadow had enveloped the ship.

"Stay in your quarters and keep out of sight," the captain ordered his daughter.

"Yes, Father," she responded still brokenhearted from the recent loss of Henry. "Are you certain we're doing the right thing?"

"No, Kera, but it's the only way," said her father as he kissed her on the forehead and left the room.

Knowing his feelings for the Spaniards, Kera was surprised to see her father make a deal with Mendivia, a man of questionable character, poor reputation and a dark nature. The weight of responsibility for the entire situation bore down on her mind as she stared into the moving shadows created by the sway of the hanging lamp. She had done nothing to warrant the obsession of the British admiral, but because of her, everyone on the ship was in danger. The guilt she felt over Henry's loss only compounded her panic, making it difficult to breathe. Lying down on the bed, she pulled the sheet over her head in an attempt to disappear from the world, but there was no escaping her burden.

Soon, the torment turned to dread as a wave of fright washed over her. It was the same fear she felt during the storm that took her mother's life. Jumping out of bed, she ran to the door; her hand grabbing the knob, but this time she chose to follow her captain's orders. Letting go, she pressed her back to the wall and closed her eyes. She would wait as her father requested and shoulder the burden on her own. Her father had enough to deal with and she refused to add to his load. But that didn't mean she couldn't have a peak. Opening the door just enough to see through the crack, she watched as the men loaded the final trunk onto the Maiden's Return.

As Captain Locke approached the trunks, his crewmen were chomping at the bit to see inside, so he ordered Mendivia to remove the locks and reveal the treasure. It only took the opening of the first chest to mesmerize the crew with its contents. The gold jewelry and royal accoutres were intoxicating as the crew took turns holding the pieces of each trunk with their own hands. To avoid any pocketing, Mendivia would not allow the small gold pieces to be touched - they were a group of thieves, after all. But they were allowed to hold the jewel encrusted gold head and neck pieces and even model them for each other.

Feeling an uneasiness, the captain ended their worship by ordering the trunks locked and stored in the hull. Mendivia retained control of the keys as he watched the heavy trunks lowered into the bowels of the Maiden's Return. Once they were safely stored, the captain requested a meeting with the Spaniard as the wind that accompanied the dark clouds changed directions and picked up in speed.

"How did a skilled sailor such as yourself run his ship aground?"

"I'm not familiar with these waters."

"And your crew?" asked Falcon, concerned by the circumstances of his shipwreck.

"All dead."

"How?"

"Accidents."

"An entire crew, dead from accidents?"

"I only began with ten."

"Still, ten men?"

"Ten men who are no longer important."

"Where did you get the treasure?"

"That's none of your concern."

"Where?" yelled Falcon, demanding an answer.

"A place where no one will ever miss it."

"These sails will fall until I know the truth."

"We have an agreement."

"An arrangement made before I knew the truth."

"That gold is going to the south of Spain."

"I'll drop it overboard before I allow it to harm my crew."

"They'll turn against you if you try."

"My crew is loyal to their captain."

"Look," demanded Mendivia. "They're obsession with the gold begins."

Captain Locke did as Mendivia suggested and looked around the ship. His men appeared pensive and preoccupied, almost absent from their surroundings. "What is happening?"

"It begins in the mind. Actions will follow," whispered Mendivia with the voice of experience.

"I do not fear my own crew."

"Mutinies have risen from less."

"The bounty on your head proves that fact."

"Do not cross me, Locke!"

"Nor threaten me, Mendivia! I hold all the cards, as well as your gold. If you want to return to your home, free of chains, then you'll tell me where you stole the treasure."

"Very well. The hull of your ship holds the treasure of royal emperors. I took it from the burial tomb of the Aztec kings."

"You stole from their sacred grounds?"

"They're dead! Why let it go to waste?"

"So are ten of your men."

"Accidents!"

"What have you brought upon my ship?"

"Enough wealth to last both of us ten lifetimes."

"At what cost?"

"That depends on how much freedom is worth these days."

"Is it cursed, Mendivia?"

"Even if the legend is real, there's not a thing anyone can do about it."

"Most curses are broken when the treasure has been returned."

"That gold is going to the south of Spain."

"On my command and no others!"

"Captain Roberts would not hesitate."

"I am not Bartholomew Roberts."

"Yet you served him faithfully for years."

"To protect my family. All the treasure in the world is not worth the life of my crew!"

"Or the mermaid who brings luck to the Maiden's Return?" responded Mendivia knowing the captain's weakness.

"Leave her out of this!"

"If you stay in the Caribbean, the admiral will have her for himself. You can only outrun him for so long."

"I'll take my skill as a captain on the open sea over cursed gold any day."

"I'm the only one alive who knows the location of the tomb and that knowledge will go with me to the grave. Be it water or earth."

"Give me the map."

"Demand all you like, but I'm no longer in possession of it."

"You expect me to believe that?"

"What good would it do me? I took the gold and left the map in its place."

"Sealing both our fate."

"We sail together or we die together," yelled Captain Mendivia over the sound of the approaching wind, then he walked to the companionway leading to the hull and disappeared from the deck. The captain wondered if it was the effects of the curse that led to the doom of Mendivia's ship, or did his sickness play a role in his lack of acuity and good judgment.

Captain Locke felt an inner sickness grow to rival the day he was taken from his family and forced into a life of piracy. He had concern for his crew, but they signed on for this and knew the risks. His daughter did not. It was his decision three years earlier that took her from her home and now he questioned if he had made the right choice.

Grabbing onto his hat, Captain Locke fought his way to the helm as the change of the wind resulted in larger swells, shifting the boat back and forth. He rang the bell alerting the crew to come top deck and man the sails as he pushed Henry's replacement aside and took the wheel. Barking out orders, he rode the fury of the ocean like he'd done so many times before, but this storm felt different: it felt personal, as though it had a vendetta. He could feel the wood twisting beneath his feet as he gripped the wheel with all his strength, trying to hold her together. Then something unexplainable happened. Just as the ship was about to succumb to the torment of the raging storm, the wind came to a sudden stop. The clouds disappeared and the moon became visible once again. The waves settled into a roll and everyone breathed a sigh of relief.

"Tis a warning that was," said Henry's replacement, surprising the captain with his observation.

"Get us back on course," ordered Captain Locke as he left the helm and walked toward his quarters. Once out of sight, he stopped and grabbed onto the top of the bulwark, steadying himself against the wall of the ship. He was no stranger to risk, but this was nothing like he'd encountered before. In a last ditch attempt to protect his daughter, he had done the unthinkable and endangered them all. The curse was real and had fallen upon the Maiden's Return. The only question left was whether or not their fate was sealed.

SANTA CATALINA ISLAND, Present-day

This time it was Rome who let go of the captain's hand. She had seen the beginning of the end for the Maiden's Return and her crew. All the pieces had now come together and she felt a profound sadness. Once again, she had allowed herself to be swallowed up in the tragic story of a family and their friends who lived centuries ago. She wished she could do more to help them, but her hands were tied as she realized there was no way to break the curse.

Mendivia would never tell them where the burial tomb was in order to return the gold and Rome highly doubted she would get a chance to look into his mind again. The gold would either stay at the bottom of the ocean or be sold by the man who held Jamie against his will. Either way, the crew would remain tied to the gold as they had been for nearly three centuries and Rome could think of no way to help Kera save her father.

"Is it the curse that keeps the Maiden's Return intact? There should be little left of a wooden ship under water for that long."

"Tis still my ship and the crew work to maintain it, but the curse may have a hand in its preservation as well."

"Is it your crew who tried to drown me a few days ago?"

"It was the ten men of Mendivia's original crew."

"They do Mendivia's bidding?"

"To this day. I intercede as a voice of reason, but it doesn't always help."

"I need to get a message to Jamie."

"One of the men who swims in the mask?" asked Captain Locke.

"One of the men?" responded Rome, surprised by the new information.

"There are two now."

"Heath. How deep?"

"Two hundred feet to the deck, give or take."

"Can you take this scarf to the one who's been down there the longest?"

"Will he recognize it?"

"He should. He bought it for me. I also added a special touch."

"It shall be delivered to the Maiden's Return."

"Thank you. I need them to know I'm alive," said Rome. "One more request, Captain... can you keep them safe?"

"I can make no promises but will continue to try."

"We'll figure this out... for your family and your crew."

"I would like to believe there is truth in that, but you know as well as I, there is nothing that can be done. Tell Kera to return to her mother and forget about me," said Captain Locke as he took the scarf in his hand and disappeared into the water.

"Then it be over," concluded Henry.

"Not even close. I guarantee Jamie's working on a plan on his end, and now that I have more detail, I can do the same."

"If I can be of help..."

"I'll call you. Right now, it's Kera who needs you the most."

Henry nodded his head in agreement and disappeared from the

island. After taking a moment to ponder the situation free of distraction, Rome knew what needed to be done next. Boarding the boat, she returned to the harbor and made her way to the dive shop to reserve some equipment. Everything she needed for the day was already rented out. Fortunately, there was another possibility and it revolved around Jonah.

Chapter Seventeen

Shipwreck of the Maiden's Return

*J*amie continued his work inside the cramped hull, removing the gold pieces, transporting them up the three sets of companionways, then handing them off to Heath. It would have been much faster to take them out as they had been stored, through the loading holes in the top deck. But he was afraid if they pulled up the removable portion of the deck, the pressure of the chasms walls would sandwich the ship together, causing it to fall into the abyss. They would do it the slow way, the careful way, until they had removed every last piece of gold.

With the video camera attached to Heath, Jamie was able to alternate trips in and out of the stairway. One load would be gold pieces, while another trip would be cannon balls. The two men had it down to a science: the science of deceit. They were a well-oiled machine, working together in perfect unison. Lazenby must believe that only treasure was being removed from the hull. The work was time consuming and dangerous, but it was the only way Jamie could think to keep Lazenby from getting his hands on the gold.

Heath's orders were to move extremely slow as he took the gold pieces from Jamie, propelled himself up the side of the crevasse and onto the sea floor. There he would load the gold in trunks then return for more. At the same time, Jamie would propel himself up with a load of iron cannon balls, weighing about eight pounds each and place them into a separate set of trunks.

The cannon balls were stored exactly as they would have been when the ship sailed the waters of the Caribbean, setting inside a long wooden plank with holes bored to accommodate their round shape. Covered in rust, the black of the iron had turned to a yellow/orange color. Even better for appearing to look like gold. They were awkward to hold onto and Jamie dropped more than one ball as he navigated through the bowels of the ship, each time wondering if it would cause a chain reaction. He even found some bar and chain shot: two cannon balls connected by a short piece of chain. These were used for busting through the enemy's masts during battle. The discoveries were a once-in-a-lifetime opportunity and Jamie had a front row seat.

The rumblings of the ship had become common place, providing moments of pause for Jamie each time he felt the ship move around him. He was not a claustrophobic man, but the fear of the ship sinking into the chasm and taking him with it was weighing heavy on his mind. Every moan and creak of the lumber was a reminder that he was running on borrowed time. He breathed a little easier each time he left the ship with a load of cannon balls.

Returning to the ship, Jamie saw something that captured his attention: a piece of fabric moving through the water toward the Maiden's Return. Floating just above the deck, the fabric fell into his hands as though someone had placed it there on purpose. Little did he know he stood in the presence of Captain Falcon Locke, a subject of his fascination for years. Jamie recognized it right away as the head scarf he had bought for Rome during a diplomatic trip to Tel Aviv. Opening it up, he examined it closer and found a message written in a black marker along the seam: "See you soon, Rome. P.S. Don't lose the scarf."

Jamie had to take his own advice to conserve air and gas when all he really wanted to do was begin shouting and jumping for joy. Rome was alive. She had beat the odds. Needing to hide the scarf from the camera's view, Jamie propelled himself toward the figurehead connected to the bow of the ship and tied the scarf securely around the mermaid's neck. He would have loved to take more time to revel in the happy moment, but he had to get back to the hull before crossing paths with Heath and his camera.

Unfortunately, his dive partner would have to wait to hear the news, but it would be well worth it in the end. Although Jamie had to stay focused on the plan, he couldn't help but wonder what Rome was planning. Knowing her as well as he did, he had to be prepared for anything, especially after finding out she'd bested the three gunmen trying to kill her.

KEEPING to the task at hand, Heath placed his latest gold pieces into the first full trunk and closed the lid. As he picked up a padlock, he noticed the mysterious phenomenon he'd been warned about moving toward him through the water. Supposing them to be the ghosts who tried to drown Rome, Heath felt the first wave of panic ripple through his body as he did the math. Rome was near the surface and barely survived. He was a hundred and seventy feet below.

In desperation, he scanned the sea floor but could find nothing to use as an anchor. As expected, the force hit him hard, driving him away from the trunk and into the crevasse. The ghosts continued to spin him in every direction until Heath was so disoriented he had no idea which way was up.

Slamming him into the side of the chasm, the ghosts continued to abuse their enemy, causing a shower of rocks and debris to fall toward the deck of the precarious Maiden's Return. Thrown against the wall again, he lost his dive light, leaving him in the dark with no frame of reference. Jamie's advice to not breath heavily continued to roll through his mind as he fought to escape the gang of ghosts, only to be shoved back into the face of the crevasse, this time damaging the video camera. Concern for the state of his hoses and equipment was paramount in Heath's mind as he continued to collide with the rock, unable to protect himself from their strikes.

Turning his head, he caught a welcome sight: a light on a direct intercept course. Feeling a strong hand wrap around his upper arm, Heath finally had the help he needed to escape his attackers. With Jamie's arrival, the spirits left the crevasse and raced toward the trunk of gold.

Propelling themselves up to the sea floor, they watched the lid to the trunk slowly open and several small pieces of gold float out the top. Heath and Jamie pushed themselves through the battering ghosts like quarterbacks running the ball straight into the defensive line. Grabbing onto the floating pieces of treasure, they shoved them back into the trunk then closed the lid. With no other option available, Heath laid his body over the unlocked trunk and grabbed onto the handles, refusing to be moved as Jamie tried to protect him from the angry ghosts as best he could. It was a losing battle until the unexpected arrival of an opposing force.

Heath and Jamie watched the two sides fight it out. It was a water show of special effects unlike anything they'd ever seen. Eventually, one side split off, followed by the remaining force in the opposite direction. Heath floated off the trunk and patted Jamie on the back, showing gratitude for his help. Jamie returned the sentiment with a thumbs up, then they checked their gauges and each other's equipment to make sure everything was still in working order. Finding everything to be satisfactory, they found a hand held dive light and awkwardly attached it to Heath's suit then went back to work.

JONAH'S HOUSE

Rome arrived at Jonah's and parked the motorcycle at the top of the hill. Martin was there to see her and they greeted each other with a big hug and a genuine thank you. They were on the way to bum a ride from his neighbor to their favorite fishing spot. Rome offered them a ride in exchange for an introduction to his friend, the marine biologist. She told him of her need for diving equipment and he was happy to make the exchange.

Martin helped Jonah into the side car and handed him all the fishing equipment, then gave the bike a push. Rome fired it up halfway down the steep driveway and waited for Martin at the bottom to jump on back. Off they went with Jonah as their guide, giving directions as clearly as if he were seeing the road with his own eyes. He knew the island like the back of his hand and his navigation was flawless.

Within fifteen minutes, they arrived at Orlando's home. Martin leaped from the bike and came to Jonah's aide, helping him out of the sidecar. Together, the three of them walked toward the door of the beautifully-located beach house. The setting was more than picturesque as Rome stared out at the ocean, waiting for someone to answer the door. She could only imagine waking up to such a beautiful sight each morning. Her thoughts soon turned to Jonah, who had just as beautiful a view but would never see it with his own eyes again: a fact he never seemed to let dampen his spirits. Soon the door opened and a woman in her early forties greeted Jonah with a welcoming hug.

"This is Rome, a new friend of mine, and this is Mary, Orlando's daughter. And you know Martin, of course."

"Yes. Come in, please. We just finished an early lunch, but we have extra. Would you like something to eat?"

"No, thank you," replied Jonah. "Martin and I are about to catch our lunch."

"You have a beautiful home," complimented Rome as they made their way through the house.

"Thank you. My father retired here and I decided to join him."

"I can see why," responded Rome as they entered a large lanai on the side of the house.

"Jonah... welcome," said Orlando, doing the best he could to speak despite the effects of the stroke.

"My friend here's in need of your help."

"No," said Orlando, shaking his head in response to Jonah's request. "Can't."

"Nonsense. You're as useful as I am," responded Jonah in an attempt to jokingly reassure his friend. "Rome London, meet Dr. Orlando Melgosa, one of the greatest marine biologists on the planet."

"Once, maybe," said Orlando, correcting Jonah's introduction.

"It's a pleasure to meet you, Doctor."

"He prefers Orlando," said Mary.

"Before you two get started," interrupted Jonah, needing an excuse to remove Martin from the conversation, "might we do some fishing off your dock while you chat?"

Orlando nodded his head in approval and Jonah turned to leave the room, followed by Martin. Nervous about losing her translator, Rome caught hold of Jonah's arm before he escaped the lanai. "Wait. You're leaving?"

"The fish be calling us."

"How are we supposed to carry on a conversation?" whispered Rome.

"With your mouths," responded Jonah, then with a wink he turned to Orlando's daughter. "If it isn't too much of a bother, Mary, how about something cool to quench the thirst of two lowly fishermen?"

"I was in the middle of pouring some juice when you knocked on the door. Follow me, gentlemen."

Rome watched them leave the lanai, wondering how she would understand Orlando's side of the conversation without help. As she turned back toward the brilliant scientist, he pointed to the chair next to him, inviting her to sit. Rome did as he requested and got right to the point. "I have a friend who's in trouble and I need to contact him. Unfortunately, he's diving and has no access to a telephone. All the scuba equipment has been loaned out at the shop and I'm wondering if you would have what I need for a deep dive."

"You won't," paused Orlando trying to find the words. "You won't find... better."

"I'm happy to pay whatever it costs."

"Your friend...?"

"What about him?"

"Missing?"

"He's the one that went missing several days ago with two others."

"Diving?"

"Yes. He was on a dive trip."

"He found... her."

"Found who?"

"Ship... wreck."

"Are you talking about the Maiden's Return?"

Orlando nodded his head and leaned in toward Rome. "Aztec... treasure."

"You've seen it. You know it's down there. Why haven't you announced your discovery?"

Again, Orlando shook his head in disagreement, his expression growing serious.

"You have everything you need for the exploration."

Orlando quietly groaned in frustration as he lowered his head, wishing he could speak what his mind wanted to say. Fortunately, Mary entered the room carrying a pitcher of juice and three glasses on a wooden tray. "Let me help you, Papa," she said as she placed the tray on a small table and began handing out the glasses. "When he discovered the shipwreck, he returned to study her and found there to be an eerie feeling about the Maiden's Return, a presence of sorts. He believed it was a warning to never return."

"It's rare to find a superstitious scientist."

"For many years, Papa has studied our Aztec ancestry. It may be a small percentage of our DNA, but it's a part of who we are. He truly believes the Aztec treasure will only bring harm to those who claim it for themselves."

"Orlando, you had to know that somebody would eventually discover it."

"Your friend?"

"He's being forced by a very bad man to dive for the treasure."

"Warn... him."

"That's why I need to use your equipment. I also need to return the treasure to the Aztec burial ground, but I haven't figured out how."

"How? Even archeologists have found no remnants of the Aztec emperors' remains or burial sites," explained Mary.

"It's true. And I don't have a map," said Rome before being hit by a powerful epiphany. "But I've seen it." Suddenly, her thoughts turned to her time with Mendivia as she relived his memory. She remembered him unfolding the map and laying it on the table as he made plans with his crew. She spent most of the time studying the map while listening to their conversation. The image had been burned into her memory and she felt confident she could redraw it and then locate the burial tomb. "I know how to get there. I know where to return the gold!"

"Take it... take it!" said Orlando with enthusiasm.

"Papa wants you to take his boat to recover it. All the equipment you will need is aboard. We took it out yesterday with some friends so all the toys are charged and in working order."

"Are you sure?"

Orlando reached out his hand and took hold of Rome's. Squeezing it tight, he looked her in the eyes with all seriousness. "Your... destiny."

"All I can do is try." Suddenly, Rome's romantic idea of returning the treasure and freeing Kera's father and crew became a heavy weight on her shoulders. She had yet to rescue Jamie and here she was planning to return a stolen treasure to a remote burial tomb in Central America.

She had come to Providencia to find her friend, a plan that seemed cut and dried on the beach of Kauai. Since then, she'd been drugged and kidnapped more than once, survived two days in a remote village, lost Heath to violent drug runners and was nearly drowned twice, once by a group of angry ghosts. Needless to say, her time in the Caribbean was not going as smoothly as she had hoped.

"Are you all right?" asked Mary, pulling Rome out of the daze that enveloped her mind.

"Sorry."

"Jonah has been aboard our boat many times. He can help in Papa's stead."

Thank you," responded Rome as she stood up and shook his functioning hand. "Thank you so much. I promise to return her unharmed."

"Do what you need to do," responded Mary as her father shook his head in agreement.

Rome left the house and walked toward the dock, conflicted as to what her next move should be. She couldn't just pull up to Lazenby's boat and demand the gold. Nor could she get close enough to dive for it. She could call in the US Navy lieutenant who gave her his card, but they had already searched Lazenby's boat and came up with nothing. If they went in with guns-a-blazin,' innocent people could get harmed or even killed in the crossfire. The thought of losing either Heath or Jamie would be more than she could bear. And what of the gold? It would be confiscated, leaving Captain Locke and his crew still captive to the treasure's curse and Kera and Henry unable to move forward.

Pausing on the beach, she closed her eyes and inhaled as deeply as she could, breathing in the good air then letting out the bad.

"They're both still alive."

Rome opened her eyes to find Kera standing next to her. "I hear Heath's diving with Jamie?" asked Rome, looking for a confirmation.

"They remove the gold as we speak," replied Kera.

"Come on," said Rome as she ran toward the dock to interrupt Martin and Jonah's outing. She needed to get to Jamie as quickly as possible if she had any hope of helping them or returning the Aztec gold.

JONAH, Rome and Martin returned home with fish in hand and parked the motorcycle. Entering the living room, Jonah sent Martin to the back of the house to prepare the fish on the barbecue. Once out of sight, the boy snuck back toward the door to listen in on the conversation as Rome gathered Bev and Sheldon together for a huddle of sorts.

"Heath's in great danger and we need to act quickly," began Rome.

"Did the men who abducted you finally talk?" asked Bev.

"No. And they're not going to."

"How do we act quickly when we don't even know where he is?" asked Sheldon.

"Heath's being held with my friend, Jamie, and the two others who were taken a week ago."

"That's more than you told the police," concluded Sheldon.

"Quite a bit more," agreed Rome, glancing at Kera and Henry.

"Why would you lie?" asked Sheldon.

"I didn't lie. I just withheld some details. The men who have Heath are very dangerous. They'll destroy the evidence before the police can rescue anyone."

"What evidence?" asked Sheldon.

"She means they'll kill Heath and everyone else," clarified Bev.

"How do you know all of this?"

"I've seen first hand what they're capable of."

"It's one thing to know the type of men we're dealing with, but how do we find them?" asked Jonah.

"I know where they're being held."

"How?" asked Sheldon.

"I... figured it out."

"With help from beyond this island," said Jonah.

Rome paused for a moment, staring at Jonah. This new revelation was unexpected and Rome wasn't sure what else to expect from her new friend.

"Whose help?" asked Sheldon.

"An anonymous source or two."

"Can we trust these 'sources?'" added Sheldon.

"Absolutely."

"Clearly, I'm not the only one who has an appreciation for intensifiers."

"Obviously," agreed Bev with a touch of sarcasm.

"Did I miss something?" asked Rome.

"You were saying?" responded Bev, forwarding the conversation.

"Your friends are returning to the enemy's boat with their first load of treasure," announced Kera, appearing with Henry within the walls of the huddle.

"If I may point out... I'm a butler. You're a travel writer, Beverly's a gorgeous, top-notch guide..."

"Thank you, dear."

"And Jonah here is a brilliant doctor. What do we know about going up against a group of armed criminals?" asked Sheldon.

"We did it at the castle," Rome reminded him.

"We had no choice. If the Columbian or US Navy knew the details you've uncovered, then the odds would be in their favor," suggested Sheldon.

"I won't reduce Heath or Jamie's lives to a ratio. The man calling the shots has been committing serious crimes for years and has never been convicted. Not once."

"So what's the plan?" asked Bev growing more intrigued by the second.

"If I know Jamie, and I do, he's already set events in motion. But that doesn't mean he can't use some help from the outside. I need to make contact with him."

"How?"

"They're being held aboard a yacht about three miles north by northeast."

"So you want to sneak aboard a yacht full of armed gunmen to have a chat with your friend?" asked Sheldon, seeking clarification with a touch of skepticism.

"More like below the ship."

"Go on," responded Bev eagerly.

"The reason Jamie was kidnapped in the first place was for his diving ability. Lazenby is making him recover stolen treasure from a shipwreck two hundred feet down."

"And how do you know that?" asked Sheldon.

"The location of Lazenby's boat coincides with the coordinates where Dr. Orlando Melgosa discovered the shipwreck a few years ago."

"Orlando found the Maiden's Return?" responded Jonah with great surprise.

"Why didn't he recover the treasure for himself?" asked Bev.

"The gold comes with a different set of problems."

"Such as..."

"It's believed to be cursed."

"Curses don't actually exist," exclaimed Sheldon.

"Oh, but they do," remarked Jonah.

"From what I've heard, this curse is real. Jonah's friend, Orlando, has offered us the use of his exploration boat."

"Which means..." enquired Sheldon.

"We have access to diving gear and much more."

"What do you want us to do?" asked Bev.

"I need to enter the water close to the dive spot so I don't use up all the oxygen propelling myself toward the Maiden's Return. You guys will steer the boat toward the direction of the South'n Hunter and when we pass by, I'll drop into the water."

"We'll need a distraction so they don't see you," suggested Bev.

"Good idea," agreed Rome.

"Then what?"

"I should have enough in my tanks to rendezvous a ways from Lazenby's ship."

"When are we performing this 'mission impossible?'" asked Sheldon.

"They will be returning to the water soon," warned Kera, helping Rome with her timeline.

"It has to be now. They're about to re-enter the water."

"How do you know that?"

"A little bird told me."

"Of an anonymous nature?" responded Sheldon.

"It is."

"I'll ask to borrow the neighbor's car," said Bev as she quickly turned to leave. "Then change into something more appropriate."

"Forgive me if I'm not as exuberant as the two of you," remarked Sheldon.

"You need to trust me on this. It's the only way we're going to save Heath."

"Then I better change into something more appropriate as well," said Sheldon just as an incoming call sounded from his pocket. Examining the caller, Sheldon's demeanor quickly changed. "I need to take this." Walking away from the crowd, he answered the phone, leaving Jonah and Rome alone.

"Exactly what kind of voice does this little bird sing with?" asked Jonah, fishing for a confession. "My eyes may be blind, Rome, but that doesn't mean I do not see."

"What about Martin?" responded Rome, completely changing the subject.

"We can drop him off on our way to Orlando's."

"We have one shot at this, Jonah. Nothing can go wrong."

"We should let Martin know we're leaving. He'll need to gather his fish."

Rome and Jonah made their way through the house and out the back. Although she was confident in her plan on paper, she also knew anything could go wrong. Not only had she put Heath's life in danger, but now she was asking three of her friends to endanger their lives as well. This had to go well or she wouldn't be able to live with herself.

Once they reached the patio, Martin was nowhere in sight. Rome noticed the barbecue was cold and the fish were still in the cooler. She found a note on top of the cooler that read: "Borrowed the bike to check on my aunt." As soon as she finished reading it out loud, they heard the motorcycle fire up and head down the mountain.

"One less thing to worry about," said Jonah.

"There's a twelve-year-old driving a motorbike around the island without a license. That doesn't worry you?"

"Not compared to what we're planning."

"True, but that's not the point."

"It's all relative."

"He could get hurt."

"But he won't."

"How do you know that?"

"I don't. But I believe it."

"Let me guess... it's the island way."

"Now you're learning. And we have a boat to catch," said Jonah as he wrapped his arm around Rome's and left the patio. Walking toward the driveway, Rome couldn't help observing Sheldon's animated movements as he continued his conversation. It looked serious, leaving her to wonder if it had something to do with Heath's shipping company.

With a quick beep of the horn, Bev rolled up the driveway in the neighbor's car. Rome walked Jonah to the vehicle and got him settled as she watched Bev approach Sheldon, wrapping up his conversation. Something was definitely going on that had them both worried and she expected them to fill her in when they returned to the car, but she was met with nothing more than commitment to the task at hand. Quickly, the amateur team made up of a writer, a guide, a blind doctor and a butler, jumped into the car, ready to come to the rescue of their friends.

Chapter Eighteen

The South'n Hunter

*J*amie returned to the surface between the two hulls and gave the thumbs up for the men to start the winch. He watched as the cable began to move, pulling the basket full of treasure-filled trunks from a hundred-and-seventy-foot depth. This would be the first of only two loads to rise from the Maiden's Return, a fact Jamie would keep hidden from his captor. Lazenby had to believe there were more loads of treasure waiting to be transported in order to keep everyone alive and to buy Jamie the time he needed to enact his plan. The deception had to be flawless if they had any chance of escape.

Most importantly, Lazenby could never find out the trunks surfacing were filled with cannon balls, while the gold rested in a separate set of trunks on the sea floor. The entire plan was a gamble, but Jamie had no other choice.

Heath pierced the surface of the water just in time to switch his face mask with Jamie's then watched him grab onto the moving cable that carried him through the hatch. Heath followed Jamie's lead and after a couple of attempts, finally seized the cable with his right hand. Once he cleared the hatch, Jamie grabbed onto his free hand and helped him land his foot securely on the deck. Exhausted, Heath removed his mask and collapsed onto a crate, never happier to breathe fresh air and feel the security of something solid beneath him.

A couple guards approached from behind and removed their near empty tanks as Lazenby crossed the floor, followed by his two bodyguards. Clapping his hands slowly and loudly, Lazenby applauded Jamie's success with a touch of mockery. Although he watched them load each piece of gold, he wanted to be present when the trunks surfaced. His hands had begun to shake in Jamie's absence and he was sweating profusely as he walked toward them, wiping his forehead. "You missed your calling, Webb. With your set of skills, you could make a lot of money in the smuggling industry."

"I'll stick with the good guys."

"Your loss."

"I'll get over it," replied Jamie dishing out an equal amount of sarcasm.

"What was cuttin' out the video feed?"

Jamie removed his glove and examined the camera attached to the face mask, finding it to be damaged but still in working order. "Must have happened when I slammed into the side of the chasm."

"What happened down there?"

"Remember that bad feeling I had when I first opened the trunk? Multiply it by a thousand."

"We're not goin' there, Webb."

"You asked."

"So how much is left?" demanded Lazenby, changing the uncomfortable subject.

"Four loads, maybe five."

"Which will bring us to the end of our joint enterprise."

"And where does that leave us?"

"You done good so far. I'll give you that."

"No one needs to get hurt, Jack. The kids haven't seen anything and there's no proof you kidnapped us."

"So we all just walk away? No harm, no foul?"

"Exactly. You get your gold and we get to go on living."

"Like it was nothin' more than a vacation."

"That's right."

"Until you get back to D.C. and start stewin' on it. I know you, Webb. You're calm, but persistent. One day you'll be sittin' at that important desk of yours, pushin' those important papers and somethin' will snap inside ya, replacin' the blood in your veins with a lust for justice. Then you'll come for me. I wouldn't be able to sleep knowin' that. And I love my sleep."

"At least let the kids go," chimed in Heath, surprising both Lazenby and Jamie.

"What do we have here?" asked Lazenby as he moved past Jaime and squatted down next to Heath. "You got somethin' to say, Jones?"

"If there's even an ounce of humanity in you, you'll let them go," responded Heath.

"There's no humanity in business."

"Not your kind."

"You and me... we're not so different. We both get paid to transport stuff."

"I ship by the rules."

"Ya sure about that?"

"Of course."

"How? You don't inspect your cargo."

"It goes through several inspectors."

"Who can easily be bought," implied Lazenby.

"I don't believe you."

"A by-product of the ivory tower."

"You don't know me, Lazenby," said Heath.

"I know your type."

"And I know yours," responded Heath defiantly.

"I think I'll hang onto you for a while, Mr. CEO, and show ya what it's like down here in the mud. Maybe even find some shark infested waters for when I'm done with ya."

"Here it comes," yelled one of the other guards, referring to the basket rising from the water.

Lazenby moved to the open hatch and welcomed his long-awaited prize as one of his men stopped the winch and let the water drain from the basket. Using a crane to move it onto the deck, Lazenby and his men watched in anticipation as it pivoted through the air. Once it came to rest, his men opened the side panel and began unloading the trunks. They were heavy and required two men per chest. The lids were secured with locks so they could only imagine the extent of the contents. Feeling satisfied, Lazenby turned to Jamie and ordered him back into the water.

"I need to use the bathroom first."

"Fine. I want this done by sundown. I'm ready to get back to civilization."

"I thought you lived in New Orleans."

Lazenby laughed a fake laugh as he walked away from the gold and back to the stairs. Once he was out of earshot, Jamie leaned down to Heath. "Distract them with conversation." Then Jamie, still wearing his wetsuit, crossed the deck in the opposite direction toward the bathroom.

Once he entered the hallway, he bypassed the bathroom door and headed to the supply room. Utilizing his misshapen paperclips, he unlocked the door and quickly made his way to the previously discovered C-4, detonators and blasting caps. Removing the tools from the two bags that hung around his waist, he filled them with the right amount of explosives to do the job and a small 9 millimeter handgun, then grabbed two candy bars and two knifes and left the room. As he walked past the siblings' room, he tapped his knuckle to the door as he slid the candy bars and knives through the crack. "Are you two all right in there?"

Quickly, he got the response he had hoped for from Talin. "We're okay."

"See ya both soon."

"Okay, Mr. Webb," came a little voice from behind the door.

"Very soon."

Jamie stood up and left the hallway. He walked to the cot along the wall of the large deck and covertly placed the handgun beneath the pillow. "Hurry it up, Webb," ordered one of the guards ready with his tanks. "I'm coming," responded Jamie, ready to wrap up his time being Lazenby's puppet. One way or another, the nightmare would end before sundown, just as Jack had requested.

While putting on his fins, Jamie quietly instructed Heath. "Descend slowly and don't look for me. I have some business to take care of beneath the boat. I'll catch up with you." Heath understood the type of business he was referring to and shook his head in agreement.

"I need a handsaw. I've got a piece of lumber blocking the hull that I can't get around," said Jamie. One of the guards responded by pulling a hacksaw out of the tool box and handing it to him. Although it was designed to cut through metal or plastic, Jamie examined the teeth on the blade and determined it would cut through wood. "It'll work."

Jamie signaled to the man near the winch to drop the basket, and as it descended, they both hung on for the ride. Once in the water, Jamie handed Heath the hacksaw then watched as he descended.

Turning back toward the bottom of the boat, he began strategically planting the explosives along the bottom of the two hulls. He still wasn't certain as to the sequence of events that would need to take place to get Leta, Talin, and now Heath, into a lifeboat and safely away from Lazenby's ship, but he needed options and blowing the boat was one of them.

Dr. Orlando Melgosa's Exploration Boat

Rome and her crew boarded Orlando's exploration boat and were immediately impressed. She was equipped with everything they could possibly need: a winch, a crane, scuba gear, floats, nets, a rubber dinghy and plenty of scientific equipment. The piece of equipment that caused the most enthusiasm for Rome was the DPV —diver propulsion vehicle or sea scooter as most people know them.

The size and weight of it told Rome it had the capability to reach the two-hundred-foot depth of the Maiden's Return. It would provide extra propulsion to get her there faster and use less of her own energy, which meant her air supply would last longer. Since she needed to travel a longer distance to return to Orlando's boat once they moved away from the South'n Hunter, the sea scooter would allow her to make good time on a gradual horizontal ascension. She checked the battery level and it looked good.

Fortunately, both Sheldon and Bev were very familiar with boats and knew exactly what to do the minute they boarded. Rome helped Jonah to the seat next to the captain's, so he'd be available to answer any question Sheldon might have. Bev untied the ropes from the mooring cleats and rolled them up as Sheldon started the engine and steered her out to sea, heading for the coordinates provided by Kera. Bev quickly helped Rome on with her scuba gear and the rest of her equipment; three miles doesn't take long to cover in a boat.

"We still haven't figured out how to get you and the sea scooter in the water without them seeing you," said Bev.

"The DPV probably weighs around fifty pounds. Light enough for me to pull it off the back of the boat."

"We'll still need a diversion."

"Something that would give us an excuse for stopping the boat."

"I am wearing a swimsuit under my shorts."

"It's going to take more than your amazon legs, Bev."

"I can help," said Martin as he burst onto the deck from beneath.

"Martin? What are you doing here?"

"I overheard you talking at the house and I want to help."

"What we're doing is very dangerous," said Rome. "Lives are at stake."

"We can't endanger the life of a child," added Bev.

"I am only a child by age."

"Exactly," agreed Bev.

"I want to help rescue my bosses."

"How can you possibly help?"

"A boy falling off the boat would be a good reason to stop."

Rome and Bev looked at each other as they considered Martin's plan. "I can't believe we're actually thinking about this," said Bev.

"We are kind of desperate."

"I'm a good swimmer," inserted Martin.

"And I've been trained in lifesaving... in case something goes wrong," said Bev.

"What if they start shooting at us?"

"What kind of people shoot at a kid?"

"The same people who kidnapped 'em."

"You have a point."

"I know Leta and Talin. Please, I can do this," begged Martin.

"There's his boat," said Rome as the South'n Hunter came into view. "Are you sure about this, Martin?"

"Consider it part of the island guide package."

"Oh, he's smooth," said Bev.

"Just doing my job, ma'am."

"You ever want a guide job in Australia, look me up."

"Fill Sheldon in about Martin," requested Rome as she attached several accessories to her belt, including a dive slate.

"He's never going to go for this," responded Bev.

"You're right. Keep him in the dark."

"It'll be more spontaneous."

"And more believable."

"What kind of girlfriend does that make me?" asked Bev, feeling a little guilty.

"The kind that knows her man."

"We're coming up on the boat," yelled Bev. "Are you ready, Martin?"

"Yes."

"Sheldon's going to come at her from an angle, so pretend to fall off the starboard side."

"Okay," said Martin excitedly as he started for the side of the boat.

"Put this on," yelled Bev as she tossed a life jacket to the boy.

"Keep an eye on him."

"You can count on it," she said as they picked up the sea scooter and moved it toward the opening at the rear of the boat.

"I can push it in by myself."

"Good luck, Rome."

"Thanks. You better get within earshot of Sheldon so he can stop as soon as Martin goes overboard," recommended Rome as she crouched down and hooked the strap on her belt to the pop out clip on the sea scooter. Then she turned the switch to the on position.

Bev stood up and hurried toward the front of the boat, watching Martin as she went. She felt the boat begin to slow as it turned to pass the South'n Hunter. Nodding to Martin, she watched as he fell into the water between Orlando's and Lazenby's boat. "Man overboard. Stop the boat!" she yelled throwing Jonah and Sheldon into panic mode.

"She's supposed to go overboard," responded Sheldon, shutting off the motor.

"Not Rome. Martin."

"Martin? What's he doing aboard?" asked Jonah.

"He's our diversion."

"You're using a child as a diversion?" Sheldon yelled as he ran toward the side of the boat, grabbing a life preserver attached to a rope along the way.

At the same time, Rome pushed the sea scooter into the water and pushed the trigger but nothing happened. She remembered Orlando's daughter telling her that everything was charged, so she continued to try.

In the meantime, three of Lazenby's men exited the ship and watched from the balcony at the stern of the lower deck. Their rifles were concealed behind them, ready to be used at the first sign of trouble.

Using a British accent, Bev made contact with the enemy as Sheldon worked to pull Martin aboard. "Everything's all right. We just lost... our son, overboard. Fortunately, he's a good swimmer. So how's your day going?"

Choosing not to respond, Lazenby's men watched suspiciously as Sheldon pulled the boy toward the boat. Although his near drowning performance was a bit over the top, Martin was the perfect diversion and kept the men focused on his rescue.

"Start the boat, Jonah," Bev whispered loudly enough for him to hear, knowing Rome would need some noise to drown out the sound of the sea scooter once she got it started.

Jonah guided his hand along the controls until he came to the familiar ignition. Soon the boat motor was running.

"It certainly is a beautiful day," yelled Bev, making polite conversation to give Rome time to get the sea scooter to work. "The water's perfect for an afternoon outing. And would you look at the color. Just gorgeous!"

Coughing from inhaled water, Martin allowed Sheldon to pull him onto the boat as Bev wrapped him in a towel. Looking toward the back of the boat, Bev saw no sign of Rome or the DPV, so she leaned over to Sheldon and whispered in his ear. "Get us out of here."

Still hyped from the endorphins produced over Martin's rescue, Sheldon hurried to the wheel and left the South'n Hunter in her wake. Bev waved goodbye to the men on the deck while robustly drying the boy's hair.

"We did it, ma'am."

"You were a perfect diversion, Martin, but don't ever do that again."

"Now what?"

"We anchor at the rendezvous point and wait for Rome."

"That's it?"

"I saw a deck of cards below. Fancy a hand?"

"What are we playing for?"

"What do you got?"

"The best guide services on the island."

"This trip just got interesting," said Bev as she followed him below.

BENEATH THE SURFACE, Rome took a moment to relax from the

adrenaline rush of trying to start the sea scooter. She's not sure why it wouldn't start or why it did start, for that matter, but was happy it finally did. Looking around, she was surprised to see a diver descending from the bottom of Lazenby's boat. Her first response was to assume he was the enemy. She would know soon. There was no turning back. On the other hand, it could be Heath or Jamie heading back to the shipwreck. The only way to know would be to catch up with the diver and have a look. "What's the worst that could happen?" she thought to herself then quickly dismissed the question as ridiculous. An interception was imminent as she steered the sea scooter in his direction.

Seeing a diver approach from the side, Jamie stopped his descent and prepared himself to meet one of Lazenby's men. His reconnaissance had uncovered no underwater cameras attached to the boat but maybe he missed something. If they knew about the explosives then his plan was over. So were their lives.

Surprisingly, he recognized a familiar face through her mask. It was Rome. An occasion like this would normally call for a more personal greeting, but they were too laden with equipment to pull off one of such magnitude. Instead, Jamie took hold of the sides of her head and moved his mask close to hers as she gabbed onto his forearms. Rome closed her eyes for a few seconds, squeezing his arms tightly to make sure he was real. Opening her eyes, she found him still in her sights.

They had to move on from the moment, but neither wanted to let go first. Fortunately, they were two peas in a pod when it came to carrying out a plan. Their mutual nod signaled it was time to get down to business.

Rome pulled the dive slate from her belt and wrote the first sentence: "What's the plan?" Jamie took the dive slate in hand and twisted the knob to advance the scroll, giving him a clean writing surface. "How much do you know?" Rome read the message and followed the same procedure to respond. "Maiden's Return - Aztec treasure."

"You got the message," scribbled Jamie.

"From Ross."

"And others?" asked Jamie, confirming he knew about her gift.

"Ghosts make good spies," penned Rome, validating his belief.

"Was counting on it."

"How long?"

"A year into dating."

"Why not say?"

"Yours to tell."

"What now?" asked Rome.

"Get gold, blow ship."

"How can I help?"

"Boat with winch."

"Got one."

"Impressive."

"Go big or go home."

"I rubbed off."

"In a good way."

"Plan's dangerous," jotted Jamie, turning the conversation serious.

"Figured."

"Can go either way."

"I believe in you."

"In you too," wrote Jamie, then he advanced the scroll after she read it and continued to take the conversation in a personal direction. "Always have."

Rome read it and nodded a 'thank you' in response. Taking the dive slate back, she returned to the business at hand. "What's next?"

"Watch for boom," wrote Jamie as he pointed up to the charges located along the bottom of the South'n Hunter's two hulls.

"Soon?"

"Hour or so."

"Then what?"

"Come and get us," wrote Jamie then he scrolled up and included, "and the gold."

"To return it?"

"Where?"

"Aztec burial ground."

"How?"

Rome pointed to her head letting Jamie know she had all the answers. "I know where," then she scrolled up. "Not sure how."

"Leave to me."

"Happy to," jotted Rome, relieved to have a professional's help to return the treasure.

"See ya soon," wrote Jamie, noticing the camera hanging from her belt. "Camera?"

Rome shook her head in agreement and handed him the camera. "Don't lose it."

"Safe with me."

"We all are."

"Dive slate?"

"Take it."

"Thanks," mouthed Jamie then he gave her a quick salute and left her floating.

Rome watched as he propelled himself deeper and deeper. She wanted so much to be descending with him, but that was not the plan. She had expected to meet them both at the bottom and even get to see first hand the infamous Maiden's Return, but that was not to be. Her chance meeting with Jamie was better and would save her a lengthy return.

Suddenly, it dawned on her that she didn't ask about Heath. Not once. No inquiry as to how he was doing or where he was. As she pulled the trigger on the sea scooter and propelled herself through the water, her mind continued to process what appeared to be her lack of concern and why. She loved Heath with all her heart, but current circumstances had taken precedence. She would chalk her absence of thought up to current events. She had no doubt her focus would return to her boyfriend once they swooped in for the rescue. For now, however, there was a comfortable familiarity in working with Jamie.

After all she'd been through, Rome could use a little comfort.

APPROACHING THE MAIDEN'S RETURN, Jamie used the camera to capture the haunting beauty of the lost ship. Heath was at the helm holding onto the wheel as though he were sailing her across the bottom of the sea. After taking a few pictures facing the bow, he noticed the head scarf was no longer wrapped around the mermaid's neck. Descending to the deck, he found Heath with the scarf wrapped around his utility belt, the ends floating behind as though caught in the wind. Jamie grew worried that Lazenby had seen Rome's message, but Heath motioned to the video camera temporarily attached to a rope, pointing away and swaying with the water's movement. Heath opened the end of the scarf and held the writing for Jamie to see. "See you soon, Rome. P.S. Don't lose the scarf."

"Sorry," Jamie wrote on the dive slate then cleared the writing and continued to communicate with Heath. "She's alive." Jamie could tell by the look on his face that he was both happy she was alive but disappointed he didn't tell him. "I forgot. That's all," wrote Jamie then he handed him the dive slate to respond.

Heath pulled the scarf from his belt instead and pointed to her inscription. Then he took the dive slate in his hand and wrote, "When?"

"Just did," scribbled Jamie. He could see the letdown on Heath's face increase but had no time to explain. Lazenby would expect to be seeing them in action and that's what needed to happen. "Let's get to it," wrote Jamie, then he floated back up to the sea floor to place the dive slate in one of the trunks of gold as well as Orlando's camera and the scarf.

Alone with his thoughts, Heath reattached the video camera to his face mask as he waited for Jamie to return and make his way into the hull of the ship. Questions begged for answers as he processed the fact that Jamie and Rome made physical contact with each other but didn't include him. "How long had they planned to meet?" he wondered. "How many times had they met? Why hadn't anyone filled him in? Didn't they trust him enough? How could she not trust him? Did she pass on a message for him? Did Jamie forget to share it or did she forget to even ask about him?"

With each new question his chest grew tighter. It was a familiar feeling that took him back to the day he left Rome at his Tasmanian castle, expecting she would return to her life with Jamie. The last thing he wanted was to experience that kind of pain again, but he could already feel it settling in.

Turning his attention to the treasure, Heath went back to work, a familiar activity and the one thing amidst the chaos that he understood.

ROME SURFACED within sight of Orlando's boat and removed her mask. She couldn't see anyone aboard and began to get nervous. "I'm back!" she yelled. Martin hurried from the cabin and alerted the others as Rome closed the gap between her and the boat. Together, Sheldon and Bev lifted the sea scooter up then helped Rome into the boat.

"We didn't expect you back so soon. Is everything all right?" asked Bev.

"We made contact at a higher depth," responded Rome as they helped her off with the tanks. "Jamie's going to blow the ship and we're going to come to their rescue."

"What kind of rescue involves blowing up a boat?" remarked Bev.

"We didn't have a lot of time to discuss the details."

"I'm with Beverly on this one. How will they survive?" asked Jonah.

"Jamie knows what he's doing."

"How's Heath?" asked Sheldon.

"I only saw Jamie, but Heath's fine."

"Is that what Mr. Webb said... 'fine?'" enquired Sheldon further.

"I've never liked the word 'fine,'" mentioned Bev.

"Doesn't really say much," added Jonah.

"Definitely lacks description," agreed Bev.

"Unless, of course, you're referring to china," pointed out Sheldon.

"Are the bad guys Chinese?" asked Martin.

"Not the country, the dishes. Fine china," inserted Jonah.

"He's fine! We'll see him soon," said Rome, bringing an end to the vocabulary tangent.

"How much longer before the fireworks begin?" asked Sheldon hesitantly.

"Forty-five minutes, give or take."

"What can we do to prepare?" asked Bev.

"We'll need the winch hooked up to the basket and ready to go."

"We may be needing the first aid kit," suggested Jonah. "It's usually well stocked."

"I'll get it," volunteered Martin as he ran from the back of the boat.

"Probably good to have several life preservers nearby," added Bev.

"Let's do it," said Rome.

Sheldon and Bev began readying the boat as Rome worked to remove the rest of her equipment.

"I'm curious about your relationship with Jamie," said Jonah out of the blue.

"What about it?"

"Have you always just been friends?"

"We dated for a couple years."

"That's a long time."

"Yeah."

"Why did you end it?"

"What makes you think I ended it?"

"Did he?"

"It was mutual."

"Breakups are rarely mutual."

"I may have gotten the ball rolling," she said, removing her fins and unzipping her wetsuit.

"After you met Heath?"

"Where are you going with this?"

"You didn't ask your friend about Heath, did you?"

"He's fine."

"That's not what I asked."

"Are you trying to diagnose me, Doctor?"

"Just a question."

"I forgot. I had other things on my mind."

"Planning a rescue mission can take up a lot of processing space, but that's not why you forgot."

"I'm in love with Heath, Jonah."

"You also love Jamie."

"As my best friend."

"I find it interesting that you're sharing your life with Heath, yet he's not your best friend."

Rome sat quietly pondering Jonah's observation as Martin approached with the first aid kit. Leaving Rome behind, Jonah walked with his young friend toward the front of the boat to take an inventory of the contents while the others made preparations.

Standing up, she pulled on a pair of shorts over her swimsuit while continuing to contemplate Jonah's observation. Heath was the man she planned to spend the rest of her life with, but she did see his point.

"We could use some help," hollered Bev.

Returning her attention to the rescue, she opted to tuck Jonah's advice away for future use. For now, she had bigger fish to fry in the present.

Chapter Nineteen

Shipwreck of the Maiden's Return

Within the span of a day, Jamie had held more Aztec artifacts than most curators dream of in a lifetime: large pendants and neckwear, earrings, bracelets, upper calf cuffs and armlets, crowns, headbands and headdresses—embedded with jewels of all types—solid gold figurines that once rode high atop the emperors' staffs and shields made of silver and beautifully engraved with gold. They even found a few wooden Obsidian swords, the Aztec weapon of choice.

Under normal circumstances it would have been inspiring, but the darkness surrounding the gold had taken its toll physically on both Jamie and Heath. They felt an ongoing sickness in their guts that was unexplainable. With only one wooden crate remaining, Jamie left the ship, signaling that he needed a break. Heath disconnected his camera and hooked it onto a rope swaying from the mast. Turning back, he watched Jamie pick up the hacksaw and a crowbar and propel himself toward the tip of the bow. Following suit, Heath pulled the proper tools from the canvas bag then worked to remove the ship's wheel.

Freeing it from the base, he propelled himself and the wheel out of the cavern and onto the sea floor just as his partner returned carrying the mermaid figurehead. Jamie nodded his head in approval at what Heath had accomplished and he returned the sentiment.

Laying the artifacts near the gold, they floated back to the edge of the chasm and looked down at the distant glow of the ship. Jamie took the lead and stepped off the cliff first. Heath followed as they both descended to the deck. Once Jamie disappeared into the bowels of the Maiden's Return, Heath reconnected the camera then patiently waited for the next piece of treasure to make an appearance, all the time watching the movement of the water around him.

Using his hands, Jamie pulled himself down through the three companionways to the lowest deck and opened the last of the trunks. Expecting to see more of the same, he was amazed to find only one item: a life-size replica of a man's chest and back made of pure gold. It reminded him of armor worn by a Roman legionary around 100 A.D. The chest design was chiseled, showing the detailed pecks and the six pack across the abdomen. The front and back of the armor connected at the shoulders by hinges and were secured with a strap around the two sides of the waist.

With difficulty, he lifted it from the box. Due to the density of gold and the effect it has on gravity, Jamie recognized the challenge it would have been to bear this type of weight in battle—much heavier than the iron armor worn in Europe and England. "The emperor who wore this must have looked like Hercules," he thought to himself, secretly wishing he had the opportunity to try it on himself.

Swimming out of the hull was the roughest exit by far. Dropping the armor several times, he continued to adjust his grip. Like a bull in a china shop, he ran into obstacles along the way, snagging the steps and any other protruding part to the ship as he moved it inch by inch. Breathing heavy from the exercise, he worried about the level of his tanks as he reached the ladder to the second deck. "One more deck to go," he thought to himself. But his excitement would be short lived.

Just as he pulled himself and the armor onto the second deck, the water began to move. He knew what was coming. Wrapping his arm around one of the steps leading from the second deck to the main deck, Jamie prepared himself for another beating by the invisible force. Determined to keep the remaining piece of the treasure, he pressed it between the ladder and his chest, hanging on with all the strength he had left.

The force came at him from every direction, pounding his body and pulling against the armor. The first thing to go was his dive light, leaving him in the dark, the only illumination left coming from the square opening in the deck above him. He wanted to yell, to scream for help, but there was nothing anyone could do. The only thing he knew was to ride it out as he'd done so many times before. But this attack was different. The force was brutal. He could hear the ship moaning from the turbulence and feel it twisting back and forth. She could break free at any moment, and if Jamie couldn't make it to the top of the stairs and out the final hatch, he'd be along for the ride. Within seconds, a muted crack of the lumber, followed by a jarring of the ship, alerted Jamie that her descent was imminent. The only way to save himself was to drop the last of the treasure and try to escape the force attacking him. A thump on the top of his head changed his mind.

Looking up, he saw Heath, head first through the hatch, being pounded by the ghosts as he stretched his arm toward Jamie. Help had arrived. Jamie pushed the armor against the force and into Heath's capable hands, who pulled it through the hatch and out of sight.

With all the energy he had left, Jamie grabbed onto the next step with his empty hand and began to pull toward the light of the hatch. Step by step he pushed against his invisible enemy until he came within reaching distance of the main deck. But before he could make it through the final hatch, the Maiden's Return gave away. Jamie's time was up. He did all he could to make it out, but it wasn't enough. His last thoughts were of Heath and his two fellow captives, knowing they would never escape Lazenby without him. He had failed them all.

About to let go and allow the invisible force to have its way with him, Jamie felt a hand wrap around his wrist. Heath had returned. Reaching up Jamie secured himself to his rescuer as the Maiden's Return pulled away. Once outside the ship, he felt Heath let go of his wrist, allowing him to float free of his wooden coffin. While basking in the rush of endorphins brought on by his near death experience, he momentarily lost sight of his objective. The relief he felt was euphoric as he closed his eyes in an attempt to slow his breathing, unaware of his partner's struggle.

Heath worked to rise with the armor, his legs kicking at their maximum just to keep him from sinking deeper into the chasm. No matter how hard he tried, he'd never make it to the sea floor by his own strength. Wrapping one arm around the gold chest, he turned on his dive light, hoping it would get Jamie's attention. No response came. Heath began to wonder if he had lost consciousness due to oxygen toxicity or narcosis... not a good thought at two hundred feet below.

A decision needed to be made. Their lives were more important than the artifact he was trying to save. Just as he was about to let go of the gold, Jamie came into sight, grabbing onto the armor. Using all the strength their legs could muster, they began to ascend while watching the Maiden's Return disappear into the abyss, the luminaries attached to the mast still visible as it slipped into the darkness. She would no longer be a risk or an intrigue to future divers or seekers of treasure. There was a quiet sadness to her disappearance as Jamie bid a final goodbye.

Once they reached the sea floor, they secured the armor with the rest of the gold, loaded the cannon ball-laden trunks into the basket, then began their slow ascent. Surfacing on the outside of the boat, Jamie signaled to Heath to pull off his mask. "Thank you for saving my life down there."

"Consider it payback."

"Once we board the ship, things are going to go fast, so be ready for it," said Jamie.

"Ready for what?" responded Heath, beat from lack of sleep and physical endurance.

"I have a pistol under the pillow on the cot. Do you shoot?"

"At clay pigeons off the boat."

"These targets will be shooting back."

"We're actually doing this," exclaimed Heath.

"We won't get another chance."

"Is there some kind of signal?"

"Signal?"

"A code word to go for the gun."

"You'll know when to start shooting."

"Humor me."

"What's your favorite food?"

"Anything off the barbie."

"Barbecue it is."

"Is what?"

"The code word."

"So when I hear barbecue, I go for the gun?"

"Yes."

"Where will you be?"

"Not sure at this point."

"Barbecue," repeated Heath, feeling less than prepared for what was about to happen.

"Let's do this," said Jamie as he swam around the hull and into the center of the ship. Heath followed and they met up beneath the hatch. This time he allowed Heath to grab the moving cable first, which he did on his first attempt and disappeared through the deck.

Diving below the surface, Jamie took one last look at the explosives he'd set along the two hulls. Satisfied that no one had found them, he swam toward the moving cable and grabbed a hold with one hand, holding his mask with the other. Things were going just as he'd planned until he entered the ship to an unexpected sight.

Both Talin and Leta were kneeling in front of Lazenby's two bodyguards, guns pointed at the backs of their heads, while Jack stood in the middle. The rest of the guards were scattered behind them and to the sides, weapons drawn.

Jamie let go of the cable and joined Heath facing the opposition. On Lazenby's signal, two of his men removed the divers' tanks, then returned to their previous position.

"You must think I'm stupid, Webb," said Lazenby, pointing his trembling hand at the opened trunks full of cannonballs.

"I was trying to protect you, Jack."

"Recoverin' sunken treasure's no crime."

"That gold's cursed and if we bring it up, we're all dead men," warned Jamie, causing the guards scattered around the deck to look at each other with concern. "Do your men even know how the six divers died down there? I do. I saw what killed the last two."

"Don't listen to him!" ordered Lazenby, wiping the sweat from his face. "He's sick from the nitrogen."

"Did he tell you why he wanted the gold brought up in locked trunks? To keep you from stealing it."

"Lies!" screamed Lazenby, pulling a 44 Magnum Semi Auto handgun out of the belt holster of the bodyguard next to him and pointing it at Jamie. "I know what you're tryin' to do, Webb."

"Your men deserve to know the truth about the gold. If you don't believe me, ask him."

"The curse is real," confirmed Heath, nervously watching the pistol shake in his captor's hand. "There's your proof. The fever's already begun."

Noticing his men were getting nervous, Lazenby reached in his pocket, pulled out the Aztec arm band and erratically waved it in front of their faces. "There's more where this came from. Pure gold. Plenty to go around. We'll be rich beyond our wildest dreams."

"He'll kill you all before he shares the treasure," warned Jamie, causing an even greater stir among the guards.

"The only killin' to be done is mine to do... and I'm startin' with her." As he stepped toward Leta pointing his gun, Talin sprang to his feet and tackled him to the floor. Lazenby hit the deck hard, flat on his back, his head bouncing off the steal. The impact caused him to let go of the gun which sailed across the floor in Jamie's direction.

Retrieving the enemy's 44, Jamie pointed it at Lazenby's two bodyguards. "No one touches him," he said while the six other guards chose to wait it out.

"Shoot him!" Lazenby screamed between blows. "That's an order!" But there was no stopping Talin's rage. With one hand around his kidnapper's neck and the other fist swinging, Leta's brother delivered some long-awaited justice.

Knowing Jamie's legendary background, the two bodyguards were more concerned with keeping themselves alive than rescuing their employer, so they continued their standoff. Neither one wanting to pull the trigger first, until a tooth from Lazenby's mouth skipped across the metal decking. Sliding the pump action on his 12 gauge shotgun, one of the bodyguards aimed it at Leta's head. "Stop or she dies!"

Maintaining eye contact with Lazenby, Talin let go of his neck and signaled surrender by lifting his hands in the air.

"Get him off!" yelled the bodyguard, motivating two of the guards to go after the young captain.

"Looks like you were right, Jack. I did rub off on the kid," commented Jamie, adding salt to his nemesis' wounds.

Just as Lazenby lifted his head, Talin hit him hard with a final blow, right before the guards yanked him off. The blow was so hard and so unexpected that he dropped his gold armlet. Dizzy from the beating, he scrambled to grab it as it rolled across the floor. Silence fell over the deck as everyone watched him scamper after it until the arm band rolled through the open hatch. Lacking all rational thought, Lazenby dove in after it... a surprise to his men who looked back and forth at each other wondering what to do.

"Don't do anything crazy while we're gone," said Jamie to the guards while handing the 44 to Heath, then he followed Lazenby through the hatch.

ONCE JAMIE GOT his bearings he could see Lazenby swimming straight down in pursuit of the gold armlet. Using his fins for speed, he quickly closed in on his long-time enemy, while the armband continued out of reach. He knew they'd never recover it, but Lazenby was undaunted. His obsession with the gold had depleted him of all common sense. In jeopardy of losing his life, he continued to push through the water until he started to slow.

Swimming past him, Jamie gave the 'thumbs up' symbol to surface, but Lazenby refused to change course. No longer able to hold his breath, he started to convulse. With zero sympathy, Jamie watched the life drain from his enemy's battered face, his eyes turning to glass. Jack Lazenby had come to the end.

Running short of breath, he pushed himself away from Lazenby, but before he could start for the surface, he saw the entity from below fast approaching. Jamie had nothing to anchor himself to and knew he couldn't outrun it. All he could do was ready himself for impact. Much to his surprise it never came. Instead of attacking, the force pushed the gold armlet toward him as though it were a gift. Reaching out, Jamie gently took hold of the armband and thanked the force by nodding his head. Then the entity disappeared as quickly as it had arrived. Using his fins to rapidly propel himself upward, he burst through the surface and inhaled, filling his lungs with as much air as they could hold. The cable was still pulling the basket from the bottom, so he grabbed onto the cable and rose through the hatch.

Lazenby's crew showed signs of uncertainty when Jamie returned alone until one of the bodyguards foolhardily assumed the leadership roll. "Where's Lazenby?" he asked, armed for combat and prepared to use Talin and Leta as bargaining chips.

Jamie could see the overconfidence in his eyes as he walked past the two bodyguards towering over Leta and Talin. "Jack's no longer with us," he answered while connecting with Leta's eyes, letting her know the time had come to do what needed to be done to survive.

"Nothing has changed. You'll retrieve the gold for us," demanded the body guard.

"Get it yourself," responded Jamie just as the basket full of cannon ball-filled trunks passed through the hatch and continued toward the pulley.

The guard grabbed onto Leta's hair and pressed his gun against the top of her skull.

"Change your mind, Webb, or she dies first."

Staring at Leta, Jamie watched her slowly pull the knife from the side of her shoe. "You can try, but I think she's got the upper hand."

Finding her target, Leta looked back to Jamie for the courage she needed then thrust the knife deep into the center of the bodyguard's foot. Talin followed by driving his own knife into the thigh of the second bodyguard, then fought him for his shotgun. The siblings' surprise attack, combined with the basket colliding with the pulley throwing sparks and squealing, set Jamie's plan into motion. Dropping to his knees, Jamie grabbed Leta and yelled, "Swim as far from the boat as you can!" Then he pushed her through the hatch into the ocean below.

Surprised by the instant chaos, Heath tossed Jamie the 44 then ran for the cot. Grabbing the gun from beneath the pillow, he dove behind some metal barrels and returned fire while Jamie got Talin to safety. "Get off the ship!"

Talin crawled through the array of bullets and dropped through the hatch as Jamie fired toward the guards as a diversion. With the siblings out of harms way, Jamie had one more person to save. Diving behind the barrier that Heath was using for cover, he quickly removed his fins. "Run for the hatch. I'll cover you!"

"What are you going to do?"

"I'm going to stick to the plan. Now move!"

"What's the plan?"

"To blow the ship."

Just then the basket broke loose from the cable and wedged itself cockeyed in the open hatch, blocking their exit from the boat.

"We're not getting out that way," said Heath, removing his fins.

Looking around, Jamie noticed they were close to the companionway leading to the top deck. "Head for the stairs. I'll cover you." Heath did as Jamie ordered and ran through the gunfire toward the stairs. Just before he reached the stairway, a bullet sliced through the top of his arm, causing him to dive for cover.

It was Jamie's turn, so he laid down fire as he ran toward their only escape. Heath covered him from inside the companionway until Jamie burst through and raced up the stairs. Heath followed Jamie across the top floor to a small deck at the stern of the ship where they could see Leta and Talin swimming in the distance. "What happened to the code word?" yelled Heath.

"Barbecue!" yelled Jamie as they leaped over the railing, plunged into the water and began swimming as fast as they could. Before they could reach a safe distance, the guards began laying down fire from the ship, leaving Jamie no other option. Too close for comfort, he pulled out the two detonators and pressed the buttons. The ship blew instantly as they continued to swim, dodging the flying debris. Soon they met up with the siblings who were treading water while watching the ship burn.

"You did it, Mr. Webb," said Leta as she wrapped her arms around his neck.

"We did it."

Talin shook his hand as soon as his sister let go. "Thank you, Mr. Webb. You're our friend for life."

Suddenly, a boat horn could be heard and the four of them turned in the direction of the welcoming sound.

"Perfect timing as usual, London," said Jamie as he waved his arms in the air for them to see. Heath watched Jamie's reaction to Rome and truly understood what Rome meant when she said they worked well together. He'd seen it before in Australia, but this was a whole new level.

Soon the boat pulled up next to the motley gang and Rome pulled Leta aboard as Heath and Jamie helped push from the water. Rome wrapped her in a towel and the safety of her arms as she watched Bev help the older brother aboard. Waiting for Talin to join his sister, Rome's main focus was Heath. The anticipation of holding him in her arms again was almost more than she could stand.

"Your turn," said Jamie to Heath just as Sheldon reached the back of the boat in time to help him aboard. Jamie followed close behind, eager to celebrate their survival with Rome.

"Looks like that first aid kit will come in handy, Jonah," hollered

Sheldon as he rushed his wounded friend past Rome to a seat next to the blind doctor, then helped him out of the top half of his wetsuit. "I also brought you a change of clothes."

Before Rome could get to Heath, Jamie pulled her into his wet arms, unaware they had Heath's sole focus. Feeling his tight embrace, she returned the hug full throttle. It was the ending she had hoped for, the opportunity to hold her living, breathing, best friend.

"Thank you for coming," whispered Jamie, his lips touching the surface of her ear.

"There's nothing I wouldn't do for you."

"Right back at you."

"What's this?" asked Rome jokingly as she pulled away and ran her hand along his newly grown facial hair. "I'm not used to that scratching my face."

"Part of being a pirate."

"And where might be the loot, Captain Webb?" said Rome, mimicking a pirate accent.

"On the sea floor. I just hope we didn't drop Lazenby's boat on top of it."

"The way this trips going, I wouldn't be surprised."

"I don't want the kids to know about the gold."

"I'll take care of it. The winch is ready to go."

"I'll suit up and head back down," said Jamie as he turned toward the tanks near the end of the boat.

As Rome turned back toward Heath, she recognized a look she wasn't familiar with.

There was a sadness in his eyes as he stared at her in silence. Returning a look of concern, she made her way toward the newly-formed medical station. "Martin, would you take Talin and Leta below? Get them water and something to eat?"

Rome waited for Martin to leave with the siblings then sat down next to Heath. Desperately, she wanted to give him a hug that rivaled the one she gave Jamie, but she could only watch as Jonah stitched up the deep gash in his arm completely by touch. "You're doing an amazing job, Jonah."

"I used to joke about being able to do this blindfolded. Looks like the joke's on me."

Rome watched Heath deal with the pain like a trooper, sneaking a kiss onto his cheek. "Thank you, Heath."

"I haven't done anything."

"You've done everything."

"That would be you and Jamie. I'm just along for the ride."

"You saved me from drowning and stuck by me no matter what."

"Does that mean I get the girl?"

"You already got the girl," confirmed Rome as she attempted another kiss.

"Hold still. I'm almost done," advised Jonah.

"You and Jamie are like bookends. A matched set," noted Heath. "After watching him in action, I don't know why you'd choose me over him."

"Jamie's skill set is impressive. On top of that, he's an amazing human being. But he's not the man I'm in love with."

"And what type of man would that be?"

"Someone who's been drugged, kidnapped and beaten, all in less than a week. And for what?"

"You know the answer."

"You made me boots out of a tarp, Heath."

"But will I be enough for you?" he asked, already believing the answer to be 'no.'

"Let's do this, London," yelled Jamie from the rear of the boat right before he placed his mask over his face.

Frightened by the questions he was asking, the last thing she wanted to do was leave his side. "Just a minute." She needed more time to make Heath understand, to erase whatever foolishness was going through his mind.

"Go. He needs you," he said, treating it like nothing more than a business decision.

With no other choice, Rome left her boyfriend's side. Heath watched as she skillfully used the crane to lift the cage over the side of the boat and began lowering it, giving Jamie the thumbs up and go ahead to step off the boat.

"Don't jump to conclusions, my friend. It's the truth that matters," advised Jonah as he tied off the last stitch.

"I've been watching the truth unfold firsthand," responded Heath as he rose to his feet. "My eyes are wide open, Jonah."

"Your eyes may be open, but there is more than one way to see."

"Thanks for stitching me up. You do good work."

Rome turned to check on Heath but only caught a glimpse before he disappeared into the cabin, so she returned her attention to the winch and watching the depth meter tick by. It would take some time to reach a hundred and seventy feet, enough time to find Heath and continue their conversation. Turning from the winch, she ran straight into Sheldon and Bev, approaching from behind.

"What are you going to do with the treasure?"

"Return it."

"To...?"

"The Aztec burial tomb."

"Where would that be?" asked Sheldon, continuing with his inquiries.

"In the remote mountains of southeast Mexico."

"I don't know how much treasure's down there, but presumably it's more than will fit in a backpack."

"He's right, Rome. How are you going to get all that gold through the rough terrain of a rainforest?" asked Bev.

"I haven't had time to think that far ahead."

"I wouldn't even guide people through that mess," mentioned Bev.

"Jamie will know what to do. In the meantime, can you keep the kids inside the cabin until we secure the gold?"

"No worries," responded Bev as she walked away.

"Heath needs my phone to make some business calls. Let me know if you need any help," said Sheldon as he joined Bev on her way toward the front of the boat.

She did need help, but not from the living. Rome watched them walk away, knowing they were right. She hadn't given much thought to the practicality of her plan. She also had concerns about Mendivia and his men as well as Captain Locke and crew. "Henry? Are you near?" She waited for a response, but nothing came.

"The one you seek is below," came a voice from behind speaking Nahuatl, the language of the ancient Aztecs. Rome had heard it before in her travels of central Mexico and knew it was still spoken today by nearly one point five million of their descendants. But this time she understood it perfectly.

Rome turned to face the back of the boat and found a tall man with an impressive build standing before her. He wore a white, wrap-around skirt, reaching just below his knees with a wide band at top and a white, seamless shirt with sleeves, open in the front. "Henry is detained. He thought his captain may need help."

"My name is Rome."

"Yes, I know. I am Teno of the Aztec Empire."

"You're the one Moctezuma entrusted with the map."

"It is my failure that led to the discovery of the sacred tomb."

"Dying was not your fault."

"I live with the regret."

"Not for long," promised Rome.

"You seek to return the gold."

"We do, but I have concerns, especially with the curse."

"The strength of the curse is dependent on who bears it. The gold merely amplifies what's in the heart of man. If the heart is turned inward, the gold becomes a thirst that cannot be quenched, a lust impossible to satisfy."

"It can't be that simple."

"Simple it is not. In our day, the men chosen to carry the emperors' remains and adornment, to the burial tomb were put through many tests before given the honor of escort. Only those found with selfless hearts were allowed to transport the gold."

"That can be a hard characteristic to find," expressed Rome.

"One who has truly given his heart to another carries a selfless heart. Once he's given his heart away, he's less likely to think of himself, and in turn, use the gold for his own gain," clarified Teno.

"... truly given his heart away," repeated Rome a bit stunned as she thought of both Heath and Jamie's ability to avoid the curse, as well as Captain Locke and Henry.

"Each emperor's headdress, collar piece, shield, staff and jewelry were designed, built and dedicated for him and him only. Every piece fashioned from the purest of gold and embellished with the finest jewels. Before the ceremony, the gold was consecrated by the hands of the priests within the walls of the Temple House, a structure near the great temple. It was a striking sight to watch them placed on the new emperor for the first time as he stood atop the temple. Seeing the sunlight reflect off the gold made him appear nearly godlike. Following his death, each emperor's adornment was placed in the tomb, never to be worn by another."

"If the curse is all about obsession then what happened to the men who sacrificed themselves after delivering the treasure to the burial tomb?"

"The spirits of the escorts are bound to protect the gold. They can't take a man's life, but they can create circumstances to hinder his success."

"So now we're adding another set of ghosts to the mix?"

"More reason to break the curse."

"I saw the map in Mendivia's memories. I know where the tomb is located."

"The mountain has been sealed."

"Sealed? How?"

"Two hundred years ago, a large earthquake destroyed the tomb, burying the emperors' remains."

"Then what do we do?"

"The only other way to break the curse is to return the gold to its original state."

"I don't understand."

"Return it to the earth."

"Bury it? I like that solution. Nice and easy."

"No. You must succeed where Fernando and I failed."

"You and Teno were supposed to destroy the map, not the gold."

"Destroying the map was the only way to protect the location of the gold. If the map had been destroyed, the treasure would still be hidden."

"So you're telling me to toss the gold into a live volcano?" asked Rome growing a bit distressed.

"The gold must become one with the earth again to free them from their obsession."

"Molten hot lava should definitely work."

"Return it to the earth and all will be made right," said Teno before disappearing from sight.

"Jamie's going to hate this idea," said Rome out loud. "Not to mention, Heath." Just then the winch reached the one-hundred-and-seventy-foot depth. Figuring the cable would need room for sway, she let it go another thirty feet before stopping the winch.

Now all she had to do was wait for Jamie to return then reel in the catch of a lifetime: a haul worth tens of millions if not more. Looking to the upper deck, she saw Heath slowly pacing around as he took care of business using Sheldon's cell. She loved how he wandered when he talked on the phone. It was just one of his little quirks. Rome hoped they could get back to normal now that the crisis with Jamie had come to a successful end, but he seemed changed somehow and that had Rome worried.

Their first vacation had come to an end before it even began. Most likely, they would fly back to Hawaii, then go their separate ways. Heath would return to running his business and she expected a call from her editor at any time, asking when she would be coming back to the office. She wondered when they would find time to see each other next. Feeling a need to rest herself, Rome sat down next to the winch and closed her eyes, for the first time in a week. It felt good to close her eyes in relative peace.

HEATH HAD his hands full as one phone call led to another. Being absent from contact had taken its toll and he was paying the price by playing catch up. Just as he finished one call and was about to place another, Sheldon approached with a glass of water. "I need a moment of your time, Heath."

"Get in line," he responded half jokingly, exasperated by the many fires burning.

"It's in regard to the British author."

At that point, he had Heath's full attention. "How's the search?"

"It appears our young friends have hit a bit of a snag."

"A snag?"

"They spent the night incarcerated."

"They were arrested?"

"Something to do with stalking, illegal entry and misrepresentation involving counterfeit police credentials. Miss Lemmons's father, a solicitor, made arrangements for their release this morning."

"How bad is it?"

"The publisher is pressing charges."

"And the good news? Please let there be some."

"They got the name and contact information for the boy's father."

"I can work with that."

"You'll probably need to do it in person."

"Add it to the itinerary."

"You're handling this better than I thought," said Sheldon happily.

"After what I've been through this week…"

"Understood."

"Now about that itinerary?"

"Let's start with England. I'll know more after this next phone call."

"And Ms. London."

"She won't be joining me."

"Obligations at work?"

"We're both busy people, Sheldon."

"Who love each other. Don't lose sight of that, Heath," his friend suggested. Sheldon would like to have continued the topic of conversation, but he was interrupted by the ringing of the phone. To pacify his butler, Heath nodded in agreement then answered the incoming call. As Sheldon walked toward the stairs, he caught sight of Rome on the deck below, her head nodding up and down as she tried to sneak in a few minutes of sleep.

Once again, she had gone beyond the call to help those she loved. Just a month ago, she had rolled into Heath's life at the perfect time, saving his business as well as opening his heart. Although the circumstances of their relationship were challenging, they were perfect for each other and Sheldon couldn't be more happy for his longtime friend. He only hoped they could make it work.

Chapter Twenty

Feeling a splash on her face, Rome pulled herself out of a deep sleep to find Jamie flipping water at her from the back of the boat. "Bring her up, Rome," he hollered as he crawled onto the boat.

"Funny. Very funny," responded Rome, wiping the water off her face as she moved to the winch, started the motor and flipped the switch to reverse. The weight of the gold caused the boat to lean slightly, knocking everyone off balance and Rome into Jamie's arms. She got her bearings and stepped away, rotating around to help him off with his tanks. Glancing up, she saw Heath staring at the two of them while talking on the phone. The look on his face was unsettling. Rome motioned with her arm, inviting him to join them and he signaled back by lifting his index finger, indicating he would join them after the phone call ended. Happy he was coming, she still couldn't shake the look she saw on his face.

Jamie continued to talk, oblivious to Rome and Heath's communication until he sat down to remove his fins. "Is everything all right?"

"Everything's fine."

"What's wrong?"

"Heath seems different."

"He's been through a harrowing experience."

"What did they do to him?"

"That's for him to tell."

"The male race and their egos!"

"I will admit to knocking him out."

"You did what?"

"I brought him back."

"He was supposed to be safe with you."

"I knocked him out to keep him safe."

"Great!"

"I doubt what he's feeling is from the physical abuse. He thought you were dead, Rome."

"For how long?"

"After our meeting in the water, I found him with your scarf. So pretty much the entire time he was with me."

"Why didn't you tell him after you saw the scarf?"

"I was preoccupied."

"He must feel like the third wheel."

"I know that feeling from my visit to the castle."

"I seem to be batting a thousand these days."

"He'll work it out."

"I hope you're right."

"Give him some time," said Jamie as he stood up and unzipped his wetsuit. "Right now, the only thing I want to do is get out of this wetsuit. And then I'm going to burn it."

"I know the perfect place for that," responded Rome, hoping to ease Jamie into the idea of dumping the gold into hot lava.

"Bonfire on the beach?"

"Live volcano."

"Funny," laughed Jamie as he stripped down to his swim trunks.

"I'm serious. We have to dump the gold into a live volcano," said Rome quickly, then waited for a response.

"That's your brilliant idea?"

"No, it's Teno's."

"Who's Teno?"

"The Aztec guy who was entrusted with the mission to destroy the only map to the emperors' tomb by tossing it into a live volcano."

"Why didn't he just start a fire and burn it?"

"Do I look like an expert on ancient Aztec customs?"

"You talk to the dead. That's as close as it gets."

"You have a point," conceded Rome, enjoying the banter that was a standard part of their relationship.

"I'm assuming Teno's not alive," enquired Jamie.

"Hasn't been since the 1500's."

"Why does it need to be a live volcano?"

"'Return it to the earth.' That's what Teno said. It needs to become one with the earth again in order to free the ghosts obsessed with it."

"Were these ghost on the Maiden's Return?"

"Until you took the gold."

"That would explain the invisible force attacking us."

"It's the curse. We have to destroy the gold to set them free."

"The only live volcano close enough spewing hot lava would be on the big island of Hawaii."

"Isn't there an active one near Mexico City?"

"Popocatépetl is active, but it's only smoking at this point."

"It's needs be lava, so it has to be Hawaii."

"You know it's a tourist attraction, right?"

"I am a travel writer, Jamie."

"We'll have to do it at night."

"Any thoughts?"

"Helicopter's our best bet. We gotta to be in and out quick."

"I'm good with that."

"First, I need to clean up this mess with the State Department."

"What are you going to tell them?"

"The truth."

"Which part?"

"That I was rescued by my ex-girlfriend who talks to ghosts," Jamie said jokingly.

"There's a certain lieutenant in the Navy that would love to hear that one."

"They'll have to investigate the wreckage. Bodies will need to be recovered and identified if possible. Plus, I'll need to give a statement about Lazenby and his obsession with the treasure. A treasure that was never found."

"We don't have that much time."

"I'll make it work. I've been down this road before."

"Where are we going to stash it in the meantime?"

"We can't let it out of our sight. After I contact Ross I'll make a call. I know who can help make this happen."

"Can you trust him?"

"He's the type that doesn't ask questions," responded Jamie as the basket holding the gold broke through the surface of the water. "And he owes me a favor. A big one."

"I'll stop the winch," said Rome as she hurried toward the control. "Get the crane arm in position."

Jamie extended the cable from the crane to the basket and hooked on using a heavy-duty shackle. Then he returned to the crane and put enough tension on the cable to provide slack for Rome to unhook the winch. Taking control of the treasure-filled basket, Jamie moved it through the air as Rome's focus turned toward the upper deck. Again, she found Heath leaning on the railing watching her and Jamie at work. The look on his face had not changed.

Rome gestured with another wave and this time he turned toward the stairs. Relieved that Heath would be near when the gold arrived, she took a deep breath and waited for him to get there. They all needed a moment of closure and she couldn't think of a better time than this.

Again, the boat shifted as the basket full of trunks came to rest on the boat deck. Heath arrived just in time to help them remove the trunks and place them around the ship, spreading the weight more evenly. They were heavy beyond belief and it helped to have all three of them moving each trunk together.

Just as they had everything set, the water surrounding the boat became chopping, but no wind accompanied it. Rome had a bad feeling as she made eye contact with both Heath and Jamie, then instinctively grabbed onto both of their hands. Dark clouds closed in as the water grew more turbulent until ghosts began to shoot through the surface. Their numbers seemed endless as they continued to rise. Soon, the three of them were surrounded by spirits, hovering over the water, facing them down.

Looking around, it was easy to see they were divided into groups. Rome recognized Captain Mendivia and his men, as well as Captain Locke, Henry and the crew of the Maiden's Return.

"Captain Locke. It's good to see you again," said Rome, starting the conversation.

"Captain Locke?" whispered Jamie into Rome's ear. "As in the Maiden's Return?"

"Yes."

"And you as well," responded Falcon Locke, relieving Rome with his kind tone.

"Is it you I have to thank for the armband?" asked Jamie enthralled by the legend standing before him.

"It is."

"Enough with the pleasantries," demanded Mendivia. "We would have stopped you below if Locke and his men had not interfered."

"Thanks for that as well," mentioned Jamie.

"You won't get away with stealing our treasure," yelled Mendivia.

"A treasure you stole in the first place," responded Rome.

"Discovered."

"What's the point? You're no longer able to enjoy it."

"You must leave this place at once!"

"We're going, but we're taking the gold with us."

"We'll follow it to the ends of the earth."

"The earth's round, remember?"

"There is no distance great enough," remarked Mendivia, growing frustrated with Rome's cavalier attitude.

"You won't like where we're taking it."

"We've spent the better part of three centuries at the bottom of the ocean. What could be worse?"

"I hope you like it hot."

"There is no stopping them," inserted Captain Locke. "I have tried to reason with my men, but they cannot let go either."

"And what of you?" said Rome, turning to the group behind them. From the look of their dress, they were the ghosts of generations of funeral escorts. Some were wearing skirts, their chests bare, while others had fabric extending beneath one arm, stretched across the chest and tied over the shoulder.

"We each made an oath with our respective emperor," replied one of the pallbearers.

"We will not break it," replied another as they all spoke up in agreement.

"Any thoughts?" asked Rome, quietly to Jamie and Heath.

"I got nothing," responded Jamie.

"And you?"

"You're the captain," replied Heath.

"I'm the captain? That's your advice?"

"It makes sense. Go with it," added Jamie.

"Your boat, your rules."

"I think it's more complicated than that, Heath," she whispered.

"Do you have a better idea?"

After a brief pause to consider Heath's advice, Rome returned to the conversation. "As the current captain of this boat, I deny any of you permission to come aboard."

"You may deny us permission to board, but you can't keep us from following the gold," responded Mendivia.

"I can live with that," responded Rome as she watched them sporadically disappear from sight.

"They're returning your call from Singapore," said Sheldon as he burst onto the scene.

"Strange weather we're having," he continued, unaware of what just took place.

Heath let go of Rome's hand and replaced it with the phone as he walked away. Sheldon followed leaving Rome alone, still holding

Jamie's hand. As she tried to pull away, she realized it was Jamie holding her hand, not the other way around.

"Jamie?"

No response.

"Are you all right?"

Still no response.

"Come on. Snap out of it," encouraged Rome as she stared into his eyes, gently slapping her open hand against his cheek. Concerned for his well-being, she continued to call him back from wherever he had gone until movement ended his distant stare. Blinking several times as he refocused, Jamie turned to Rome. "They were all down there. The whole time I was down there. I was surrounded by them," said Jamie. Taking in several deep breaths, he leaned down and grabbed his knees.

Rome slid her hand over his back in support then leaned down to his ear. "If it's any consolation... I'm still not used to seeing them either." Then she returned to the trunks and started covering them with small tarps. Looking in the basket, she saw a couple of extra items. "I see you kept some souvenirs. Isn't that the mermaid figurehead from the Maiden's Return?"

Surprised by Rome's question, Jamie stood up and asked, "How do you know that?"

"I saw it on the ship."

"When?"

"Let's just say my gift magnified while in Tasmania. I can now see into a ghost's memory when we touch," answered Rome as she and Jamie slid the heavy, waterlogged figurehead to the deck and pushed her aside.

"You touch them?" enquired Jamie, leery of the idea.

Rolling her eyes at Jamie rather than responding, they returned to the basket. "Let me guess, the ship's wheel is Heath's."

"You know your man," joked Jamie as they set the wheel safely aside.

Needing a break, Rome sat down on top of a tarp-covered trunk and made herself comfortable as Jamie joined her. "How does it feel to sit on a bench worth millions?"

"You need to talk to him," said Rome, ignoring Jamie's lighthearted comment and changing the topic of conversation.

"Talk to who?"

"Heath."

"I'm sure we'll say something before we go our separate ways."

"No, I mean talk to him," inferred Rome.

"About what?"

"I need him to feel like he made an impact. Like he contributed."

"I could never have pulled off the switching of the gold or getting Talin and Leta off that boat without his help. And as much as it pains me to admit it, he saved my life."

"How?"

"I was being attacked by the ghosts... again. But this time the force broke the ship free from the walls of the chasm holding her in place. I couldn't get out. If Heath hadn't reached in and grabbed my arm, I would have died... trapped inside the Maiden's Return."

"That makes two of us. I was drowning and Heath got me to shore."

"You're one of the best swimmers I know."

"Not when a group of angry ghosts are pulling me under."

Rome and Jamie sat in silence for a few moments as they contemplated their own mortality. It had been a whirlwind week for Rome and even longer for Jamie. To have survived all they had gone through was nothing short of a miracle.

"I'll talk to him," said Jamie, respectfully.

"While you're doing that, I'll have Sheldon take the boat back slowly."

"You want me to do it now?"

"Yes, and put on a shirt first. That's the last thing he needs to see," said Rome, pointing to his chiseled chest.

For fun, Jamie responded by flexing his pecs and biceps as Rome rolled her eyes and turned to leave.

"Where am I going to find a shirt?" called out Jamie as she kept walking. "My butler didn't bring me a change of clothes."

Rome shook her head as she climbed the stairs to the upper

deck, smiling at Jamie's familiar sense of humor. Once she reached the top, she crossed to the opposite side and stood next to Sheldon and Heath, who were staring off into the sunset. "Am I interrupting?"

"Not at all," replied Sheldon, standing in the middle of Rome and Heath. "I assume we're ready to return to shore."

"Take it slow, so we don't draw attention."

"You got it."

Heath and Rome stood in silence as Sheldon left the deck. Rome moved toward Heath, filling the space between them. "So how are things in the world of shipping?"

"You don't want to know."

"Back to the real word, huh?"

"After the week we just had, I don't mind one bit," said Heath, creating a lull in the conversation.

Rome wondered if it was too soon to bring up his time with Jamie but decided to test the waters anyway. "Do you want to talk about what happened on Lazenby's boat?"

"Maybe later," responded Heath, purposefully bringing an end to the topic of his abduction.

Again, they stood in silence as Rome wondered where to go from there. She knew the obvious destination but wasn't sure how it would be received. "Jamie and I have a plan to get rid of the gold."

"Get rid of it?"

"It needs to be returned to the earth in order to free the spirits of Captain Lock, his crew and all the other spirits effected by the curse."

"What does that mean?"

"According to Teno, we have to dump it into a live volcano."

"You're joking, right?"

"Nope. The closest one is in Hawaii."

"And Jamie's on board with this?"

"It took some doing, but he agreed to handle the logistics."

"He's good at that."

"He knows people."

"You're both welcome to stay at the beach house while you wrap it up."

"Aren't you coming with us?"

"I have to get to England to clean up a mess and a few more shipping ports after that."

"I thought I traveled a lot."

"Then it's back to the office for a while."

"How long's awhile?"

"I've got a lot on my plate right now."

Rome paused on purpose, waiting to see if Heath wanted to plan a future rendezvous, but nothing came. Nor did he enquire as to her plans following the disposal of the gold. Uncertain as to what was going on with him, Rome decided to give him some space. "I should go see if Bev needs any help."

"Rome?" said Heath, stopping her from leaving the deck. "We may have to put off that 'starting point' we discussed at the castle."

"All right," responded Rome tentatively knowing in her heart that it was far from okay. Stopping at the top of the stairs, Rome decided to take control of the conversation. "No, Heath, that's not all right. If this is about my search for Jamie, just say it."

"The only thing Jamie has to do with this... is that I'm not him."

"I never asked you to be anyone but yourself," argued Rome as they walked toward each other, meeting in the middle of the deck.

"You told me in Tasmania how hard this would be and I didn't believe you."

"So now you want to give up?"

"I'm in love with you, Rome."

"And I'm in love with you."

"But is that enough?"

"We knew this would take work, Heath, but you made me believe it was possible."

"I still want to believe that."

"It's a choice. A choice you already made."

"Maybe you were right about the extreme circumstances."

"Don't do this, Heath. Talk to me," implored Rome, her eyes filling with tears.

Seeing the effect their conversation was having on Rome, Heath decided to back off. The last thing in the world he wanted to do was cause her pain. "I'm sorry, Rome," he said, taking her hand in his. "I think I just need some time to unwind. To process everything that's happened this week."

"I get that. We all do. So we're okay?"

"Just give me some time."

Relieved, Rome wrapped her arms around him and held him as tight as physically possible, happy that his arms embraced her as well. They took a quiet moment to hold each other until the ringing of the phone ended their time together.

"I should get that," Heath said pulling away from her. "This is Heath."

Taking hold of the handrail to the stairs, she turned back for one last look, hoping to find him staring at her. That was not the case. Heath had already returned to the business of shipping. Leaving him alone with his work, she descended the stairs to prepare for their return to shore.

The call was short but just what he needed to end his conversation with Rome. Confused and brokenhearted, he wanted nothing more than to return to the safety of Forest Gate and lock himself away behind the castle walls. Unfortunately, the castle would never be the same without Rome residing within those same walls, even if it were just on occasion. But he had to do what he felt was best for her and at that point it was allowing the love of his life to be with Jamie, the man he felt she was meant to be with. The only way he knew to handle the situation was to throw himself into his business, the same thing he did after the loss of his father. And that's what he planned to do.

REACHING THE DOCK, Jamie and Heath both jumped out and tied the ropes to the mooring cleats, then Jamie helped Leta and Talin off the boat. "We're going to get you checked out at the hospital. Your parents will meet you there."

"Thank you, Mr. Webb," said Leta as she wrapped her arms around his waist.

"Thank you for your bravery. Both of you."

Leta walked to Heath and wrapped her arms around his waist as well. "Thank you too."

Talin shook both of their hands and the look of respect from their eyes was something the young man would hold onto for the rest of his life. "Did you find the gold Lazenby was looking for, Mr. Webb?"

"No. Just a whole lot of cannon balls."

"What about the armband?"

"An antique we found on the ship. Probably worth a hundred bucks. We had to make him believe we found the gold to keep everyone alive."

Bev walked up behind them and wrapped her arm around Leta's shoulder. "Let's get you to the hospital," then she and Sheldon escorted the siblings to the car.

Jamie approached Heath as they waited for Rome and Martin to help Jonah out of the cabin. He extended his hand and Heath respectfully took hold. "Thanks for the help. I couldn't have saved their lives without you."

"It was an experience I'll never forget. A real eye opener."

"That ship's wheel will look great in the castle."

"Yes, it will."

"Can't wait to display my mermaid."

"Her name's Karukera. Kera for short."

"I like that," said Jamie as he moved to the edge of the dock to help Jonah out of the boat. Martin jumped onto the dock and Heath extended his hand to help Rome. She happily took hold and stepped off the boat as well.

"I guess I better head to the police station and get this over with. Does anyone have a ride?" asked Jamie.

"It just drove off," said Rome.

"Guide me to the side of the road and we'll be picked up in no time," said Jonah.

Heath took his hand and they walked toward the road where

Jonah stuck out his thumb and waited for a car to pass. Two cars stopped right away and that was enough to get them all to where they were going.

At the police station, Jamie made all the necessary phone calls and told them as much as they needed to hear. The responsibility fell on them to form a search and rescue team to retrieve the bodies and examine the wreckage of the South'n Hunter, now at the bottom of the sea. Jamie was happy to wash his hands of it, especially since there was no one left alive to counter his story. After being handed his belongings, he left the police station and went his merry way.

Arriving back at Dr. Orlando Melgosa's exploration boat, Jamie plugged in his phone to charge, then opened the trunk that held the underwater camera he borrowed from Rome. The pictures contained on its memory disk were priceless, the only visual evidence of the Maiden's Return. He would protect the disk as carefully as the treasure he was fostering.

An hour later, Jamie called his friend, the one he would ask to help him dispose of 'the package.' Although he trusted him with his life, he chose not to burden him with the added temptation. It was a short call, but arrangements were made. He planned to stay on the boat with the gold until his friend's arrival. "What to do till then?" he asked himself mentally. He knew the answer before he asked himself the question. Sleep. Putting his feet up on the couch, he laid back and took a long overdue nap.

Chapter Twenty-One

Waking up after a restful night's sleep, Rome looked at the time and realized she had been asleep for ten hours. She couldn't believe her eyes, so she refocused on the frigate clock and discovered she was accurate. Crawling out of bed, she left her room and entered Heath's, expecting to find him still in bed as well. But the bed was made and the room appeared to be void of his belongings. A slight panic began to set in as she hurried to his closet only to find empty hangers. She found nothing in the drawers or anywhere else she searched. Heath was gone. He had left without a word or even an explanation.

Rome sat down on the foot of the bed and stared at the wall. "Breathe in the good air, let out the bad," she told herself as she followed her own orders. The deep breathing helped to calm her as usual while she retraced the happenings of the day before. Heath had gone to bed early once they returned from the police station. He had to be physically spent from his time with Lazenby. She followed shortly with plans to continue their discussion started on the boat the next day.

Now morning had arrived as mornings always do, but there would be no talk between them. "Wait a minute," she said as she stood from the bed. "He might be waiting for me in the house." With renewed enthusiasm, Rome ran from the room and continued down the trail to Jonah's backyard patio.

"Good morning, Rome. How did you sleep?"

"Have you seen Heath?"

"Seen Heath?" enquired Jonah, referring to his lack of sight.

"I mean... is he still here?"

"No. He took the watersport you borrowed from the yacht and left for San Andres three hours ago. He mentioned needing to return it to the rightful owner."

"Is he coming back?"

"He left this note for you," responded Jonah as he felt around for the envelope on the stand next to him, then presented it to Rome. Holding it in her hand, Rome couldn't find the courage to break the seal.

"Aren't you going to read it?" asked Jonah.

"What makes you think I'm not?" she responded robotically.

"I haven't heard you open it."

"Nothing gets past you, does it?"

"Not the important stuff."

"This trip has tested our relationship, Jonah."

"Did you both pass?"

"I think I'm holding the answer in my hand."

"The truth may be painful, Rome, but it's the only way forward."

Rome turned her back to Jonah and walked to the edge of the patio looking over Providencia. She knew he was right about the truth but wasn't sure if she was ready to face it. Heath already shared his desire to put their relationship on hold, but Rome thought they moved past that. She was certain that he would snap out of it and all would be back to normal. Their normal.

Rome closed her eyes as she slid her finger beneath the seal. Finding the courage to look inside, she found a single key, no doubt the key to his beach house, and a piece of paper folded in thirds. She pulled out the paper and carefully unfolded it as though it were a bomb waiting to detonate. "My dearest, Rome. This week has opened my eyes to many things. Nearly losing you twice scared me more than I expected."

"An okay start," she thought to herself, then continued to read. "Spending time with Jamie and seeing you two together has also opened my eyes. Maybe with time we could have made this work, but for now I need to do what I do best... focus on the company. Best wishes to you and Jamie on the final leg of this great adventure and any future endeavors. I have no doubt you're in safe hands. Love always, Heath."

Folding the paper back into thirds, Rome pressed it tightly to her chest as she stared out at the ocean. It was a clear morning and she could see a great distance until a wash of tears clouded her view. She pictured Heath bouncing across the water on his way back to San Andres, trying to make sense of his decision, trying to convince himself that this was the right course of action. But in Rome's heart, she knew it wasn't the right path.

Somehow in the chaos of the Caribbean they had switched the roles they played in Tasmania. Just a few weeks ago, Rome was the one who wanted it to make sense on paper, to understand the logistics of a romance that would span the globe. But after their time together in Nicaragua, she let go of all the reasons why it couldn't work. She knew in her heart of hearts that he was the one for her. Now the tables had turned and they were viewing their relationship from opposite sides.

Suddenly, laughter could be heard coming from inside the house. "Sounds like Bev and Sheldon have returned," remarked Jonah. Rome quickly wiped the tears from her cheeks then turned just in time to see them enter the patio

"What a beautiful morning for a stroll along the beach," announced Bev.

"With the woman I love," added Sheldon.

Bev immediately noticed something was wrong by the look on Rome's face. Letting go of her boyfriend's hand, she walked toward her as Sheldon took a seat next to Jonah and began a conversation about the beach they had combed. Rome turned back toward the ocean view and Bev joined her. "What is it? What's wrong?"

Rome handed her the paper and she read it once, then read it again, trying to make sense of Heath's thinking. Folding it up, she placed her arm around Rome's shoulder. "No worries, Rome, he'll come around."

"No he won't. He'll go to Sydney, take care of business, then return to Tasmania and hide away in his castle. You know I'm right."

"We all process things differently."

"That's not processing. That's running away."

"Then do something about it."

"I tried. We talked. He told me we were okay. I believed him."

"Heath was relentless in winning you over in Tassie. Now it's your turn. Go after him."

"He's gone, Bev. He left hours ago. He'll be in England by the time I reach Hawaii, then back to Australia by the time I get to New York."

"You've left out some of his itinerary."

"Where else is he going?"

"Busan and I think Japan."

"That's still halfway around the world."

"You have to catch him before he locks himself away."

"I've got to get back to work."

"You travel for a living."

"That's right," agreed Rome as the wheels started to turn in her head. "I travel for a living."

"You just need the right assignment."

"You're the best guide I've ever had."

"You guys are right for each other. I knew it the day we toured the Isle of the Dead."

"How could you know that when I didn't?"

"Like you said, 'I'm the best guide you've ever had.' Go after him, Rome."

"That's good advice."

"Here's some more… Knowing you're spending more time with your ex-boyfriend can't be helping the matter. Do you both have to go to Hawaii?"

"I need to see this through."

"Then make it quick."

"We will."

"Sheldon and I have decided to stay on the island for the rest of the week."

"What about your job?"

"I'm on extended leave."

"When will I see you next?"

"At this point, my future's wide open. If you told me a month ago that I'd be vacationing in the Caribbean with the man I love, I would have laughed out loud."

"I'm happy for both of you."

"Without you, none of this would have happened."

"I just knocked on the castle door. You guys did all the rest."

"And if we can fall in love, anything's possible."

"I should get going. I'll touch bases with you before I leave the island."

"Sounds good," said Bev as Rome turned to leave. Grabbing onto her hand, Bev stopped her before she got far. "Do you know why Heath's going to England?"

"I assume shipping business."

"To find Martin's father."

"I'm not surprised. That's so Heath."

"I'll let you know how it turns out."

"Do that."

Bev watched Rome walk away to prepare for the next leg of her adventure. She didn't know the reason behind dumping the gold into a live volcano, nor could she begin to understand it. It wasn't her choice to make, only her secret to keep. She just chalked it up to being part of the mystery that made Rome's world so unique, a mystery she hoped to someday unravel.

ARRIVING AT THE DOCK, Rome paid the driver and walked

toward Orlando's boat. Jamie exited the cabin and helped her onto the deck. "You're late."

"Did we set a time?"

"No."

"Then how can I be late?"

"Daylight's burning."

"I slept in."

"You never sleep in."

"I think I earned one morning of sleeping in."

"You're not sitting on millions of dollars in gold," said Jamie.

"True."

"I'll cut you some slack... for old time sake."

"I did rescue you."

"I'm never going hear the end of that, am I?"

"Probably not."

"Did you see Heath before he left this morning?" asked Jamie.

"How do you know he left?"

"He dropped by to pick up his ship's wheel. We had that 'chat' you wanted us to have. He'll be fine."

Before Rome could ascertain more details, a man of tall stature and Jamie's build exited the cabin and walked toward them.

"Rome London, meet Kitty," said Jamie as the man extended his hand for Rome to take hold.

"Kitty's an unusual name," responded Rome, allowing her hand to be engulfed by his.

"He had an incident with a kitten on one of his first missions. The nickname stuck," clarified Jamie.

"Let's get this done," stated Kitty with a smile, then he moved past her and left the boat.

"A man of few words."

"What he lacks in vocabulary, he makes up in resources and skill. After you."

Rome left the boat and walked with Jamie toward the two motorcycles. She waited for him to get on then straddled the seat behind him, wrapping her arms around his waist, a familiar position for both of them. Following Kitty, they left Dr. Melgosa's dock and drove down the road. Rome had no idea where they were going but trusted Jamie implicitly. Eventually they pulled into the airport and got off the bikes. Kitty started for the plane, but Rome needed some clarification. "Are we leaving now?"

"Everything's loaded on Kitty's plane and ready to go."

"I didn't say goodbye to anyone. My luggage is still at Jonah's house."

"Call your friends from the jet and have them mail everything to New York. We don't have the time."

Rome watched as Jamie followed Kitty to the plane. With no other option, she followed as well, pulling out her phone and checking the percentage of power. Fortunately, she had it charging all night which meant it would probably last the duration of their trip to Hawaii. At least she hoped so. She would call Bev from the plane as Jamie recommended, then silence her phone until she absolutely needed it. She was in Jamie's world now and would have to live by his rules until the mission was complete.

They made one stop at a small airfield in Mexico to fuel up, then began the longest leg of the flight, crossing the Pacific Ocean to Kauai. The flight took far less time than it took for her and Heath to make their way to the Isla de Providencia and she never would have guessed she'd be returning to Hawaii with Jamie rather than Heath. A lot can happen in a week.

Kitty piloted the plane as Jamie and Rome sat in the back catching up. Their current flight was far better than the last one they shared from Sydney to New York. He told her in great detail of his experience aboard the South'n Hunter as well as his history with Lazenby and his experience with the invisible force aboard the Maiden's Return, now known to be the ghosts. After a period of incessant pleading from Rome, he also shared some of Heath's experience, giving her an eye into his current mindset, but he refused to share any details of their morning chat.

Eventually, she could tell that Jamie needed some more sleep, so she made her way to the copilot's seat and began a conversation with Kitty. Most of it was one sided and she kept to world topics, but at least it was passing the time for both of them. Although she couldn't see them, Rome knew the ghosts linked to the gold were nearby from the sound of their whispers. In a way, she was glad they were along for the ride. Hopefully, it would be the last leg on a journey that spanned centuries.

Arriving on the island of Kuaui under the dark of night, Kitty made a flawless landing at the Lihue airport, then taxied the jet to the cargo facility where he parked it for the duration of his trip. It was one o'clock in the morning and there wasn't a whole lot of activity at the airport. Jamie woke with the landing and joined Kitty in putting on olive drab jumpsuits. Jamie tossed one to Rome and she slid it over her clothes as well. They waited as Kitty disappeared across the runway and returned driving a delivery truck and backed it up to the plane. Together they loaded the six trunks into the back and crawled into the truck.

On the way out of the airport, Rome noticed a fuel truck pulling up next to Kitty's plane. She marveled to herself at the level of planning that went into this mission. The ease of the entire operation was dependent on Kitty and Jamie's trusted contacts, from a friend in the air traffic control tower to the person who left the delivery truck for them to use. No one was told of the gold, not even Kitty. And no one asked. It was obvious that Jamie was part of tightly-knit network who had each other's backs no matter what.

They quickly arrived at a small airstrip nearby used mostly for helicopter tours and light aircraft, then pulled up along side a good-sized helicopter. She was an older model, privately owned Puma, originally designed and used to transport troops and cargo. Even under the night sky, Rome could tell the helicopter had seen combat. Jamie slid open the doors and the three of them struggled to load each of the six heavy trunks into the cargo area. Kitty jumped in the pilot seat and fired her up as Rome and Jamie secured themselves in the back, putting on their helmets for communication. Concerned about the extra weight and how it would effect the aircraft, Kitty made the necessary adjustments as he lifted off the runway.

Rome's heart pounded as they left Kuaui and headed for the Big Island of Hawaii, the doors wide open, taking in the fresh ocean air.

She looked at her teammates' calm demeanors and couldn't help but be impressed. They had spent years on covert missions, so this was nothing more than run of the mill for them both. Beyond that was Jamie's willingness to see this to the end and help a group of spirits finally make their way home. Jamie glanced over at Rome and found her looking at him. He smiled and gave her a thumbs up and she returned the gesture. Tonight she was one of the guys and she liked how it felt.

Kitty let them know they were nearing the Kilauea Volcano so Jamie unbuckled his safety restraint and began removing the locks on the trunks. This was the first time Rome had seen the treasure and it took her breath away as he opened the lid. Staring at the beautiful headdresses, shields and neck pieces, she questioned whether they were doing the right thing, but looking up she saw Kera and Henry sitting in the seats facing them. They were along for the ride and Rome was grateful for their presence, a wonderful reminder as to why it needed to be destroyed. Kera knelt down next to one of the trunks across from Rome, and Henry did the same thing on Jamie's side of the helicopter.

Soon the bright red color of the lava was visible beneath them as Kitty lowered the chopper to the crater, leaving enough space for the helicopter's safety. The last thing they wanted was to explode the fuel tanks or melt the three sets of tires they'd need for landing. The rotaries kept the smoke away from the chopper, but the heat from the lava added to the urgency.

Pushing with all their might, Rome and Jamie worked to inch the first trunk to the opening. Rome's strength paled in comparison to Kitty's and Jamie was taking on more than he should. Quickly, Henry and Kera came to their aid and pushed from behind, helping them to shove it from the helicopter and into the lava below. They watched with curiosity as it disappeared into the hot magma, then turned back for the second trunk.

Following the same procedure, the four of them used every bit of strength to slide the second trunk out the door. They repeated the process three more times until they came to the sixth and final trunk: the heaviest one on board containing all the small pieces of jewelry as well as a few large items. Try as they might, they could barely budge the trunk. They had to get some weight off. Rome opened the lid and together they grabbed handfuls of bands, earrings, necklaces and threw them into the hot lava. Henry and Kera joined in and Jamie watched with amusement as pieces of gold jewelry floated through the air and out the door. Half empty, they were able to push the last trunk from the helicopter, returning the gold to the earth where it belonged.

After Jamie and Rome returned to their seats and belted themselves in, Rome wanted to give her best friend a thank-you gift. She took off her helmet and signaled to Jamie to do the same. Then she reached out and took hold of his hand, allowing Henry and Kera to become visible to his eyes. Both Karukera and Henry mouthed the words "thank you" to Jamie, then smiled at Rome before they disappeared. Moved emotionally by his brief encounter, Jamie turned his attention toward the open door. Even now, the idea of displaying his emotion was not acceptable. Still hanging onto Rome's hand, he saw a spectacle that rivaled the ghost sighting he experienced on Orlando's boat. In awe, he watched hundreds of spirits, once attached to the gold, experience a newfound freedom as they disappeared into the starry sky. Rome's eyes were more focused on Kera and her father being reunited after so many years. Captain Falcon Locke was finally free to return to the love of his life, Wanahani. And Kera and Henry were free to pursue their love as well. The view couldn't have been better. Rome and Jamie had seen what few people have the opportunity to see and that would change them both forever.

Returning to Kauai, they landed the chopper where they found it, piled into the delivery truck and left the small airport. On their way back, Kitty made a planned detour to Heath's beach house where Jamie bid his longtime friend goodbye with a hardy handshake. Rome, however, refused to let him leave without a hug—not that it took much convincing—then he was gone. She knew nothing more of him than his name, but that's how they liked it in their world.

Rome removed the key from her pocket and they entered the

house. Turning on the lights, she found herself standing in the same room where she began more than a week ago. Her Hawaiian vacation was over and she felt a deep sadness for what could have been. Jamie, on the other hand, went straight for the fridge and cupboards, pulling out items for a possible meal and placing them on the counter. Rome had stocked the kitchen with a few items from the local convenience store, making it an odd assortment of food. As a confirmed bachelor, Jamie could make a pretty impressive meal out of almost anything and Rome was glad he was there. Not only was she starving, but she needed the distraction. More than that, she needed a friend.

THE NEXT DAY found Rome walking along the beach, the same beach she was strolling when she met Kera for the first time. She was bound and determined to have one restful day before her midnight flight back to the bustle of New York City. She had heard from Bev that morning and received good news about Heath's progress in London. It seems the mysterious author never received the letter from Martin's mother, nor did he know he had a son. His publisher chose to bury it thinking it was someone trying to extort money from his client. Martin's biological father had already boarded a plane headed for the Caribbean and Heath booked him a room at Jonah's. The perfect mediator. "Chalk one up for the good guys," she thought to herself as she stopped to pick up an orange scallop sea shell.

Bev also mentioned that Heath shared the story of the Maiden's Return and the cursed Aztec treasure with the author, minus Rome's ability to communicate with the ghosts, and the author wanted to retell the experience in fiction.

The only thing missing was not hearing it directly from Heath. Rome would have loved to hear the excitement in his voice as he relayed the details and shared his hopes for Martin and his father.

Wiping the sand from the crevices of the shell, she heard Jamie call her name as he jogged toward her. She'd never been a fan of running, especially when there were more enjoyable ways to exercise that don't lead to early joint replacement. Circling around, Jamie slowed to a walk next to her. "This sure beats running through D.C."

"To say the least."

"So what's your plan for the rest of the day?"

Rome thought about it but had no plan to offer. "I'm wide open. How about you?"

"Since we slept through breakfast, I say we pick up lunch at that food shack on the way home. Then maybe an afternoon nap in the hammock?"

"You had me at food shack."

"Of course, I did," joked Jamie. "Any idea where your editor will send you next?"

"I have some suggestions. How about you?"

"I'm headed to Tokyo."

"So soon?"

"I'm playing 'back up' on a security detail for a week-long summit."

"Wait a minute," said Rome suspiciously. "Are you sharing classified information with me?"

"Only seems fitting since you showed me your secret."

"I can't believe they're throwing you back in so quickly."

"The summit's a big deal."

"So they need the best."

"I'm not running the show. Just there to help," he said taking off in the opposite direction. "I need twenty more minutes of cardio. See ya up there."

As Rome turned to watch Jamie run down the beach, it felt routine, as though nothing had changed. But things had changed. Her world had been transformed over the past month or so since Heath entered her life. "A month or so," she thought to herself, questioning how her life could be turned upside down in such a short period of time.

Her loyalty to persistent planning had crashed and burned somewhere along the way, leaving her with a list of unanswered questions and an uncertain future. Combine that with the fact that her gift had ramped up to a whole new level and Rome had her work cut out for her.

The only two stable elements left in her life were her job, a career she loved, and her family, the one thing Heath didn't have. Rome completely understood his decision to revert to the family business. It was safe and there's much to be said for stability when the storms of change and uncertainty are whirling like a hurricane.

The ringing of her phone brought Rome out of deep thought as she accepted the call. "Hi, Mom." Expecting to be lectured for not returning her calls, she was surprised to hear that her mother was calling from an airplane about to take off for Okinawa. The call was short and one sided as her mother spoke briefly of an emergency situation that needed her attention. The connection ended before Rome could get any details, leaving her confused and concerned. The upcoming weekend was her parents' anniversary, but they had no plans of traveling abroad. And why Okinawa? Rome's curiosity quickly turned to guilt as she realized her mother had been calling for help and she had ignored her calls.

Being the guru of travel, she quickly estimated when their plane would land on the Japanese island: about twenty-one hours, give or take. Hawaii was closer to Okinawa than New York which meant she could be there in roughly twelve hours once she boarded the plane, putting her on the ground before her parents arrived. Her only wild card in the plan was Angelica Fontaine, Editor and Chief at *Trekking the Globe*. Rome's only hope was to sweet talk her longtime friend into one of two options: extending her vacation time or a writing assignment in Asia, specifically Okinawa. She was somewhat familiar with the island from an article she wrote five years earlier, but there was much more to the travel destination than what she covered.

This would be the fourth island to impact Rome's life in the past five weeks... a strange coincidence... but no stranger than Heath, her parents and Jamie being in the same part of the world at nearly the same time. The safe route would be to head home to New York City and wait for them to call. But Rome had kicked safe to the curb after her time in Australia and proven it on the Isla de Providencia. She had a relationship to save with the man she loved and her plan was to think outside the box, which in reality was no plan at all... exactly what it would take to rescue Heath from himself and put Rome's world back together.

The End

Hand in Hand

BOOK THREE IN THE ROME LONDON SERIES

Okinawa, Japan, 1945

An eighteen-year-old student, forced to serve as a nurse by the Japanese military during the Battle of Okinawa, saves the life of a downed U.S. Naval pilot. Caught in the middle of a war between nations, they must rely on each other if they have any chance of survival.

Okinawa, Japan, Present Day

Rome arrives on the island with a long to-do list: write an article on Japan's vacation paradise, find out why her parents rushed to Okinawa, locate Heath and get their relationship back on track. What could possibly go wrong?

About the Author

Xann-shapella Smith had the opportunity to study playwriting and screenwriting at Brigham Young University and has brought her plays to the stage on many occasions. Her love for great storytelling has produced scripts that span many genres, including: drama, romance, comedy, fantasy, adventure and science fiction. Transitioning from screenwriter to novelist has given her another outlet in terms of storytelling, affording new possibilities and expanding the range of her audience. Excited about the second installment in the Rome London series, she looks forward to taking her readers on future adventures.

Xann resides on a small farm where the beauty and solace that surround her provide the perfect atmosphere for creating stories as far as the expanse of her imagination. Writing has been one of the great loves of her life and telling a good story is one of her passions. Xann-shapella's writing is a skill that rewards her in abundance each and every day and a passion she loves to share with people everywhere.

For more books and updates:
www.xannsmith.com

Made in the USA
Monee, IL
25 March 2021